A DIFFERENT KIND OF KENT

A Different Kind of Kent

Writers of Whitstable

ISBN 978-0-9935492-1-2

A CIP catalogue record for this title is available from the British Library.

Published in the UK in 2017 by Coinlea Publishing
www.coinlea.co.uk

Typesetting: Coinlea Services
Cover design: David Williamson
Cover illustration: Lily Mari Williamson age 6
Editing team: Lin White, Joanne Bartley, John Wilkins
Illustrators:
Maggie Johnson piii p206 p231
Simon Bennett Hayes p8 p195
Kristy Widdicombe p28 p137 p219
Lin White p60
Ellen Simmons p71
Helen Howard p99
David Williamson p113

Contents

Foreword

by Matthew Munson

Matthew Munson is an author, a disability advocate and a photographer. He lives in Kent and has published three novels: two fantasy, and one science-fiction, which is the first in a new trilogy.

I adore short stories; genuinely adore them. There's an immediacy about the stories, where ideas and concepts are focused into a set number of words, that allows for an exploration of ideas, themes, and personalities.

It also takes a particular kind of skill to create a short story. There's an exquisite brevity of words that enables writers to pack as much of a punch as someone might try to include into a full-length novel, and that punch might be emotional, psychological, spiritual … well, the list goes on.

When we look the history of the short story, it's often been considered the poor relation of the fiction world, with people thinking that they should have to buy full-length novels all the time because that's what's done. Utter tosh and rubbish, of course.

I was first introduced to the world of short stories by Jeffrey Deaver, he of *The Bone Collector* and other novels featuring Lincoln Rhyme. He is something of a hero of mine, in that his writing style is clear, inventive, witty, and making you constantly second-guess whether you know what the ending's going to be. I like that in a writer, and I had avowedly followed his books for years – and then, some time ago, I realised that he had published a couple of volumes of short stories.

I was surprised, to say the least, because I'd had the view of short stories that I've just mentioned above (don't worry, I'm rather embarrassed about it now). Why would Jeffrey Deaver bother with this medium of writing when he could be focused on another novel? Why?

Well, I can tell you why: because they were damn good, and the stories needed to be heard in precisely that format. They were perfectly formed and entirely right to fit into a book of short stories, and it opened my eyes to knowing that there were many good writers of the style out there.

I soon began avidly collecting short story collections; Steven King, for example, is a prolific writer of shorter fiction, using both his own name and the pseudonym of Richard Bachman. Sir Terry Pratchett launched a book of short stories not long before his death, and they were wonderful; I almost wept with the sheer joy of knowing that STP was joining the fray.

I've tried writing short story fiction in the past, and haven't always been that successful; occasionally I've created something that I'm proud of, but they're few and far between. As I said, short story writing is an art, and the writers in this collection have got that skill in spades. I suspect that at least part of the reason is because they're mutually supportive of each other and have an effective critiquing system in their writers' group.

I'm a huge fan of writers' groups. I've belonged to one for a long time and, whilst I don't go every week, I'm in frequent contact with the regular members, and we share news, information, and ongoing critiques of our work. You see, that's the benefit of these groups; when they work well, they work very well, and I can't speak highly enough of Writers of Whitstable – for a group to create such a professional book (and this isn't even their first) is a thing of beauty. You can sometimes come across books from writing groups that are a bit wafty in quality, but trust me; I've seen the book, and wafty it ain't.

Good writers' groups are social, objective and constructive, and provide a sense of rigour to your style. There are two camps in the writing world: those who believe it's a competition and those who believe it's a community. In a competitive view, we're all trying to outdo each other, so we are often guarded and cloistered behind our walls. But, if being a writer is about joining a national and international community where we can learn from each other and improve together, then we can all benefit from mutual support. The beauty of a writing group is that it's a built-in community of people like you, eager to improve their craft and help you improve yours.

Sherrie Flick is something of a prolific short story writer; she's written a flash fiction chapbook called *I Call This Flirting*, and a novel called *Reconsidering Happiness*, and this is what she has to say about how she constructs stories:

> *I write very-short short stories; 2,000 words or less. In these stories I try to condense a vivid sense of the world into a small space. I compare the process to shoving an angry black bear into a lunch bag, without ripping the bag.*

One of the most fundamental differences between the short story and the novel is *not* word length. A novel is not a short story that kept going, though a lot of short story writers dream of writing such a story. Neither is a novel a string of stories with a random collection of connective links, sub-plots, and inside jokes and comments. One of the first things the writer learns is how amazingly little room there is in a good novel for padding – for 'stuff' that floats around the outside of the story, artificially puffing it up. In a good short story, the meaning is rather more tightly controlled in the main details of the text. A scene in a short story – and there may be only one – operates with a lot more focus and concentration.

So, the belief that the short story is a poor relation of the novel persists, but it's absurd. Its roots reach back to the very beginning of literature, although the short story as we know it only came to be regarded as a distinct form in the 19th century, with works by Poe, Kleist, Gogol and Turgenev resisting established pigeon-holes. In the 20th century, the short story was the site of as much innovation and great writing as the novel. Consider Joyce, Borges, Kafka, Barthelme, Mansfield, Conrad, Carter, Kipling, Trevor, or (at the risk of repeating myself) King; any of those effectively contributes towards the great literature of the last century.

I think that a good short story is magnificent and captivating, engaging your brain in short, sharp sentences in a way that novels often don't – it's a unique art form all of its own, and we should celebrate it. That's why the Writers of Whitstable are so wonderful; they are celebrating the art form with a collection of brilliant stories – believe me, I've read every single one at least twice, and couldn't put them down. These writers deserve the kudos that comes with bringing this collection together; they are talented individuals who are working collaboratively to bring this collection to life. I applaud them, and I urge you to pick your time to read these stories carefully – you'll be cursing yourself if you have to put the book down and come back to it later.

Breath of Fresh Air

by Nick Hayes

He held his breath as the news came on. It wasn't good news – in any sense. First there had been Brexit – a disaster in waiting as the xenophobes took over the asylum. Now, across the water, the radio waves brought the impossible. It was possible – President Trump.

He let his breath ease out from his chest. The day suddenly felt a lot gloomier. In the eighties he remembered going to bed in fear of the mushroom cloud. His dreams had been haunted by the hideous consequences of fallout. What would be the fallout of this latest election? he mused humourlessly.

With the mess in the Middle East growing and Russia flexing its muscles, the luxury of a peaceful Europe and a stable globe began to look a lot more fragile. But what could he do?

As he dressed, tended to the children and sparred with his wife, he had few moments to ponder on his helplessness. He was just a teacher in a secondary school in Canterbury. What difference could he make? There were days when he could barely get the children to eat their cereal, let alone change the global political climate.

He shook his head as he ushered the children out the door and into the car. His wife urged him to get moving but he paused on the drive for a second. In the winter sky the sun was shining brightly despite the chill. He squinted at the sun as his wife's words faded into the background. He gazed at the brightest light and thought for a second he saw something...

'Let's go!' She tugged at his arm and the moment had passed.

He suddenly realised he had been holding his breath again. Gathering himself together he blew out a long stream of cool air. He was back in the present.

He couldn't bear to listen to the radio on the way to the children's party. While the world was going to hell in a handcart, he was going to the Bowling Alley to celebrate his little daughter's birthday with her school chums. The fact that all the lights were green on the way gave him scant satisfaction.

The Bowling Alley was a perfectly depressing venue for such a day. It lacked any natural light. It lacked any fresh air. The colour and cheer the interior design once had, had long since faded. The sounds of the balls colliding, and the squeals of children, echoed harshly around the space. The refreshments brought little relief for agitated adults. This was an attraction locked in decades past.

Of course, the children saw none of this and happily converged on the lanes to play their game while the adults organised presents and squash. He could feel a heaviness as he sipped on the coffee and tried to shrug off the gloom of the day's news. His wife was attending to a crying girl who had dropped a ball on her toe. He was alone with his thoughts.

He was taken back to the sun. There was something there, he knew there was. He wasn't able to articulate to himself just what he saw. His eyes had been dazzled. Everyone knew you shouldn't gaze at the sun so what was he thinking of?

Precisely as he grappled with these thoughts, he felt a breeze pass over him. Sitting in the middle of the venue, locked away from the outside world, away from nature, detached from the elements, he felt the soothing caress of a breeze. This was no draft; he was far from any exit. This was a breeze that swept past him and away into the cosmos.

He was frozen as his sensations prickled. He frantically looked around him to see if anyone else had reacted. There had been nothing. He knew what he had felt – he looked about him for vents or openings or fans or anything. He could find nothing.

First the sun and now the wind, he thought to himself. While he had started the day with gloom, he felt strangely calmed by the weirdness. He felt that somehow he had embarked on a journey and presently only he was on board. There was a pool of calm after the breeze. All the sounds and fuss of the bowling drained away and he savoured the kiss of the breeze.

Then it happened and he knew things wouldn't be the same again.

There were ten alleys at the venue and the bowlers suddenly all approached to bowl at exactly the same time. All shapes and sizes, the bowlers each steadied themselves and like some bizarrely choreographed dance simultaneously let the balls fly. Each ball swept down the alley at the same unnatural speed and with the same conclusion – each set of pins was toppled in a deafening clatter. The screens called out Strike ten times. Strike! Strike! The hall was in joyous uproar!

He needed to clear his head – there were adults tending to the hooting children but he needed space to think. What was going on?

Outside the Bowling Alley, he expected the fresh air to shake him back to normality but he was greeted with complete calm. There was a peculiar stillness despite the proximity to the beach and seafront. This time he almost expected it. The breeze came and swirled around him. He smiled to himself and waggled his fingers through the strange air.

And it happened.

Outside in the car park there was a vast expanse of sky visible in each direction. In the sky, there now emerged the largest flock of birds of every description. This was no swathe of starlings but contained blackbirds, sparrows, sea gulls, crows, magpies and woodpeckers in some sort of huge super flock. The birds were in the air and swooping and swirling in an amazing dance of delight. Those people outside were swept

7

up in the wonder of the display.

Seconds later, this stupendously diverse collection had completed their aerial performance and set themselves down on the rooftops. That was when they opened their hearts and sang the most sensational chorus over the streets of the town. People stopped and sighed in awe. The sound was magical.

Things were clearly moving now and he mounted the steps to the beach expecting to see something wonderful. He was not disappointed. The sea was becalmed like a sheet of polished marble. Yet those out dog walking and promenading were not taking in the calm. They were pointing to the ripples that broke the glassy surface.

Never before and never again would dolphins leap from the ocean like this. The beautiful beasts leapt and span for the audience on land. Elsewhere, smaller fish broke the surface and jumped into the air as if to mimic the diving dolphins. Back and forth they swam, in and out the water, the silence broken only as the leaps broke the surface.

It was certainly moving now. As he walked back, everywhere people were talking to each other and shaking hands. There were tears in their eyes as they recounted what they saw. People weren't just chatting but they were connecting. Strangers were hugging each other and sharing their tears – all along the seafront and in the streets and in the car park. Everywhere he looked he could see people in touch with one another.

The birthday party was soon to come to an end and he unlocked the car in readiness to receive them. The breeze swept a final time. He smiled and slipped inside the car. He flicked on the radio.

There was good news. News about some strange happenings. People were singing on the news. People were crying with joy. This was going to be a good day.

A Certain Purple Hue

by John Wilkins

'I can tell you what the first job I ever had was. It affected my whole life.'

'More than marrying me?' said Sara, my wife.

'If I hadn't got that job, I might not have married you.'

'Oh, c'mon, Tim!' she said, followed up with her arched eyebrow look, which meant Sara wouldn't buy it, not without a good story to back it up.

'It's true, Sara.' Then I looked away from her to Emma, our fifteen-year-old daughter, as she glanced up from her mobile phone that she clasped with both hands; as if that would hasten the hoped-for text from her boyfriend. I pulled up a chair and sat down opposite her at the kitchen table.

'I think I've upset your mum, Emma.'

'So you're telling us that you getting that first job helped you marry Mum? I want the full story, Dad. The whole picture – nothing left out,' Emma replied. 'That's if you can remember that far back,' she added.

'Yes, I can, thank you – it's a memory that I won't ever lose,' I said hoping to put her in her place.

'You're privileged, Emm – I haven't heard this one before,' Sara interjected, before Emma could tease me any more.

'Pour me another glass of wine, Tim, I think I'm going to need it,' Sara added.

'Can I have one too, Dad?' Emma ventured.

'Oh, let her just this once, Tim. It is a special day,' Sara pleaded on Emma's behalf. I knew I couldn't win.

'Well, only if both of you don't interrupt me while I'm telling the tale,' I said, knowing they wouldn't push me much further with the teasing. They both knew how far they could go.

'Err… Once upon a time…' said Sarah, interrupting the images that had started to appear in my head as I recalled the day I wanted to tell them about.

'Thank you, Sarah. Just because you know there is a happy ending! I'll start with how I found out about the job in the first place. In the newsagent's window in the middle of Harbour Street, there was a card with *help with errands wanted – apply within.*'

I settled into storytelling mode.

I needed a job to get pocket money – no one was just going to give it to me. This could be the way to get some cash.

First I had to deal with the girl behind the counter, who was two years above me at school. She thought she was superior, I thought she was gorgeous, so we had to get past the staring at each other bit first before she told about the job.

'Teresa and Simon are looking for somebody – my brother used to help them out but he's got a part-time job at Tesco's now and he gets staff discount,' she told me and then she handed over a card with a name and telephone number on it.

'Thank you,' I said, hoping that I could go now and get the job.

'They need somebody who's reliable and can start straight away,' I heard her say as I left the shop. I rode back home on my bike as if my life depended on it. I went around to see them the same afternoon.

The house was one in the middle of a terrace called Corn-wallis Circle. It was the only one with a deep purple painted door and a Victorian brass door knocker in the shape of a dragon's head. The curtains in the adjacent front window had very different patterns from those that my parents had – when you looked closely it seemed there were faces all looking at you, but when I went closer they seemed to fade and the outline of eyes looking back out made me jump when I heard the door open.

A woman stood there in jeans and a yellow tee shirt. She had brown hair and lots of freckles. What fixed me on the step staring at her was the gaze she held. I couldn't move, not until she wanted me to.

Before I managed to say anything, she spoke. 'The shop told me you are interested in helping us out. Tim, isn't it?' Her voice soothed and commanded at the same time.

I said yes before I realised. She turned into the house leaving me to follow her into the tiny hall and then turn right past the stairs underneath an arch, and then I was in a study area with books surrounding a round table. The kitchen facilities were the other side of the table looking out on a short narrow garden crammed with trees and ferns with a round pond in the middle.

She introduced herself as Teresa and then I heard a door open and a man came in from the garden. I was introduced to Simon. He was very tall with sandy hair and round glasses which he peeked over the top of, as if to say he didn't believe what he had just been told.

'Let me introduce you, Tim. This is Simon – he needs you to do the errands and other tasks that I refuse to spend my time doing,' Teresa said with a laugh. Then she winked at him and he turned red in the face.

I had never met anyone like them and I wanted the job badly. So I offered to start straight away – that Saturday afternoon. I didn't think twice.

'Great!' they both said together. Simon said, 'There is some shopping if you don't mind that.'

My first errand was to go and collect some cheese they had ordered from a shop in Harbour Street. When I told them I had come to collect an order for Teresa, a brown carrier bag was put in my hands very quickly with a smile and the request made that I give Teresa and Simon their best wishes.

They were a lovely couple, Simon and Teresa. Simon had retired early from a high-pressured job in the civil service, and didn't seem unhappy with his decision. Teresa, well there was a mystery. She made jewellery, earrings, to be specific. She mounted them neatly on boards covered in a soft grey material, I think because that made the colours of the earrings really stand out. They were much sought after when she had stalls during the summers in the harbour market at the Oyster Festival and in the winters at the Whitstable Castle craft fairs.

She also gave tarot card readings when most of the earrings had been sold. There was a legend that if you wanted to contact anyone who had passed over, then you asked Teresa. Her customers claimed it was just like dialling a number on your mobile because she was so effective in reaching the 'other side'. She gave an immediate answer to any question you might ask in private sessions.

The biggest mystery about the two of them was how they got together in the first place. She was the artist with a degree in fine art from the old Canterbury Art College. Simon was the retired career civil servant with the chess board always on the kitchen table, while he attempted the daily chess puzzles in the newspapers I fetched for him.

I ran regular errands for them. My mum was pleased I was helping them – they paid me, so she didn't have to give me pocket money and put further strain on her modest income. Sometimes Teresa sent me to George's to get card and glue so that she could make up the display cards for her earrings. I could stare for ages at the coloured stones she used, at least until Teresa broke the spell they held me under every time I looked at them.

I had my favourite colour, which I was drawn to without fail every time I saw the earrings – they were in a special frame on the mantelpiece in their sitting room at the front of the house. It was a deep purple, unlike any other purple I had ever seen, and I saw something different every time I looked at it. She only ever made one set of earrings using that colour, at least that I knew of. Both Simon and I held the same opinion about those earrings. We told her that they were so special, that they should be priced to reflect their unusual quality. Presented in the sort of display box that was kept on the mantelpiece, they might fetch a very good price indeed – if she offered them to one of the upmarket boutiques in Harbour Street.

Teresa didn't agree. She had a very clear idea about the earrings and what should happen to them. The morning Simon and I begged her to sell them at a price that we thought reflected how unique the purple colour was, Teresa was very definite about the future of the earrings. 'I am never going to sell them, Simon,' she told him, in a way that made me feel it would be stupid to even contemplate selling them.

'Well, what are you going to do with them then?' Simon asked her.

Teresa looked at Simon – it was a while before she spoke. I remember her looking down before she replied. Looking back, I think now that she wanted to draw on some strength to confront our wishes for the earrings, in a way that would discourage us from any further debate. She achieved that aim when she did speak. 'After I'm gone, Simon, you will keep them to remind you of the first smile I ever gave you.'

Then without acknowledging Simon's reaction at all, she turned to look directly at me and explained what she wanted me to do. 'Tim, you can come back and visit Simon. When you have met the girl you want to marry, you must ask him to give you the earrings so that she can wear them on your wedding day. I will know if you have found the bride who is right for you.' She laughed for a while, presumably at the expressions she saw on our faces.

'Oh well,' said Simon, which I understood meant that he knew it would be useless to try to change her mind. She had made her mind up and was not going to try and make a good profit by selling the earrings.

Simon and I reluctantly accepted her terms for the future of the earrings. Neither of us wanted to consider a time without Teresa. From that day on until I finished running errands for them, I looked at those earrings with all sorts of half formed dreams in my head.

I ran errands for quite a while for Simon and Teresa, but the day came when I left Whitstable to go to university. Although I kept in touch, my visits were less frequent as my life moved on and eventually I settled for a career in London, and moved away completely. I still came back down to Whitstable, and always I asked how they were doing. I was sad when I heard Teresa had died.

When I came down with the girl I hoped to marry (Sara, your mum) to introduce her to my parents, we stayed at the Marine Hotel in Tankerton. I had a restless night and so I left Sara, and walked along the slopes on my way to buy a paper. It was the sort of errand I used to run for Simon and Teresa, I remembered, when I bought the paper from the mini market by Tankerton Circus, after picking up the fresh rolls from the baker's across the road next to the barber's.

As I came out of the mini market I saw a woman walk past me. She was wearing Teresa's purple earrings. I knew the colour. I snatched a second glance. Were they Teresa's earrings enriched with a certain purple hue? I had to see Simon. I had felt a shock – as if someone had walked over my grave – that was how my mother would have described the sensation that gripped me.

I felt cold and yet I was sweating. I needed to see Simon – it was the time of day he was usually up and ready to challenge the chess puzzle in the daily paper that I used to deliver to him. It was more than a mile but I ran there without even noticing how far it was. I ran all the way to Simon and Teresa's house, to find Simon sitting there looking at the purple earrings in the setting I remembered them. He looked up at me and his words sent a chill through me.

'Teresa told me you had found the right woman, Tim.'

I knew then for certain that Sara would be the woman I would marry.

Laughter on the Marsh

Springtime in Oare

by Kim Miller

The tide's in, the sun's out and I'm going to join them.

I practically plunge out of the door, as spry as the new spring. As the warm air hits the bare skin of my arms and its fragrance hits my nostrils it's confirmed – climatic kindness has returned.

I set off down my road excited to see how the flora and fauna are flourishing in the new season I hope this lovely day heralds.

St Peter's charming, ancient church seems happy with the sun on its stone and I jiggle my way through the slightly sticking gate into a churchyard that must surely have one of the best views from any churchyard in the country; and it's certainly got its glad rags on today. Miles of marsh with shimmering creek and boats and Whitstable in the distance with the North Sea beyond.

After this diversion I press on down the road past bud-bursting hedgerows. The fresh, green verges at their feet are sprinkled with bright Celandine and, my favourite, Greater Stitchwort, unpretentious and cheerful with the breeze bouncing them about in the springy foils of grass.

At the summit of the short incline the view spreads out from my feet: green land and the shared blue of sky and water. I'm fond of the pylons here, firmly planted and elegantly strung, individually standing their ground and collectively determined to push on into the distance. The off-shore wind farm just down the coast is all imposing spikiness, but the huge poles and sails have industrial elegance too.

The land feels ancient here with roads and lanes crossing the fields like old tracks; you're in the fields, not peering at them over hedges, and always aware of the visible distance and the invisible distance beyond.

At the cottages the road bends, then shoots out straight in front across the marsh to the Swale. The soft undulations of the fields are replaced by an iron-flat land of water and wildlife. Bird hides dot the landscape and are well used by bird watchers (along with the paths and verges), to set up their equipment.

The bird population is fantastic and attracts serious bird-watchers who dress themselves and their equipment in matching waterproof camouflage. But tripods and lenses as long and as thick as your arm aren't a necessity. Naked-eye amateurs like me can get lots of pleasure from identifying a curlew or from the breath-holding glamour of a big bird of prey that never becomes matter of fact.

A shoulder-high tangled line of bramble stops and is replaced with a cow's face which proves, with another couple of steps, to be part of a small herd of cows in the corner by the wire fence. I assume they're waiting for lunch and not especially for me so I give them a cheery 'hullo' and pass by.

The frogs are going mad! They are Hungarian Marsh Frogs, also known as laughing frogs. Bigger and brighter than native frogs, with voices to match. Talk about a chorus; they can be heard throughout the day and in the evening whenever you're outside in the spring. It's a surprise and a delight every year to find that I haven't misremembered this joyous racket and have several weeks of it to look forward to.

A few years ago the Kent Wildlife Trust introduced Konik ponies to the marshes and I can see them a hundred yards or so off to the left. I stop to watch them for a while with a moorhen and a swan in the dyke for company, neither of them having any interest in me or in each other.

On the opposite side of the narrow road a retirement bird-watcher shares my view of the cormorants and coots and we nod and half smile; his companion reads a book in the car.

The clarity of the air and the pin-sharp sunlight are highlighting every reed, bird and boat. The water goes on and on, estuary becoming sea and fading into the sky so I can't tell if it falls off the edge of the world or goes on forever.

It's the first day for a while the weather hasn't been too cold to put my hands in the never-ending, polished glass gush of the artesian well and have a couple of mouthfuls of the silky, shining water.

Shaking the water off my hands I head for the rise of the road over the sea wall. The estuary is immediately in front of me, the pressing tide filling all the space it can, the fields of Sheppey opposite. The line of the causeway is marked by an avenue of tall rustic posts; some have a characterful skew as though drunk on brine. The sun behind the sea wall makes a moving silhouette of a woman and a dog heading away from me, the dog running off in front of her and back again.

I scan the surface of the water hoping for the bobbing head of a seal, which I have been lucky enough to see from this spot before, but not today.

The breeze lightly ruffles the water's surface, it's gently tousled but not whipped up, the colour isn't varied by white tips, or shadows made by tiny waves. I've been here for some time now as I always am. I find it so hard to leave the special light and sound this place has whatever the weather. A few inches of exposed wet causeway concrete tells me that the tide is on the turn – I know I can't stay forever so force myself along the path eastwards on the sea wall.

There's a bird hide on the sharp corner, looking out into the collaborating blue of sky and water, that, like all the hides, is crying out to be settled into with a cheese and pickle sandwich and a thermos.

The frogs are off again! Building from a single call and answer to froggy surround sound; not the prettiest noise but full and abandoned and grin-inducing. This landscape excites or pleases or impresses me with something every day. The sky, too, is vast and always gorgeous, lively or dramatic with stunning light and a before and after of coming and going weather.

Wispy-topped stalks waft and lean in the slightest breeze creating coppery air-fluff above a ribbon of ink alongside the grass path that follows the creek back to the village. The confluence of Oare and Faversham creeks makes a headland, known as Hollow Shore, containing a boat yard and the Shipwright's Arms – ancient, beamy and a CAMRA favourite.

Thames barges are a fine and common sight on these waters and today I'm pleased to see two of these spirited 'grandes dames' moored together on the opposite bank, sails furled and tall masts jabbing at the heavens like spires.

The flat land to the right is still flooded from the excesses of the winter and is enough to support a couple of swans; the sun on the water and their deep white is simply beautiful. Watching them I wonder, not for the first time, about their feet that get such publicity, paddling madly beneath the surface. Unconvinced, in the light of their enormous feet, I have tried to look into it and can find no evidence to support the claim – it seems they lazily waft their legs about, just as you would imagine, if other ideas hadn't been put in your head!

The village rises up keeping its centuries-old lookout for friends and foe coming across land and water. The tide is certainly in retreat now from these farther reaches of the creek, and the faintly disturbed layer at the top appears detached, like a metallic plate sliding across the surface of the main body of water, adding drama but having little effect on the line of moored boats. With no wind to speak of there's no clanking rigging today, no noises carried from the motorised world, just bird sounds and my footsteps on the crunchy path that leads to the gate.

Crossing the corner of the field to the village street, the Castle Inn, an unpretentious pub, greets me and the Three Mariners, historic and with a reputation for its food, is only moments further on. Though hungry and thirsty, I stop at neither today and lose some of my breath going up the hills to home and a date with a large glass of iced squash, a bit of lunch and the fabulous view that will tempt me out again and again.

The Beast of Blean

by James Dutch

I'd already told Finn several times to stop bothering me. I was trying to clear up, make lunch and get Katie's stuff ready for Baby Ballet; to call it ballet was ridiculous, but it tired her out and made sure she had her all-important afternoon nap – she was such a determined, active toddler. Anyway, Finn kept on and on – *Mum, can I go in the garden and play football? Mum, where's my football? Mum, can you unlock the back door? Mum, Mum, Mum!*

I'd snapped and told him to be quiet or there would be no television later. He'd done his pouty bottom lip and puppy dog eyes, and I forced myself to stop for a moment – he was only five after all. I unlocked the back door, got his football from the cupboard under the stairs, kissed his head and told him not to walk any mud back indoors. It had been raining overnight and our shaded garden had become somewhat swampy, as it backed on to one of the little streams running through the woods.

I checked in on Katie – she had removed all her toys from the toy chest and was now inside it, gleefully gumming on a plastic penguin – and returned to the kitchen. As I began washing the dishes I could hear Finn kicking the ball and cheering himself on, and it made me smile. He was a good boy, just like his dad in so many ways; but thinking of my husband was still painful. We'd lost Jeff the previous year – he had just started working for a tiger conservation group in Bangladesh, helping them set up a new project in the Sundarbans mangrove forest, when a tiger had attacked and killed him. They had hunted down and killed the tiger they thought was responsible for the attack, but that had made it even sadder for me. Throughout all my sorrow, grief and anger, I had never blamed the animal; it was just doing what came naturally. I wiped my eye with the dry part of my forearm and smiled at the sound of Finn's running commentary.

Finn had been terribly upset, he was only four at the time and started having nightmares about tigers and lions trying to attack him ever since. I told him, the only big cats around here are securely locked up, but he remained unconvinced. There are three animal parks nearby; over the years we'd had memberships at each one, but my favourite was Wingham – I really enjoyed that one. I loved the penguins, but Jeff would always be gazing off in the opposite direction towards the tigers, whispering big cat science in Finn's uncomprehending ear. He had mixed emotions, all too aware of the need for conservation, but deeply sympathetic toward the imprisoned king and queen of the jungle.

After Jeff died, Finn wasn't ready to see wild animals in the flesh – even if they were behind bars. In fact, it had taken me several months just to persuade him that it was safe to go into our garden; he'd been terrified that something was going to be lurking in the woods, waiting for him to turn his back. Before Jeff died, the two of them would spend hours together in the Blean – making dens, watching the huge nests of wood ants, tracking make-believe beasts; it felt like an extension of our home, our family belonged there.

It was just as I was trying to recall which of the other wildlife parks had tigers when I heard a muffled crashing sound, like someone falling fast through the branches of a tree in full leaf. It was followed by a dull thud, and then a pitiful, half-strangled mewling which stood the hairs on the back of my neck to attention. In my mind, I saw an image of my little boy falling out of a tree, but it was an unlikely vision – Finn was not a climber. I shouted out to him: 'Are you okay, love?' The silence which answered was worse than any amount of crying. I dried my hands quickly on the tea towel before rushing through the living room towards the back door. I glanced over at Katie, who was now sitting on the rug, play-reading her favourite book, *The Tiger who came to Tea*; a cold shiver ran up my neck and tightened my scalp.

I opened the back door in time to see Finn's football come to the end of its roll on the grass. My eyes darted frantically around into each dark corner of the garden, searching for Finn. Under the tree. In the play-house. Down the side of the shed. But other than discarded toys, there was no sign of him. My heartbeat fell into a heavy, sluggish beat that reverberated through my chest, and I couldn't breathe. Clutching at the door frame to steady myself, I caught a glimpse of movement in the shadows. I focused like a hawk, details sharpened by adrenaline; my breathing became shallow and fast, and the blood in my veins felt like it was being drawn from my body. The tip of a thick, powerful tail flicked high, then low towards the ground with muscular fluidity, before disappearing through a freshly torn gap in a shaded part of the hedge. I heard a low, rumbling, breathy growl. I know I did.

I screamed Finn's name and ran at the hedge, on the way collecting a red and white plastic golf club, which had been abandoned on the patio and in my instinctive rush seemed the only suitable weapon along my path. I dived into the sticky, brown earth and crawled on all fours through to the other side of the privet and through the shallow, boggy ditch following a sweet, musky smell into my own private nightmare. Full of rage, fear and self-doubt, I shouted for Finn again. Had I really seen what I thought? It wasn't possible, surely. Finn must be playing… 'Finn!' I called, trying to stop myself from shrieking. 'You know not to come out of the garden!' But I was struggling against my instincts, and the rational, thoughtful part of my brain had been bypassed – I began to run into the wood, my slippers doing as their name promised along the leaf-strewn track, until my mind caught up with me, and I remembered Katie, unsupervised.

I realised then that I couldn't smell anything other than wet woodland, and began to doubt if I had picked up a scent earlier, or whether it was my subconscious recalling a fascinated Jeff saying *their urine smells like buttered popcorn!* I let the plastic golf club drop to the ground, picked my way back along the track in a blinkered daze, and pulled myself back through the hedge into the garden where I found that Katie had crawled out of the back door and was happily chewing her book on the damp grass.

The police arrived at the scene quickly, but remained unconvinced by my story. *There are no tigers in Blean woods, Madam. Are you sure you're quite all right, Madam? Do any of your neighbours own cats, Madam? Is there someone who can look after your daughter for you, Madam? Are you taking any medication, Madam?* I was sitting there, mud-smeared and shivering, wondering why there were so many questions. One of the police officers had a cursory glance around the garden and hadn't found any trace of a tiger, but I pleaded with them until, with an eyebrow raised to his colleague, he went out again for another look. Still nothing, apart from a hole in the hedge and a mess of smeared mud – *like something was dragged through*, the officer remarked.

Still, a young child had gone missing. A helicopter with thermal imaging cameras was deployed, and police with dogs stumbled through the woods like a colony of clumsy ants, but they found nothing before the evening closed in and the search was postponed until first light. But I couldn't just do nothing. That night, I stood in the freezing cold at the back of the garden, panic rising in tides over a shore of hopelessness. I called out for the blackness of the woods to return my child, but his name was swallowed up by a deep, knowing silence. When I could no longer feel my feet, I knelt, and when my throat became too hoarse to continue, I clapped my hands to create a homing signal. No one came.

In true local newspaper tradition, it was a man out walking his dog who found one of Finn's trainers the following morning less than a mile from our house. The police closed off a large area of the woods; tracking experts were consulted and the local wildlife parks, after counting and re-counting their big cats, volunteered their most knowledgeable staff to help police. But after a few days, there was still no trace of a big cat and, apart from that one muddy shoe, no sign of my son. The search was scaled down, previously diverted police resources were sent back to traffic duty, bar brawls and white-collar crime – although they told me that they were *still doing everything we can, Madam*. People began to lose interest, and eventually, Finn's disappearance became yet another tragic, soon-to-be-forgotten story.

I didn't shout loudly enough about it. Maybe I should have, but I still had Katie to look after, and I needed to try and keep my sanity. There was no evidence of a tiger, other than in my witness statement, and the police began to ask me lots of questions – questions that made it clear they wavered between suspecting me of having a mental illness or of somehow harming my son; the house was searched three times and I felt like I was under constant scrutiny. The detective in charge suggested, while smiling sympathetically, that the manner in which my husband was killed could have been instrumental in my conviction that a *wildcat* had taken Finn. I hated the detective for that comment.

The six months immediately after Finn being taken were the worst of my life. I was consumed by a relentless grief, a hollow feeling in the centre of my chest. Every time I tried to sleep, every time I closed my eyes, I would see Finn's big brown eyes looking up at me, begging to let him play in the garden. And every time, I heard myself relent to his pestering – it was my fault. Then there was the press attention; journalists crawling like maggots around the smell of death, the smell of a story; their persistence felt like a chronic illness that I'd never be able to shake off. I gave one press conference early on – a plea for help finding Finn, but a subsequent comment piece about missing persons, their loved ones and press conferences written in one of the national papers, titled '*The Killers Who Say Come Home*' made my lips tight.

Katie kept me going through it all. Her dark, intelligent eyes, her joy at seeing me each morning, her constant, wonderful, illogical babbling. She became the only ray of light during those dim times; to say that she was my reason for living would not be an exaggeration. After a while, the media circus began to fade away, and I started to actually open up and engage with my counsellor. We moved house of course, Katie and me, but only to the opposite end of Canterbury – I couldn't bear to move too far from the place Jeff and Finn had both loved.

All that happened sixteen years ago. There's still not a day that goes by without me thinking of Finn, and I still taste the fear and feel the chest-crushing panic whenever some incon-sequential little nothing stirs up the embers of memory and I unwillingly recall that specific moment I realised he was gone. Through it all, I hope I did a good job raising Katie. It was hard to let her grow up without constantly keeping check on her, and there were sad times, too. She would often gaze at the framed photographs of Jeff and Finn and ask who they were, and why their pictures were in our house. I would sit her on my lap and tell her about her wonderful father and angelic brother – and about tigers. It seemed important; somehow their story would be incomplete without mention of the powerful beasts. These conversations were often tearful, but did my best to fill them with joy. By the age of six, Katie had started bringing a tissue with her whenever she wanted to talk about Finn and Daddy, and used it to pat my cheeks, soaking up my saltwater sorrow.

Time passed, and my beautiful little girl turned into a young woman. She's still the same dark eyed, intelligent, energetic girl she's always been, always burning bright – passionate about animals, volunteering for this or that, dragging me along half the time, too: clearing litter from the River Stour, coppicing at

Larkey Valley Wood – we even did a bat survey last year. This morning I dropped Katie off at the college car park – she fizzed with excitement as she practically skipped into the building – and then I drove to a quiet side road and, with a mixture of pride, grief and happiness, let the tears come. Very early on in life, Katie had direction. She knew what she wanted to do, and had been making plans for the past few years; today she began a course in Animal Biology and Wildlife Conservation at college. After that, she plans to go to university to further her studies. I've stopped asking her to consider other things, or to get an alternative qualification *to fall back on* – yes I really did say that to her, and it still makes me cringe. Because her answer is always the same – it's the one she's been giving me for the past ten years: 'I'm going to work with tigers, just like my daddy!'

Losing Faith, Finding Hope

by Jeffrey George

Never look back

Steve smiled at the twenty-something on reception at Margate's Turner Contemporary, and she blushed. He sauntered across.

'Is there another guided tour today?' he asked, noting her name-badge.

'Er, no,' she said, gazing up. 'The next is on Tuesday.'

He grinned. 'Will you lead it?'

'No, I'm Wednesday.'

'Well then, Lucy Wednesday, I'll see you at...'

'Eleven.'

He spun around and flip-flopped towards the exit, imagining her cute eyes, framed by that dart of an impish hairstyle, following his departure. The automatic doors swished open, and he left the art gallery without looking back. He never looked back, not any more. Down the steps, his chest out, stomach in, he gazed across the bay. Tall, toned and tanned, he ambled along the harbour arm. A kid on a scooter whizzed past, and Steve winked at the child's mother as she scuttled after him. I need real ale, he thought.

'A pint of Canterbury Millers, please.'

'Good choice,' came the gruff reply.

More shack than bar, Steve mused, but well-kept barrels and a welcoming smile.

'There you go, sir. That'll be three pounds fifty.'

Steve handed him a fiver and said, 'Keep the change.'

'Very generous, squire. Thank you.'

Steve sat at a large wooden bench outside and laughed: generous! He simply didn't want the outline of coins spoiling the fine line of his Bermuda shorts. He eased back and planted his size-eleven feet wide apart, commandeering his side of the bench. Fading sunlight glinted off the incoming tide that lifted the half-dozen boats from their sandy slumber. Soulful notes of a jazz guitarist carried from the Fisherman's Arms. Steve watched two women stop to scan the bar, and the salty smell of the sea yielded to the scent of CK One.

'Fancy a cider?' one asked.

'Why not, it is Sunday.'

Indeed, Steve thought, he didn't normally do Sundays. Why mingle with the masses when every day is a holiday for someone who doesn't need to work, every encounter an opportunity for someone so single? And everywhere he looked, he found only possibilities.

'The cider's fresh from the barrel,' he said and beamed. 'You'll love it.'

'Oh, right,' the blonde said, removing her sunglasses.

Steve's blue eyes warmed to the glint from hers of hazel. Contact: that's why he never wore shades. She smiled and entered the bar. Her friend winked and followed. He ruffled his short black hair, glad he'd tinted away the grey. How many decades since he'd last flirted? How smooth was he for a sexagenarian? The word made him grin, then frown; how successful would he be? Well, you never know, he thought, and slyly popped a Viagra. When the two women returned, he stood up.

'Hi, I'm Steve.'

'Angela,' the blonde replied and held out a tanned, ringless, wrinkled hand.

'Liz,' the brunette added, propped her walking stick against the bench and accepted his handshake.

'Please, join me and tell me how you find the cider?'

As they chatted, Angela offered a playful smile, but instead of encouraging Steve, it scared him. Back home, he desired intimacy. Now, close to success, his confidence waned. Mad: out on the pull at his age.

'You're very fit,' Angela said.

'Thank you: running, yoga. You're trim yourself.'

'Spin classes, that's where we met.'

'And that's where I twisted my ankle and fell. The instructor was dying to get me flat on my back,' Liz said and grinned.

Steve enjoyed her wicked sense of humour and wondered where it might lead, but didn't allow his hopes to soar, even though she'd reached across to touch his hand. What about Angela? She may be in her fifties but still radiated feminine allure. No, he was just a lonely fool, and his grey matter was slowing as badly as his jogging. More likely, it was ale hitting the spot, Liz's crocodile charm and Angela's social smile.

But Liz said, 'Do come to our place for early evening cocktails. Angela makes the most exquisite martinis.'

A drink in a bar was fun, but their place? Theirs? He considered making his excuses, thanking them for their company, but a vodka martini was his favourite drink; had he said? What would his sons think if they saw him? Faith, their mother, his wife, had passed away a few years ago, so it shouldn't be too soon, but he doubted they realised he still had sexual needs. Steve wasn't sure his youngest, Dave, was even active. Their beautiful mistake had just turned eighteen but wasn't going steady yet. His eldest, Harry, had enjoyed a string of girls, but none lasted.

'I am partial to a vodka martini,' Steve said. 'I'd love to join you.'

Serial Monogamy

Harry threw his sports bag onto the passenger seat and jumped into his Merc. He breathed in the warm evening air: August bliss with the top down. An hour and a half's yoga with Summer Rayne, the visiting American instructor, had left him feeling alive yet chilled. He pumped the accelerator and grinned, then spotted the petite lithe blonde emerge from the gym and head for a hire car.

'Hey, Summer,' he called. 'Awesome class.'

'Glad you enjoyed it. See you again?'

'You bet,' he said, selected first and made for the exit.

He'd always thought yoga required blue-rinse hair, crossed legs and Om chanting, but Summer's classes were vibrant, dynamic and drew the hottest fittest chicks in Thanet. Admittedly, some were a few years older, others younger, but society accepted age differences more readily now. His parents had both been twenty-two when they'd met and married within the year. Harry had been keen on cute Karen and soft on sexy Sara in his twenties, but it had seemed too soon. Now in his thirties, was it time to settle down? The last couple of years, he'd started several relationships destined for short-term failure. Why? Anyway, he now had the mobile numbers of three gorgeous yoginis and he'd definitely take another class or two before Summer headed back stateside. In his rear-view mirror he watched her wave with both hands; sweet, those southern girls. Headlights shone, and a car pulled out behind. He followed the slip road towards Westwood Cross. Did he need anything from Tesco? No, straight home. He turned right for St Peters, Broadstairs.

The car behind flashed. What? He wasn't speeding. He took the roundabout and checked: a red Fiesta on his tail. Past the school, past Asda, it stayed close. Another burst of full beam. Why? He was still under 30 mph. Of course: he drove an SLC 200 sport; they were carjackers! So it didn't only happen in the US? Over the roundabout, he bounced speed bumps. Metal grated on tarmac and he cringed, but accelerated into St Peters and made a sharp right. He pumped the gas again; now he sped. An Audi hooted as he cut in front and raced towards home. The Fiesta had no chance, clogged in the honking confusion. Right, left, right: almost there.

Left into his cul-de-sac of 21 houses, he pressed the garage remote and the door rose. Why was it so dark? No headlights. Shit! Was that why they'd flashed? He eased inside, but rushed back out. Another click and the garage closed. He ducked behind his front wall and peered over. A red Fiesta entered his road and came to a halt, the engine running. A minute later it reversed out.

In his kitchen, Harry poured a generous vodka and tonic and began undoing the good of the yoga class. His phone trilled: not his mobile, his landline. No one rang that except his Dad, and it was an unknown number. Even scammers didn't bother any more. He hesitated. The call redirected to his mobile. Should he?

Samba Groove

Dave, Steve's younger son, gazed at the night lights of Ramsgate harbour, then entered The Belgian Café.

'Your round, I think,' Paul greeted, handing Dave his empty glass. 'And the mobile for that girl I told you about,' he whispered, fishing a slip of paper from his back pocket.

'Leffe blonde,' Paul said, and the others followed his lead. 'Stella, Kriek…'

Dave sauntered off to the bar, recently 18 and legal, and reeled off the list. As he waited, he glanced back at his friends.

'How can you recycle 365 used condoms?' Paul asked.

'Yuk, recycle?' one said, and the group fell silent.

'Melt them down, make a tyre and call it a good year.'

Dave snorted a laugh, even though he'd heard Paul crack that one before. Most found it amusing, and their giggles were infectious, but Kayla raised little more than a smile. That pleased Dave. He paid the barman and looked back as he awaited his change. Paul sidled around to Kayla and whispered in her ear. That didn't please Dave. A private conversation while the others recalled last Saturday's outing to Brighton, whooping, slapping backs and high fiving.

'I was up at six.'

'Me, five-thirty.'

'Only so you'd have time to comb your hair.'

'And the rest.'

'Those bacon sarnies on the pier were the best.'

'What about that tapas lunch?'

'Too many cervezas though.'

'Yeah, who fell asleep in the sun?'

'How's your tan, Paul?'

'What?' he said, turning back. 'Had the sense to take off my shades though. Andy looks like the negative of a panda.'

'Eats...' one said.

'Shoots...' added another.

'...and leaves,' Paul finished.

The group broke into laughter.

Dave returned with the first of the drinks.

'Cheers, mate.'

'Nice one.'

'The band at the tapas bar were really chilled, great sounds,' Dave said as he delivered the last pint.

'Too drawn out. All improvisation and no structure,' Paul said.

'Sort of jazz funk,' one said.

'More soul confusion,' another added and they laughed.

'It was samba groove,' Kayla said and smiled at Dave. 'They were amazing.'

'Don't mention samba,' one girl pleaded.

'Thank God the world cup's over.'

'We were never going to get out of the group stages.'

'England couldn't have beaten a team from Costa Coffee let alone Costa Rica,' Paul quipped.

The girl groaned, widened her eyes at Kayla and nodded towards the back. They scuttled off to the toilets as the guys dissected national team selection and one-dimensional tactics.

'I reckon it's...' Dan tried to interject.

'Whatever,' Paul cut across. 'We need a grass roots review.'

'A new academy.'

Dan had another go, then gave up. He seldom got to say

much, but at least he tried. Elaine never said a word. She just sat, listening and watching everyone, especially Paul. Even when they paused for her to speak, she'd take a sip of her drink and look down. Dave tuned out and thought of Kayla. He'd been one of the drivers last week, and when Paul had slipped into his drunken slumber, he'd chatted with her about work and family. It was stilted at first, but he felt they'd started to connect. He hoped so; it had been tough chatting to girls since his mother, Faith, had passed away. He'd been a bit of a mummy's boy, he knew, then suddenly she was gone. And relationships were so fragile; look at his big brother, Harry! Paul tried to help, like with the girl's number on that scrap of paper in his pocket, although she'd probably turn out to be as unsuitable as the rest. Dave didn't want to get close to someone unless... He stole a glance at Paul. He might claim to be a mate, but that cosy tête-à-tête could as easily have been putting down Dave as chatting up Kayla. Or both.

'So you like samba groove,' someone whispered in Dave's ear.

He turned and saw Kayla's smiling face.

Her restroom companion winked, eased past and said, 'Paul, I bet you can't name half a dozen England football players.'

'Come on, who can't?'

'In the women's team,' she added.

'Oh, right. Houghton, Nobbs, Carney...'

'Yeah,' Dave said to Kayla. 'Samba groove is so rhythmic and flowing, it just carries you off on a five-minute adventure.'

'Absolutely.'

'And live, it's such a communal dance experience.'

'Wow, you totally get it. I wish there was more live samba groove,' Kayla said and grinned.

'What about Cafe Loco?'

'I've heard of it. It's supposed to be awesome, but I've no one to go with.'

'Hey, I'd love to take you.'

'Next Saturday?'

'Sure thing... it's a date... right?'

Kayla smiled and Dave beamed. She kissed his cheek, then moved over to her friend, and they shared nods of excitement.

'Oh, there's Williams and that Whoopi Duggan,' Paul shouted.

'Toni Duggan, you plonker.'

Paul grinned. 'Who's that one... you know... that manager's daughter.'

'Natasha Dowie?' Dave called out.

'Yeah, Beaker's daughter,' Paul said and peered as Dave tore a slip of paper into tiny pieces.

'You're the muppet, not him,' someone shouted.

'She's his niece,' Dave corrected. 'And dropped from the squad.'

Paul looked at Kayla, then back at Dave and the scraps of paper.

Dave nodded.

Paul tilted his head. 'My round, I think.'

The Kiss (When Sally met Harry)

Stood in his kitchen, Harry took the call. 'Sorry, who is this?'

'Oh, God.'

'What?'

'We met.'

'Who are you?'

'Sally. From Pilates.'

'Right,' he said and recalled the cute young blonde, not dissimilar to Summer.

'And at folk week, in the Pavilion at Broadstairs.'

'Of course. You!' he said, and it came flooding back. Out on the balcony, she was so adorable, so kissable, so engaged to be married. 'How did you get my number?'

'Oh, I followed you. Then an online phone book; you're not ex-directory.'

Shit! Why hadn't he ticked that box? 'Where are you?'

'Close.'

His heart skipped a beat. A stalker or...?

'I'm driving to you now,' she said, and he heard a quiver in her voice.

He opened his front door. A red Fiesta pulled up. She got out.

'Why?' he said into his phone.

'That kiss.'

Outside for air at folk week, he'd approached her from behind and like a fool, kissed the nape of her neck. Exquisite, he'd said, if only you weren't…

'It stole my heart.'

He'd tried erasing the memory; she'd be someone else he couldn't bear to lose. 'You were beautiful, radiant and with someone.'

'I was. I am. I don't want to be. The wrong one. Just a kiss; it shouldn't but it did.'

Her eyes drew him in, but he hesitated.

'Oh god, I'm such an idiot.' She shook her head. 'It was just a drunken snog.'

'No. I was intoxicated, but not by alcohol. I was Bob, I was driving.'

They both dropped their phones. His shattered, the numbers for three yoginis lost forever. They kissed and he somehow felt like both a teenager and an adult. She took his hand and led him into his house, up his staircase to a bedroom she'd soon consider her own.

Aching Bones

Liz and Angela's apartment was floral and flock, a style Steve and his late dear wife hated, but the martinis were decidedly to his taste: dry and strong. By the third, they were telling risqué jokes, and Angela giggled as she served him and Liz. She came back from the kitchen with her drink and a rollie.

'You smoke?' he blurted. Of course she did, he could see that and now he'd insulted her. 'Roll ups,' he added, digging a deeper hole, and blushed.

She set down her glass, lit up and drew in the smoke. She

passed it to Liz, and his brain twigged as the sweet intoxicating aroma reached his nostrils. He took the spliff and enjoyed a lungful of top-grade marijuana. They were soon sharing a second and in hysterics, but about what? They flopped over each other on the leather three-seater. Angela stroked his cheek and kissed him hard. Liz passed the joint to Angela and took her turn on his lips. And as he enjoyed the last of the hallucinogen, they leant across him to French-kiss each other. His sons wouldn't believe this. He daren't tell them. Once he and Faith… they'd never know about that either.

Liz plucked the faintly glowing stub from his fingers, popped it into a brass ashtray and said, 'Purely for medicinal purposes.'

'Eases aching bones,' Angela added.

'Any aches that need easing?' Liz asked, and they each ran a palm up along one of his thighs.

Thoughts of Lucy Wednesday's tour of the Turner disappeared from his mind.

Standing On Your Own Two Feet

by John Wilkins

A tongue licked my face and I came back up to the surface in Squeezegut Alley, a few minutes' walk from my home in Whitstable.

I was drunk, and my senses were stuck and then loosened as I realised it wasn't anybody's tongue – it was an animal's tongue. That brought me up to the surface smartly, as I opened my eyes fully and saw a terrier in front of my head as I tried to lift it.

My head was held down by a mighty weight – the pain enveloping it was from the contents of the hip flask I had drunk that morning. The hip flask had been filled with the last of the full bottle of whisky I had decided to open earlier on a cold bright Monday. Opening a bottle of whisky at four a.m. to dull the aching pain of the argument with my son last night was all I could come up with. I was tired of it.

As I hadn't drunk a hip flask full of whisky on an empty stomach before, being revived in the alley by a dog after a wasted sojourn spent on the beach earlier didn't seem at all unsurprising; not in the least. That is how drunk I was, accepting it as normal.

Next came the dog's breathing on my face, followed by what seemed an explosion of a bark reverberating off the walls of the narrow alley, named after a policeman who got stuck there chasing a couple of boys with a fistful of stolen sweets. I was grateful when the dog was jerked back out of my face, with enough force to lift its front paws off the ground. I rubbed my eyes so that I could see who had pulled the dog away.

My eyelids couldn't open easily – because they seemed partly held with an irritating sticky tape, just breakable but itchy with the release. Then, when the stickiness went as I kept trying to blink, my eyes could make out somebody behind the dog, holding the lead in a gloved hand. A slim woman stood over me, holding the dog's tartan lead, extending her free hand to help me, as I tried to sit up. A whole universe of aches and pains became apparent as I moved. I needed somebody or something to hold on to, just to get my balance.

Then I heard her speak – I thought I could work out what she was saying now. I thought she said 'Shit!' Then the dog sat and didn't move, allowing her to squat down so that her face was level with mine.

I was being examined by a pair of hazel brown eyes that had seen a lot, possibly even somebody else who had got themselves into trouble for understandable reasons. My reasons were *understandable to me* –

'Are you okay?' A woman, dressed in jeans and anorak and walking shoes, making an effort to talk to me, came fully into focus, just as the walls of the alley warped forward and back above me. I tried to speak but she didn't seem to understand what I was trying to say. Despite the state I was in, she wanted to help me up, and out of the alley; to somewhere I could explain to her how I had finished up there, like that. It was my first reaction – why had she bothered with *me*.

She gradually supported my stumbling frame. Now I could stand up into an almost normal shape for a man of my age. My rescuer knew what she was doing; a dark-haired woman, determined to help me stand up and get me going. I sensed that she had recognised me, that we had met before. But maybe that was what I wanted to think, it was the way my self-delusion worked when I was drunk. I was beginning to come around.

'I'm Melissa, by the way,' she said as we unsteadily edged our way along the narrow alley to emerge eventually into the road at the end.

'Jake – thank you for rescuing me. I don't know how I ended up there,' I tried to say but it didn't come out much like it.

'I think it was whatever you drank from this – it smells like whisky,' she said and gave me the empty hipflask that she must have found near me when she got me back on my feet.

'It isn't my usual breakfast,' was all I managed in reply before she turned so that she stood directly in front of me on the pavement.

'I normally have a coffee in the Beach Café – they allow Rick in there,' Melissa said, as she yanked the lead. 'Won't you join me?'

It wasn't really a question, more of an explanation of what was going to happen next. I was in no fit state to argue, and I wouldn't get very far by myself. I knew that. Embarrassed, because I couldn't walk straight yet, it was wise to accept the invitation. I didn't know what made anyone so kind, the state I was in.

'Thank you, but…' was all I managed to say as I made an effort to continue on my way. She interrupted me before I could get any more words out, briskly turning and with her arm underneath mine, her momentum carried me with her – I fought to stop myself tripping over the dog's lead.

It wasn't a long way to walk to the Beach Cafe – a few minutes, even with me just becoming capable of walking straight. When we arrived at the café, she walked over to a vacant table. She looped the dog's lead under one of the table legs. The dog knew how to behave properly and sat down under the table. By this time, I was just about capable of sitting upright in a chair.

'Coffee?' she said, although I wouldn't have blamed her if she had ordered without asking me. The smell of proper coffee was probably the best way to smother the strong scent of the whisky I felt was emanating from every pore of my skin.

'Please, black would be good,' I responded politely. At least I was beginning to remember my manners. I didn't want to attract further attention from the regular patron over at the corner table shovelling down his full English.

'No argument, it's on me.' Melissa anticipated what I was going to say, before I could speak. As it turned out, it took most of the coffee before I could say enough sentences to explain what had led me to be drunk in the alley when she was on her morning walk with that dog.

'I don't normally get drunk this early,' I tried again – this time it came out so that she could understand.

'I'm sure you have your reasons,' she said. That made me think she did know me from somewhere, but I couldn't remember where. 'I know you don't get as drunk as that very often,' she said with a smile as if she did know me.

I would have remembered that smile, I thought. But I didn't – all I could think was that she had seen me as I strolled past the Continental Hotel down to the life guards' hut and back, most mornings, *sober*.

I was still dazed even after the coffee, but she persuaded me to talk that Monday morning. I rested my elbows on the table and folded my hands around the cup to take away the numbness from them and mumbled on. Sometimes she stopped me and asked me to repeat what I had said, more coherently. She was looking at my torn coat sleeve – the cuff was flopping down. The stickiness I had felt on my eyes was possibly blood from a cut on my head somewhere – it wasn't just the whisky that made it ache.

'I don't like Mondays – to begin with,' I said. It wasn't a joke, I was trying to stall for time. My head was still hoping to find out how to speak in a way that didn't present as a drunken whine.

As she didn't laugh, Melissa must have recognised on my face the signs of the internal struggle that the phrase had cost me; the way the wry arching of her eyebrow acknowledged the disowning of Mondays. She appeared to be a trained listener though, and remained quiet in a way that seemed to me as if she needed to know.

'I have a son, Luke. He lives with me in my little abode opposite the Green. I *support* him.' As I spoke the last words about Luke I was sure that she flinched at the frustration in my tone.

I was hoping I would sober up enough to tell her the full story – it wasn't a story I found it easy to tell.

'Are you his carer?' she asked. Her concern was showing me that I owed her at least a few of what I considered to be the *facts* about the situation.

'I shouldn't be. He has never stood on his own two feet. Maybe that's what I should have done – made him stand on his own two feet when he finished university,' I said as she looked at me and then gently stopped me from getting away with *that*.

'It's what parents do – look out for their children,' and then she continued, 'I should know – I have a daughter and we have our ups and downs. We moved to Whitstable to leave Natalie's problems behind her and for me to enjoy a new life. She's training to be a gardener now. She starts work on a community garden next to the playpark on a green community space in Whitstable next week. This time I hope it will *really* be the fresh start she deserves. It's what she needs to find a partner and stand on her own two feet. If I told you where she's come from, then you might think differently about the chances of your son being able to turn things round, perhaps...' She looked at me to see and waited for me to react.

I *had* listened to her, but I wasn't convinced Luke was going to turn his life around any time soon, not without some radical change. I was starting to go over in my mind what had started the argument with Luke, but it had already been erased by the whisky.

Melissa touched the torn coat sleeve to bring me back from my thoughts. 'You must be wondering why I stopped to help you? You helped me once, I lost Rick – his lead came off the collar and he headed off across the rough ground, over at Longrock nature reserve. I was calling him but he was having none of it. He found you and your dog, and then the two of them kept playing and circling each other,' she explained to me.

I couldn't remember; my dog was pleased to play with most dogs, especially when it gave her the freedom to race in uneven circles around the open rough land of Longrock.

'It wasn't long after I got Rick – he was a rescue dog – you called your dog and had something in your hand and Rick went to you. By now I could see you and Rick in the distance and you gave Rick some treat, from the same hand you gave your dog a treat. If it hadn't been for you, I might never have found him.'

I believed her. There were plenty of little white terriers around – if one was wandering around lost it was likely someone would have taken pity and taken the animal home. She was probably taking pity on me then – I was definitely lost, in many ways, that Monday.

I didn't remember capturing her dog for her, but that wasn't surprising – I couldn't remember everything about last night either. 'Well, you have more than returned the favour now,' I said.

'No, you haven't told me the real problem yet.' She knew I had to offload to someone, even if it was just to hear myself say aloud what was really wrong.

'The problem with my son is that I *keep* having to bail him out; the debt on the credit cards when he split up with his partner, buying him the car to use for work, the maintenance for the little boy, my grandson Jack. I've used up most of my savings and Luke resents me!' I said and then gave her the complete list, it was more like a litany of my bailouts than any explanation of how I ended up drunk, in the state she had found me in.

'But he accepts the help from you,' Melissa commented,

as if she wanted to know more about how I felt about him accepting my support, not just resenting my ability to give it. 'He hasn't run away from it all like they sometimes do. Have you tried talking to him, finding out what help he wants to solve his problems, other than money?' she suggested.

'Oh yes but he resents me. He tells me that *I'm* living the *good life* –because I can come and go as I please, with the free bus pass I got two weeks ago – but I've had enough. The last straw was when the gate fell off its hinges as he slammed out of the house last night. All I said was that I wanted to start charging him rent – just enough to help pay the bills. To cut a long story short, we both said things we shouldn't have, then he stormed out,' I replied.

She let go of my sleeve. 'I'm getting you and me some more coffee,' she said. As she went up to order it my mind tired again. She returned with two cups of coffee, placed them on the table and sat down. The dog obviously knew how to behave in the café; it stayed quietly under the table.

'So when he went I started on the whisky – I must have thought it was too late to bother going to bed,' I said trying to remember last night's logic.

'And you must have decided a walk down to the sea with a full hipflask would help,' she cut in to save me.

All I could do was laugh. 'So that worked, didn't it!'

I finished there, tired and no longer emotional – I had spilled out over the side to a complete stranger. I couldn't remember rescuing the dog but I was pleased a woman like her had taken the trouble to listen to me, considering the state she found me in. It felt like a cathartic experience but nothing had changed. The problem wasn't going to go away after one conversation with a sympathetic listener. Luke would reappear, and continue to take from me as long as I continued to give, *and then what*? I thought to myself.

Melissa had listened to this rant with some patience. *I really ought to say goodbye and go and think about what to do without the creative thinking inspired by whisky*, was what my mind was going over when she asked me the question.

'So, what are you going to do now? You can't rely on me to rescue you from Squeezegut Alley every time you need to get drunk – and there aren't that many who can get down there, are there?' she asked me.

I laughed with her.

'No, it's very aptly named,' I said with a slight nod.

'So you both have injured pride then, leaving an argument neither of you could solve. Why don't you let him stand on his own two feet? Have you tried?' Melissa said, pressing me to actually do something, instead of defending what I half remembered I had said to him; seeking the wisdom I had stupidly decided would definitely arrive after drinking the contents of the hipflask.

First, I became defensive and then I decided she might have a point – giving him a safety net hadn't exactly helped him to become independent so far.

'I've always tried my best to help him,' I said.

'May I tell you something?' she said, stopping me. 'Let him face his own problems without you being there.'

I still wasn't completely receptive to sensible advice in the befuddled condition I was in. I was just about able to invoke my golden rule of not making any life-changing decisions while still under the influence. My mind was beginning to wake up.

'Yes, I'll give him a chance, Melissa, and myself a break. You are absolutely right.' That was as close as I got to graciously conceding that she had made a very good point, one that I needed time to thoroughly consider. I was embarrassed not to have got anything like that as a solution.

I drunk the last of the second cup of coffee. Then I searched my pockets and after some fumbling around in a ripped coat pocket was relieved to find I hadn't lost my mobile.

I held the phone in my hand, and began to jab the screen with my finger before I asked her one more favour. That was after I looked for messages on my phone from Luke sending me a message of apology. Of course, there wasn't one, but *that* inspired me.

'I'm going to take your advice. When I've sobered up; then I will think about *how* I am *not* going to be here. Can I meet you here tomorrow?'

Melissa retrieved her own phone from a coat pocket. 'I have coffee here most mornings, about the same time,' she said as she pushed the chair back and pulled the lead to alert the dog that they were about to leave. Then she looked at me – as if she was checking to see if I was sober enough to remember what she was going to say next.

'By the way, you don't owe *me* anything – I chose to get you out of the alley. I'll be here but if you don't make it, promise me you'll text me at about this time, just so I know you are not drunk in an alley somewhere,' she said.

'Ok and you can have my number in case I don't.' I said my number and she jabbed her fingers against her phone screen.

'Thank you,' she said before she prodded her phone screen again. My phone beeped the sound it makes when it receives text. I read the message '*from Melissa*'.

'Save my number in contacts with my name,' she said with a laugh.

Then it was time for her to go. She put the phone back in her pocket and stood up, untangled the dog's lead and walked out of the Beach Café with a quick goodbye, from her to anyone who might be listening.

I went back home and sorted myself out. It took a while, but by the end of the afternoon I had made some phone calls and some plans. Luke didn't return that night – I didn't expect him to; after the arguments, he usually preferred to crash out on a friend's sofa for a day or two. That meant I had enough time to put my plans into action.

After a deep sleep, I woke on Tuesday morning – the alarm guaranteed I woke up in time to meet Melissa. By the time she arrived in the Beach Café, I was comfortable with two coffees on the table in front of me. Mine was black; I was still in recovery. My decision making had been a very sobering reflection. I didn't want her approval but I *did* want her to know what I had decided. I owed her that at least, after yesterday.

When we had greeted each other and the coffee had opened the way for our conversation to continue, I explained my plans to her. First, I told her that she had helped me make up my mind. She didn't say anything to that, so I came straight out with it.

'I'm going to support people who *really* need help to stand on their own two feet. There's plenty of them in the Calais refugee camps. My brother runs a Whitstable-based charity asking for volunteers to help them.'

There was a change in her expression; she looked very startled.

'I am going today. Luke can face up to his own problems,' I said waiting to see how she would react.

She looked at my face which was different now, with the cuts and bruises now cleaned up, the mud washed off.

She lowered her voice to make me listen closely to what she had to say. 'At least tell him before you go,' she asked me. 'I didn't mean you to make up your mind straight away what to do – I wanted you to give yourself some time to think about it,' she said.

It had never crossed my mind to consider what Luke might feel about a new approach to our problems. Without going into all the history between father and son – the absence of any faith that things would get better if we talked to each other was enough to drive me on. Listening to Melissa, I realised she had shown me a possibility that I hadn't thought of – trusting Luke to find his own way. I hadn't trusted Luke for a long time, but I pretended I always believed that he could rescue himself one day, from all his problems. So my pride didn't get hurt, I lied to myself, and told her what I wanted her to believe I thought about him. It was the best I could manage, then.

'He will survive, as soon as he realises that I'm not bailing him out any more. He can sort himself out and I'm not coming back until he's fixed that gate and I know things have changed. You are right, I should let him stand on his own two feet.' I wasn't sure if Melissa thought I was being cynical or optimistic.

When I stopped, she took her phone out of her pocket and put it on the table in front of her. I've got your number. I'll text you if the gate gets fixed. Natalie can keep an eye out when she's creating that community garden. Oh, and you can buy me dinner when you come back – if you find Luke has sorted himself out without you picking up the tab,' Melissa told me.

That reminded me to pay for our coffee. As I got up from the chair I made the promise to her.

'I will!' I accepted her terms and got to my feet, a lot more steadily than yesterday. 'Thank you, Melissa.' I left her and her smile in the Beach Café, hoping.

In my head, I was composing my goodbye note to Luke, the one that would be left on the kitchen table where he expected to find a sandwich when he came in.

Then I turned without a wobble and made what I hoped was a dignified exit.

'Good luck,' she said and I swear I heard her dog yap.

I retraced our steps back to Squeezegut Alley and looked down it, reminding myself that if it wasn't for Melissa I might have stayed there for much longer.

I made my way back home and rushed upstairs. I grabbed a change of clothing from my bedroom, then went and had a shower. When I felt refreshed from the shower, I went back downstairs and wrote on a piece of paper my message for Luke.

LUKE
I'm going, moving on – look after the house. I'll come back one day – when I do, I hope you will have learned to stand on your own two feet. It's up to you now.
Dad

The note was left in the middle of the kitchen table fixed

there by a can of beer, so that he wouldn't miss it.

~~~

I was waiting to board the ferry bound for Calais when I remembered – I hadn't told Melissa my home address.

I quickly composed a message in my head and then sent her my address in a text concluding it with:

– when the gate is fixed let me know. Thanks for this morning. Jake

She replied almost immediately, '*will do*'.

Six months passed before I received another text from Melissa.

'*Gate fixed and painted*'.

The text I sent back was confirming my promise.

'*Will arrange dinner when I arrive home in Whitstable*'. If I wasn't happy with Luke, at least I might talk to Melissa about what else I could do to build something with him that didn't end like it had done in the past.

The trip back home seemed to take a lot longer than I remembered, although my imagination about what I would find when my journey ended seemed to be expanding to include all kinds of possibilities.

'It's number 21 – in the middle opposite the swings on the Green.' I directed the cab driver as the cab arrived in my street. As he pulled up to the pavement I opened the car door and got out of the cab as fast as I could, with a ten-pound note in my hand ready to pass to the cabbie.

As he gave me the change I looked across at two boys playing football. One of them might be Jack, I thought, and then checked myself. It was Luke I wanted to see first. I stood on the pavement and looked at the doorway of my house. A pregnant young woman stood there; when she saw me, she seemed to recognise me, although I didn't know her.

Luke was painting the front downstairs window frame, and he turned around to face her when she shouted, 'Luke, somebody wants to see you.'

My son turned to her.

'Natalie, just let me finish painting – if the old man ever does come back I want him to see I've been looking after the place,' he said as he turned back to the window frame with his paintbrush. Then he turned around from it again as he heard me open the gate.

'*Dad!*' he said – he was pleased to see me. He put his hand out and I shook it. Then we hugged each other and he held me. 'It's good to see you, Luke.' I pulled my head back to look at him. He dropped his hands from around my shoulders.

Luke turned to the girl and introduced her to me. 'This is my partner, Natalie.'

Over dinner with Melissa, few days later, I learned all about how Luke had learned to stand on his own two feet, with Natalie, Melissa's daughter.

Melissa told me the whole story. I shook my head unable to believe how wrong I had been about him.

'I owe you so much. Without you none of this would have happened.' She was pleased at my acknowledgement.

'Natalie has a life of her own with a future too,' she said and smiled at me.

'There is something I can't work out. I can't remember the time when the dog I used to have helped you find your dog?' I said to Melissa as she finished the wine in her glass and then placed it back on the table in front of her.

'Jake,' and then she paused and took a deep breath. 'That's not a true story. You helped *me* home once too. I was in a bad place, not quite as bad as the one that you were in the alley. It was one night in the Oyster Arms and I had too much to drink. I was dancing on my own and inviting every man in the bar to dance with me. I wanted to forget about the relationship I had finally escaped from. When I tripped over, slipping on to the floor, you came to my rescue. The landlord found my purse and my phone when I fell over and lost my grip,' she said.

The memory returned, how I had helped her to her feet in a

very similar way she had helped me in Squeezegut Alley. She had been very drunk that night.

'And I took you home, went in the cab with you to the address the landlord found on your driver's licence in your purse. You looked so different...' I blurted out.

'We all do when we are drunk,' she said wryly and then she said, 'Anything could have happened to me that night. I was so vulnerable.'

I remembered her in the pub that night more than a year ago. How she swayed around every male drinker at the bar. Then she had danced in the small space in front of the two guitarists and the female vocalist playing vintage pop. They were waiting for someone to rescue her, and then she had slipped.

She *did* look different sober. 'I was too embarrassed to explain that was how we first met, so I made up the story about my dog,' she continued.

'I just wanted to make sure you got home safely,' I said to her.

'When I recognised you in the alley I knew it was my chance to help *you* get home,' she replied.

'And you did so much more than that,' I said, raising my coffee to her. 'Here's to your daughter, my son, and our new grandchild. But one thing bothers me. What if I had not taken your advice and Luke hadn't stood on his own two feet?'

'It never crossed my mind,' she said.

A Day Out

by Lin White

'Oh, but Mum, I wanted to spend the day with my friends,' wailed Hannah, seeing her day of freedom fading away.

'I'm sorry, darling, but you're too young to be hanging around town all day,' said Mum firmly, focusing on the saucepan she was stirring on the stove. 'I'm just glad Nana's here, so I don't have to stay home.'

Hannah's hopes raised a little at the thought that Nana would surely let her go out, even if Mum wouldn't. Nana had been distracted ever since she had moved in with them a few weeks ago, after Grandpa had died.

'What's that, dear?' Nana entered the kitchen, gazing around her as though forgetting what she had been after.

'Hannah's school is closed tomorrow,' Mum explained with a sigh. 'But she can stay with you, can't she.' It was presented as a statement, not a question.

Hannah was surprised when Nana frowned. 'Actually, I was planning on visiting Bill tomorrow. Those weeds will be knee-high by now.'

'Oh, Mum, I've told you, we'll run you down there one weekend.'

Nana stood her ground. 'It's very good of you to offer, but I have my bus pass. And I need to check on the house, as well. The post will be piled up, and there might be something urgent.'

'I wish you'd let us manage all that for you,' Mum grumbled, checking the food in the oven. 'I know you say you want to go back there, but honestly, it would be so much easier if you moved in here properly.'

Nana gave a weak smile, but said nothing. She just looked over at Hannah, whose heart had sunk at the thought of Nana living with them permanently.

Mum got plates out of the cupboard and placed them on the side. 'I know. You can take Hannah with you, then she can look after you. She doesn't get on the bus much, it will be a treat for her.'

'I get sick on buses.' Hannah made one last attempt to save herself from a day of boredom.

'You were sick on a bus once, when you were very little. I'm sure you'll be fine. And Nana can show you round where she used to live.'

Nana opened her mouth as though to say something, and then shrugged. 'I suppose I could take her with me,' she conceded. Hannah stared at her in dismay, the day on the beach at Herne Bay with her friends fading out and replaced with an image of trailing around behind an old lady and tedious bus rides.

And so it was that next morning Hannah and her Nana stood at the bus stop in Canterbury Road, along with about half a dozen other people, both men and women, all as old as Nana, or even older. 'It's the bus passes,' Nana explained. 'We're not allowed to use them before 9.30 in the morning.'

The sky was overcast, but even now the sun was trying to break through, and Hannah thought miserably of her friends and the beach. They were going to have such fun. At the age of twelve, they were just beginning to discover freedom, and she hated it that they got to go out and she had to be looked after. Didn't Mum realise she was nearly grown up now, and was perfectly capable of looking after herself? Or maybe it was Nana that Mum was worried about. Deal was a long way to go by yourself, and Nana was old. She felt a little better imagining that Nana was depending on her.

The bus pulled up at the stop and everyone got on. Nana and Hannah were last. Nana pulled her purse out of the large black bag she carried over her shoulder, held her bus pass over the ticket machine, and then asked for a day rider as well. 'What's one of those?' Hannah asked.

'It's like my bus pass – you can go anywhere you like in Kent, and ride as much as you like.' Nana handed over the change and gave Hannah the ticket. 'But yours only lasts for the day.'

Anywhere you like. But not where Hannah liked – the beach with her friends. She hid a scowl and tucked the ticket away in her purse.

They made their way to some of the few remaining seats on the lower deck of the bus. Hannah gazed longingly at the stairs as they passed them, but didn't dare suggest going up. Nana's knees would probably give out or something.

Hannah resigned herself to a day of travel and nannysitting, as they settled into seats on the lower deck of the bus. 'Not the seats over the wheel,' Nana cautioned. 'They get really bumpy.' The bus was almost full, and it picked up more passengers, all but one using their free bus passes to get around. 'Where are they all going?' Hannah asked.

Nana shrugged. 'Shopping, days out, just travelling round for the fun of it,' she suggested.

The bus pulled into Canterbury bus station about half an hour later, and everyone clambered off. Some headed towards the city centre, while others walked further around the shelter where everyone waited for their buses.

'Now,' said Nana. 'We need the Deal bus. Stand D4.'

'There's a Deal bus there already, at D3,' Hannah said, trying to be helpful. She had visions of them getting on the wrong bus, or sitting for ages waiting.

Nana laughed. 'Yes, there is, but that's not the right one. That one goes the long way round. The Number 12 doesn't leave for a while yet, but it will still beat that one to Deal.'

'Oh.' This bus business was more complicated than Hannah had thought. Perhaps she wouldn't be doing so much looking after her Nana after all.

When the Deal bus eventually arrived, it was a single decker, and only a few people boarded. Nana let her into the window seat, then settled down in her own seat with a sigh of relief.

Hannah stared out of the window, but the bus went straight down a main road, and there wasn't much to see. She sat feeling sorry for herself, lumbered with her Nana while her friends were having fun on the beach. She was just imagining Chloe and Harry chatting and laughing about how she had been left with a baby sitter, when Nana nudged her. 'Our stop next,' she said.

Hannah followed her off the bus. 'Now what?' she asked, looking around at the big houses lining the road. Deal was much like Herne Bay, it seemed. Except that none of her friends were here. And they were heading away from the beach.

Nana pointed up a side road. 'The cemetery is up there. It's a bit of a walk. I hope you're up to it.'

Hannah bit back a retort. The cheek! She followed Nana up the road. 'Shouldn't we have brought flowers or something?'

'Oh, your grandpa never believed in flowers,' Nana said. 'There are some plants on his grave, but he would just say bunches of flowers are a waste of money and a waste of flowers.'

Hannah smiled at the thought. She could just imagine Grandpa saying that. She missed him. Mum had frowned on the few occasions she had tried to talk about him. 'Don't upset Nana,' she had said. But now Hannah wondered if it was Mum who was more likely to be upset. Nana had seemed quite matter-of-fact about him.

Nana led the way into the cemetery, and Hannah looked round with interest. Row upon row of graves stretched away, some well-tended, some looking rather neglected. Nana led her way confidently through the maze to a grave that was just a patch of earth with a wooden cross at the head of it and a few flowers growing in the soil.

'Doesn't he have a headstone?' She felt disappointed that she couldn't read his name engraved in stone.

'He will do,' Nana said over her shoulder, as she stood over the grave. 'But it takes a while for the earth to settle. In a few weeks, they'll be able to set it up.'

'Oh.' Hannah regarded her Nana nervously. Didn't she care that was her husband buried there? She had worried about her Nana getting upset, but now she was starting to feel concerned about how calm she was as she set her bag down beside her, knelt down and started pulling the weeds out.

'Nana?' Hannah knelt down beside her.

'Yes, dear?' Nana pulled at a particularly strong weed, then winced and sucked at her hand. 'Thistles. How do they grow so quick?'

'I really miss Grandpa. Do you?'

Nana knelt back onto her feet and turned towards her. 'Every day,' she said with a sad smile. 'But he had a good life. We both did. We knew it was coming, and we'd made our peace with it.' She frowned. 'I need to start getting back to normal. It's hard being away from my home, on top of everything else. Your mother means well, and I know she likes having me around to look after you, but I need my own things around me, and you don't really need me, nice as it's been to see so much of you.' She yanked at a stubborn weed. 'You live so close, and yet you rarely come down here.'

'Mum says you need us to look after you,' Hannah said.

Nana laughed. 'I've been taking care of myself for long enough,' she pointed out. 'And I have all my friends here, too.' Hannah hadn't thought of that, but she supposed that it must be hard to leave the place you've lived in all your life. She wandered between the graves as Nana worked, and read some of the headstones.

Nana finished her weeding and stood up, wincing as she stretched her legs out a little. 'There. Doesn't that look better?'

Hannah agreed. 'Now what?' she asked.

'I just want to call in home, check everything is okay. It's not far from here.'

Just a couple of streets over was the small house Hannah remembered from their few visits. She stood in the living room gazing round her. All was as she remembered. Even Grandpa's chair was still sitting with his book on the arm of it, as though any minute he would walk in and sit down.

Nana walked into the room, carrying a pile of letters. She saw her gazing at the chair. 'I should tidy his things away,' she said. 'But somehow it doesn't feel right yet. Your mother says she'll help me sort his things out, but I can't bear the thought of that either.'

She finished flicking through the pile of letters, put the main pile down on a side table and tucked a couple into her handbag. 'All is as it should be. And the house can wait a few more days.' She gave a smile. 'I'm getting hungry. Are you?' As Hannah nodded, Nana said, 'Well, how about getting fish and chips on the seafront then?'

It was a few minutes' walk to the town and seafront, but Nana walked at a brisk pace, and Hannah had to work hard to keep up.

'Sorry, dear,' Nana said after a while. 'Your mother was always complaining I walk too fast.' She eased off a little.

As they reached the main shopping area, Nana held up a hand to wave to a couple of old ladies on the other side of the pedestrian area. They hurried across to speak to her. 'Betty! How are you?' said the thinner of the two.

'I'm fine, thank you,' Nana said. 'I've been missing our talks though.'

'How about a coffee now?' asked the other one.

Nana indicated Hannah. 'I can't, I'm afraid,' she said. 'I've got my granddaughter with me. It wouldn't be fair to her, having to sit and listen to us jabbering on.'

Hannah felt a blush of shame. She had been so focused on missing out on time with her friends, and hadn't even given a thought to Nana wanting to spend time with hers. 'I don't mind, Nana,' she said, but Nana put her hand through her arm and smiled.

'Fish and chips on the seafront?' she reminded her.

Hannah had to admit that food sounded a better idea than a boring cafe with old ladies, but still she hesitated. 'Are you sure you don't want to go with them?'

'I'd rather spend time with my granddaughter today,' Nana assured her. 'We haven't seen much of each other lately.'

Hannah thought of the number of times she'd gone out or stayed out late to avoid her Nana. 'Sorry, Nana,' she said.

'Ah, doesn't matter, we've got the day to ourselves now,' Nana said. 'Lovely to meet you ladies, but right now we have food and the beach awaiting us.'

Nana bought two enormous boxes full of cod and chips, and they sat on a bench near the pebbly beach in the sunshine, tucking in with the aid of the plastic knives and forks they had been given. A gull settled on the bench nearby, fixing Hannah with a beady eye, and she laughed at it. 'Look, Nana, he's after my food.'

'Yes, they're greedy birds,' Nana agreed. 'But don't feed it, or you'll have dozens after you. They're getting too bold as it is.'

Hannah pulled a face at the bird and continued eating.

'Now what?' she asked when all the food was gone.

Nana tidied the boxes away into the nearest bin. 'We can have a stroll along the seafront,' she suggested. 'Go and look at the pier? There's not as much as on your pier at Herne Bay, but I like to see the fishermen.'

As they walked, Nana told her stories about Grandpa, and how he used to fish on the pier. He had been ill for several years, and hardly got out of the house since Hannah had been old enough to know him, so she enjoyed learning about what he had been like in his younger days. And as Nana talked, Hannah started to understand that what the old lady needed was someone to listen to her stories, not someone to cook her meals or make sure she got the right bus.

'It's getting late,' Nana said at last, looking at her watch. 'And I don't know about you, but my feet are aching. We'd better look for a bus back.'

The stop wasn't far away, but was crowded with people waiting. 'Will we be able to get on?' Hannah asked doubtfully.

'Yes, there are lots of different buses that stop here,' Nana assured her. 'Not everyone will want the same one.'

Eventually a bus turned the corner – and then another and another. 'They always come in threes,' Nana said with a laugh.

'Which one is ours?'

'Well,' Nana answered thoughtfully. 'The first one is only a local bus, but both the other two go to Canterbury. The single decker is direct, and the other goes through all the little villages.'

'Can we get that one, then, please?' Hannah asked, hating the thought of the direct road that was more like a motorway. 'That would be more interesting.'

'Go on, then.'

Hannah got on, showed her bus ticket and then looked over her shoulder at Nana.

'Do you want to go upstairs this time?' Nana asked.

'Is that okay?'

Nana nodded. 'We're getting off at the bus station, so we don't need to worry about getting down the stairs in a hurry,' she said.

Hannah climbed up the steep stairs and found to her delight that the front seats were empty. She sat and gazed out, as her Nana joined her. 'I hardly ever get on a bus,' Hannah said. 'And Mum never lets me go upstairs.'

'Ah well, it will be our treat then,' said Nana, settling into her seat with a sigh of relief. 'That's the advantage of being retired. No desperate urge to be places. You can take your time and enjoy the view.'

The bus wound its way through the streets of Deal, and then out into the countryside, down narrow lanes that didn't look as though they would fit a car, let alone a double decker bus. On several of the roads, the trees hung low, bashing the roof of the bus as they drove under them.

Hannah gazed out of the window, fascinated, as she saw places she had never seen before. Usually, they travelled in Dad's car. 'This is fun,' she said.

'Yes.' Nana shifted in the seat beside her. 'I wasn't sure when your mother said you had to come with me. I thought you would be miserable away from your friends and I'd have a hard time entertaining you. But it's been nice to be able to talk about Grandpa a little. I'm always worried your mother will burst into tears if I mention him.'

Hannah blushed, remembering how she had started off thinking that she would have a terrible day. 'I was miserable at first,' she admitted. 'But really, Nana, I've had a great time. Thank you for bringing me. Perhaps we can do it again sometime.'

'Next time, you'll have to come down and visit me,' Nana said. 'I think it's time I told your mother I'm ready to move back to my own home.'

'I'll miss you,' Hannah said impulsively, although before today she had been desperate to know when Nana would go.

'But you know how to get to me now,' Nana pointed out.

'You don't have to wait for your parents to bring you.'

'They're always too busy anyway,' Hannah sighed. 'Mum would never let me travel that way by myself.'

'Oh, I'm sure she will. I'll tell her how useful it was to have you along to point out the right buses to me, and how grown up and independent you are these days.'

Was that a wink from her? Hannah grinned. 'Thanks, Nana.'

The Other Shoe

by Alison Kenward

*The story of Miss Havisham's Wedding Day, based on Great
Expectations by Charles Dickens.*

Most days I would go into her room while she slumbered and
silently put her breakfast tray down beside the bed. Then I
would draw the long drapes and carefully let the day in.

Today was different.

'Come in, Biddy. Come in. Quickly.'

Wrenching open the door, breathless and alight with excitement, she pulled me in and, just as suddenly, ran to the window
to let the day invade the room. The sun bounced rudely on
her thick blonde hair, which had escaped the plait from last
night and tumbled down her back as if to join in the game.
She ran to the dressing table where her ready jewels danced
in the sunlight.

Then she looked at me through the mirror and laughed. Her
head thrown back in abandoned pleasure, she was happy and
exultant.

Finally, she leapt to her feet in an instant and ran to me once
more, grabbing my arms, still laden with her breakfast.

'Don't just stand there, Biddy. Come in!' she gasped impatiently. 'Come, quick. Put the tray down. We must move. We
must move!'

Then, just as quickly, a thought shadowed her face and she

looked back at herself in the mirror. Her laughter slowed as she gazed at her reflection as if seeing it for the first time. Then she slid onto the stool in front of it and gazed further as if checking herself, one pale hand smoothing her flushed cheek.

And then in a more sombre tone: 'We must make me beautiful today, Biddy. Today of all days I must make him want me.'

I put the tray down and poured some coffee for her and brought it to her side.

'You will, Madam, I know it.' I said, looking at her with over-whelming affection.

And then, the feelings of pain and loss grew from the base of my heart and I felt tears sting my eyes. After today my lady would no longer need me. After today she would belong to him. I turned away and moved to the gown hanging expect-antly by the door. I smoothed the silk folds, careful not to let my tears escape.

Downstairs he was given no name. The talk in hushed tones of his reputation of greed and dishonesty had continued for many weeks previously and Cook had intimated someone should speak to her. All eyes had turned on me and I agonised for days about how to broach the matter.

Only once when I was getting her ready for a reception did I venture to speak. She was solemn and listless, having no desire to go out.

'Will you be seeing him tonight, my lady?' keeping my voice light.

She looked at me as if seeing into my anxious thoughts.

'No,' she said softly. And turned her gaze on the windows.

'No,' she said again. And then, as if more were needed, 'He is abroad.'

A silence fell and the long drapes shivered.

I knew then that she was aware of his ability to betray. I longed to protect her from harm but I said nothing.

Now the wedding day was here, all thoughts of 'abroad' were gone and she had resorted to the innocent excitable child that I had cherished all my life. I turned again to look at her. She was standing at the window looking out at the parkland below. She turned, her hair a halo of sunlight and her shoulders fragile and bare. Another leap and she scurried across to a bench in the corner and picked up her shoes.

'Look, Biddy look!' she cried with delight. 'Look how perfect they are. I shall treasure them always.'

The shoes were indeed a fine piece of craftsmanship. Heeled only slightly and made with a thick cream satin, folded and pleated with infinite care and tapering to a gentle point. And at the side of each was fastened a clasp of pearls which flirted with each other in the sunlight. She raised her left foot, intent on trying them on.

'No, Madam.' My cry was involuntary and harsh.

She turned to me, her eyes wide and her eyebrows raised high.

'Biddy,' she said in amazement. 'What is wrong with you? Why do you shout?'

I flushed deeply and apologised humbly while moving swiftly towards her to take the shoes away.

'It is bad luck, Madam,' I explained. 'The left shoe brings ill luck if put on first. And, in any case, you must dress first. Shoes must be the last thing you wear today. You might tear...'

My voice tailed away. I knew she would laugh at me and I could not explain myself. But there was an ominous threat in my heart and I took the shoes away and stowed them safely under the bed.

I went through to draw her bath, still feeling her questioning eyes behind me. The taps gushed into the cold enamel and steam rose to the high ceiling. I stayed awhile, gazing at the water swirling and bubbling below. A drop or two of her favourite oil and I returned to the bedroom. She was back at the window again, expectantly looking out as if her lover was walking to meet her. Her face played out fleeting expressions of excitement and fear all mingled in together and her breath became shorter and she turned once again, her arms outstretched to me.

'Biddy! Biddy! Why are you so glum? This is my happiest day! Be happy with me.'

The final plea was said with such imploring eyes and such an engaging smile that I tried to forget the doubt nestling in my heart and went to her with a gown.

'Your bath is ready, Madam,' I said, helping her into the warm gown and she obediently, like a small child, made her way to the bathroom and for a while I heard her softly singing as the water splashed gently and all was calm.

I had come to Satis House after leaving my grandmother's school, one dark night just after Christmas. I could no longer stay in such a place. With the demands on my time and suspicion of my actions at every turn, it became impossible to endure and I looked for a time for another post. It came by chance one day in early Autumn when my great aunt mentioned that the big house had lost a retainer and they were searching for a new maid.

I applied at once, was sent for and met my lady for the first time. She was brimming with life and could not keep still even under the firm gaze of her father. She seemed imbued with a fairy-like quality; her eyes sparkled with mischief and delight and she stared at me long and hard, finally turning to her father and saying:'We will have her, Father. She is the best.'

Once her father had accepted this inevitable choice, she ran to me and threw her arms around my neck and then, linking them with mine with a firmness which belied her fragile frame, she led me to the door and out into the garden. All the while she chatted to me, as she pointed out the marrows and the artichokes growing sturdily in the frames in the kitchen garden. And, despite my newness, I began to love her deeply even then.

As time passed I became her confidante, matriarch and advisor until the time came when suitors would call and each was discussed in length and with much laughter.

Finally, she was betrothed to a gentleman who fulfilled her

father's only aspiration, which was wealth, and arrangements were made for the wedding.

She was impatient and exasperated at the time it took and often and often would scream with impatience at the slowness of the legal administration of her dowry. But when deciding on her wedding gown and all the accessories she must have, only then she became composed and thoughtful. There were many fittings and alterations carried out but she bore them all with maturity and good will despite it being a project of mammoth proportions. Finally, the day had dawned and all was set fair for the wedding.

It was to be held in the little chapel and the reception was laid ready in the upstairs ballroom. Extra staff had been called in and the guest list ran into hundreds. Nothing was to be overlooked, for today was the talk of Kent and the gentry and well-to-do from far and wide were expected.

I went into the bathroom and collected a warm towel from the cupboard.

In a sudden moment my heart leapt to my mouth and I stifled a scream rising up from nowhere. She was lying in the bottom of the bath, her hair spread Ophelia-like and her arms floating upwards in supplication. Then just as suddenly, she rose like her own ghost and breathlessly looked at me, threw her head back and laughed until she could not speak.

'You thought I was dead! You thought I was drowned, didn't you, Biddy? Dear Biddy! You thought I was dead and gone!'

And more laughter pealed forth and wound through the corridors and out into the air.

I held the towel for her, lips tight and my heartbeat beginning to slow. She meekly climbed out of the bath, accepted the proffered towel and moved in silence back to her room. There she clambered onto the bed, her feet dangling like a child's. I began to collect her undergarments and prepared the dressing table for her hair. Now it was damp from the bath, it would make the elaborate hairdressing easier.

'Sorry Biddy,' came a small voice. 'I didn't mean to frighten you. I was just playing.'

She slid off the bed, looking at me all the while to gauge my mood.

I smiled and asked her to move to the mirror. We began the long task of coiling her hair, which was soon to receive the veil, the final accompaniment of her wardrobe.

I glanced at the clock. Twenty minutes to eight. We had one hour to get ready. Time enough.

We spoke softly and intermittently throughout. I put aside my concerns and concentrated on the complexity of each curl and layer. But the looming departure of the couple for their honeymoon abroad lay in wait and tears were never far away. They would be gone for two whole months. I was uncertain of my role during that time and wondered what changes her new husband would demand in the running of the household. The Manor House, for that was what it was formerly called, would be passed to him and there was no knowing whom he would dismiss and whom retain.

The relentless ticking of the miniature clock measured out its time as the hour was nearly upon us. At nine o'clock she must be ready to walk with her father to the Church in the grounds of the Manor House. He had insisted on an early simple service before the guests arrived to celebrate. She stood in the middle of the room, straighter than before and much calmer. The silk of the beautiful gown hugged her waist and hips and the jewels adorned her breast. We were silent for a moment, in awe of her beauty and the momentous promise she was making.

'Ready?' I said.

'One minute, Biddy.' She breathed out. 'One more glance at the table. Before we go.'

I did as she bade me and we swiftly crossed the corridor, her gown rustling as she did so, and opened the door to the magnificent ballroom. The table was decked with silver and flowers and, at its centre, stood an enormous four-tiered cake. A river of white ran away over the table and each place was laid with acute precision and the glasses jingled their greeting as she gazed from the doorway. She nodded, turned and returned to her room.

As she moved to sit for the final time in front of her mirror, I went to fetch the veil. It was a family heirloom, some two hundred years old and made in a Flemish lace with intricate patterns of birds and trees. It was so delicate that a breath might disturb it and it seemed to float in its own atmosphere as I brought it to her.

On the table was a pin that had belonged to her mother. I rested the veil carefully on her beautiful hair with whispered instruction not to move. Then I reached for the pin and as if performing a life-threatening operation, I slipped it through the net and held it in her hair. Throughout she remained very still. The clock struck the half hour. We had half an hour left.

'Satis,' she said.

'Madam?'

'It means "enough", Biddy. We have done.'

'Just the shoes, Madam.'

I went to rescue the shoes from where I had hidden them lest she break her fortune by trying them on too soon. She was silent and staring at her new image.

A knock at the door and, clasping both shoes, I went to open it.

Her flowers had arrived. One of the maids held them excitedly and nodded at me. She tried to look past me at the creation I had accomplished but I gently closed the door and turned once more to look at my lovely girl.

As she saw the flowers a tear began to fall.

'Oh, Biddy,' she breathed. 'They're beautiful. See? See how they're so delicate?'

I did see. They were like her in their frail vulnerability, their transience, their beauty.

I laid them carefully on the bench and went to kneel at her feet. The stockings hugged her young skin and the shoe slid perfectly onto her right foot. She gasped in delight.

Another knock. I put the other shoe down impatiently. I should have expected these interruptions but it was only twenty to nine. Still time. We had time.

There was a man at the door in uniform. He held a letter, sealed and addressed to her. I thanked him.

When she opened it, her life changed forever. The other shoe remained on the floor.

The Beach Hut

by Ellen Simmons

The Morgan beach hut was no ordinary beach hut.

It held no magical qualities, nor was it a place of any historical value, but to the Morgan triplets it was the most special place on earth.

Their parents had bought the little hut three years before they were born, right on the Tankerton beach front, and turned it into a haven. It changed colours over the years, the furniture and decorations replaced every decade or so as fashions changed, but the feeling remained the same. It was home.

Oscar's Memory –1961

Even in the moonlight the beach hut was easily recognisable. The alternating white and mint green stripes stood out, the flying paper fish blowing in the breeze off the North Sea, making the occasional whipping sound. It beckoned them forward.

Oscar knew tonight would be the night. His gut feeling was telling him it was time to jump over the hurdle, even if it meant falling flat on his face.

His friends brushed past him, struggling with the bags of food, drink and firewood for the bonfire, ready for the party. They weren't really allowed fires on the beach, but it was a special occasion.

'Mum is going to kill us when she finds out,' Oscar said, turning to his two siblings.

Harper just laughed. 'You mean if, not when.'

'Mum always finds out,' he argued.

'Stop worrying so much,' his brother William said as he slapped Oscar's shoulder and pushed him forward. 'We're sixteen, not six. Mum needs to stop worrying so much.'

'She won't like the fact we've brought people to the beach hut,' Oscar said worriedly. He wrung his hands together. They felt like sandpaper, grinding away at one another, so he put them in his pockets instead.

'She won't like that we've snuck out of the house either,' William commented.

Harper placed an arm around Oscar, resting her head on his shoulder.

'It's all going to be fine. I invited Alice, just like you wanted me to. Go be a man and talk to her,' she said, giving him a little shove that sent him stumbling down Tankerton slopes towards their family beach hut.

William and Harper laughed to each other at their brother's nerves. The three had been close since birth, always finishing each other's sentences and seeming to know what the others were thinking. Triplet telepathy, their parents called it.

Harper brushed her long dark hair from her face. 'He's going to mess it up.'

'I heard that,' Oscar said, looking over his shoulder.

Harper clapped a hand to her mouth while William let out a bark of laughter. Oscar just rolled his eyes and headed down the concrete steps, taking a sharp left at the front row of beach huts and pulling a key from his pocket.

Their friends were all standing on the steps, hands wrapped around their bodies as they waited in the cold air. Alice sat with her knees close to her chest, arms holding them tight against the wind. She smiled when she saw him and Oscar felt his heart stumble against his ribcage. She really was beautiful.

Most of the time he regretted telling his siblings anything. Being the youngest of the three, even by two minutes, meant Harper and William exuded some sort of right to tease him mercilessly. When they had found out he had feelings for Alice it might have been the worst day of his life. For days they had made jokes, kissing noises behind his back, sniggering like children whenever she was around. Oscar often wondered if they were six years old after all.

'This is a big moment,' William had told him when they were organising the party. 'A first kiss is never something to take lightly.'

'Who was yours with?' Oscar asked.

William paused for a moment and then shrugged. 'No idea.'

'You see how I'm not overly keen to take your advice on this one then, right?' Oscar asked, earning himself a piece of carrot thrown at his head.

'Listen wisely, little brother.'

'By two minutes—'

William made a shushing sound while Harper took a long sip of her drink, trying to hide her laughter. Oscar wanted to hit them both with something hard.

'It's not that big a deal,' he said.

Harper raised a finger. 'On the contrary, little brother, it *is* a big deal. A first kiss is always a big deal.'

Oscar sighed and hung his head. 'Not you too.'

But right then, staring at Alice as she stood and smiled at him, Oscar realised they were right. It was a big deal. Mainly because he didn't have any idea what to do. How does someone go about getting their first kiss? He didn't know.

Glancing over his shoulder, he saw Harper and William making their way towards the beach hut, arms linked as they watched him. He needed to start talking to Alice now if he didn't want them to embarrass him.

He threw the keys to the hut over to his friend Fred and then looked across at Alice.

'Fancy a walk?' he asked, wincing as his voice cracked on the last word.

Her smile widened. 'Sure.'

Ignoring the fact Harper and William were watching him like proud parents, Oscar led Alice down the last few steps until they were on Tankerton beach, the pebbles crunching underfoot as they stepped side by side in silence.

Oscar couldn't think of anything to say. Alice threw him an occasional smile when she caught him looking, but she remained mute as well.

'What made you decide to throw a party?' she asked a little while later. They had walked all the way to the Street, a narrow pathway of pebbles that appeared in the North Sea during low tide. Oscar guided Alice towards it, thinking it would be a romantic spot.

'It was more Harper's idea. She's the boisterous triplet,' Oscar said. 'I'm more the sensitive type.'

Alice laughed. It was a nice laugh, and Oscar wanted to hear it again.

'You always were the quiet one. I find it interesting,' she whispered conspiratorially, leaning in closer to him. 'What are you hiding?'

Oscar stuttered. He had never been called interesting before. He was always 'the other triplet'. His parents had been expecting twins, so when he arrived it was quite a surprise for everyone involved. William was the leader, Harper the life of the party – there wasn't much left for him to do.

They reached the end of the Street and came to a halt, the water lapping at their toes as they stared out across the sea. Oscar could just make out the lights of the Isle of Sheppey opposite.

The way Alice was looking at him made him realise maybe there was one thing he could do. Leaning forward, Harper's voice found its way into his head once more. This was a very big deal.

Back at the beach hut Oscar found his siblings waiting for him, knowing looks on their faces. Alice left his side to make her way over to her friends, and Oscar climbed the four steps to the decking where William and Harper were both sipping out of paper cups and watching him.

Harper wordlessly handed him a drink.

'Attaboy,' William said, slapping his shoulders so hard Oscar lurched forward.

'I didn't say anything.'

'You didn't need to,' Harper said, grinning. 'You've got Alice's lipstick on your mouth.'

Oscar reached up and furiously rubbed it off, but the damage was done. There would undoubtedly be weeks of teasing for this. But he didn't care.

Harper's Memory – 1972

'You're married.'

Harper couldn't help smile at the words. William sat down on the wooden decking beside her, holding out a glass of champagne, and looked out across the sea.

She took an appreciative sip and rested her head on his shoulder. Oscar, sat on her other side, took her hand in his own. The three siblings stayed this way for a few minutes in silence, watching the sunset. A little way ahead of them, down on the pebbled beach by the tide, the rest of the wedding party stood toasting the happy couple, not even noticing the missing bride. The triplets had sneaked off, William grabbing a bottle of bubbly, and met at the beach hut. They sat side by side with their feet hanging off the edge of the decking, Harper's hidden beneath her long wedding dress, content in each other's company.

'You're *married*.'

Now Harper outright laughed. She looked down at the ring glittering on her finger, the setting sun catching the diamond. She really was married.

'Yes I am.'

'That's crazy,' Oscar sighed. 'I don't feel old enough for you to be married.'

Harper watched as he loosened his tie and undid his top collar button. She hoped he would find someone soon. After a disastrous relationship with Alice that had ended two years ago, she knew her brother was a little lonely. The wedding must have been hard for him.

'Thank you for being here with me. Both of you,' she said.

The men either side of her simply smiled. Aside from her father, and now perhaps her husband, they were the only men she knew she could rely on.

'As if we would be anywhere else,' William said. He kissed the top of her head.

'I'm glad you decided to have the wedding here,' Oscar said, looking over his shoulder at the now-lilac beach hut. 'Although I'm not sure about Mum and Dad's colour choice.'

'She wanted something that matched the wedding colour theme,' Harper said, following his gaze and laughing.

'I can't believe you're leaving Whitstable,' William said suddenly.

Harper and Oscar looked over at him, surprised.

'I'm not going far. London is just a couple of hours away,' she said, giving his arm a squeeze.

'Still, we've always lived in Whitstable.'

Harper knew William had been struggling with the idea of not seeing one another all the time, but her husband's work was taking them away and she knew it was a commitment she had to make. Being married meant being grown up, no matter how much she disliked it.

'And we will again, I'm sure,' she said.

William smiled sadly and leaned his chin on top of her head as Harper rested on his shoulder. They weren't sixteen and running amok anymore, she realised. It seemed like only yesterday they were teasing Oscar about getting his first kiss, sneaking out of the house to throw a party just so he could talk to Alice.

So much had happened since then. Oscar was right, she was *married*. The thought alone felt foreign. Out of the three triplets, she would have put herself last to get married. She wanted to travel, see more of the world. To place her feet on every continent on Earth. William was the sensible one, settled and at home in the little seaside town they had always lived in. She thought he might change his ways and settle down in the matrimonial sense eventually, but he remained a bachelor.

'Another glass?' Oscar suggested, raising his empty flute.

William topped them all up and they sipped in silence. The sun was warm on Harper's face and she couldn't remember the last time she had been this content. The months leading up to the wedding had been so frantic she had considered calling the whole thing off and eloping.

'So which of my brothers do I need to marry off next then?' she joked.

Oscar immediately piped up. 'William's the oldest, it should be him.'

William shook his head. 'That's your excuse for everything.'

'Because it's true,' Oscar said.

'I'm not the marrying kind,' William shot back.

Harper knew this to be true. All through their adolescence William had never courted anyone, no matter how many friends she had pushed his way. Oscar had been the romantic one, daydreaming after Alice until Harper had grown tired and forced him into action. Something she felt slightly guilty for these days.

'I think I should stay away from dating for the time being,' Oscar said.

'Well, all right then. I'm not sure there's any woman out there good enough for either of my brothers anyway,' Harper said with a smile.

The two men toasted her words and the clink of their glasses echoed around them. Harper knew this was where she felt truly happy, beside her two brothers in the place they had called home forever. Whitstable didn't offer much in the way of excitement or intrigue; a sleepy little town known for its famous oysters and rather large retirement community, it was more calming than crazy. But Harper loved it anyway. It was where their parents had fallen in love, both moving here to focus on their writing. It was why the triplets were named after famous writers. And now she had fallen in love in that same town, by the same seaside as her parents.

There was a wonderful sense of completion about the whole affair, even if it did sting her heart a little to be moving away. She watched her new husband talk animatedly with her father down on the beach, a small grin forming on her face.

'I'm amazed you found someone Dad can have an actual conversation with,' Oscar said, following her gaze.

'Oh, I wouldn't have married him if he couldn't. Or if he didn't get along with either of you,' she said.

William and Oscar both stayed silent, but Harper could sense their teasing gaze over her head and knew they were just trying to annoy her. She was aware how well her husband got on with her brothers; it was his ability to do so that had made Harper fall in love in the first place. She needed someone who could understand the importance of the relationship she had with her siblings.

'When do you leave for Italy?' William asked.

'Monday. I still haven't packed, I've been too focussed on

everything else,' she confessed.

Oscar hummed under his breath. 'Italy for a honeymoon, it's a nice choice. Just think of all the things you will see.'

Harper agreed with him. She had always wanted to go, and at twenty-seven she felt it was time to dip her toe into the world of travelling.

'You'll catch the bug,' Oscar went on. 'You'll want to keep going until you've seen the entire world.'

Harper smiled over at her brother. That was exactly what she was hoping.

William's Memory – 2010

William felt his joints creak as he climbed the steps to the beach hut. Harper and Oscar were already there, sitting side by side in deck chairs sipping mugs of tea. There was one waiting for him, as always, on the small wooden table beside his own chair.

They looked over as he arrived, breaking out into smiles that were brighter than the setting sun before them. He hadn't seen either of them in months, Harper having been travelling through South America with her husband and Oscar moving up to Leeds to be closer to his grandchildren.

William was nervous, his palms sweating. It seemed insane to him that the two people sat in front of him, people he had known his whole life, could make him this anxious.

Down on the pebbles, new generations of the Morgan family continued to play in the dying sunlight, lit up like fire with long shadows as they shrieked and chased one another around, their parents observing from deck chairs and in turn Oscar and Harper watching them. They were the old generation now, William thought with a sigh. His brother and sister were grandparents, and he was Uncle William.

'I thought you weren't going to make it,' Harper said, nodding her head towards the mug of tea.

'I didn't put up with five hours of screaming children not to see both my siblings,' Oscar said with a smile.

William returned it, tugging his cheeks up but knowing it didn't reach his eyes. Immediately his siblings caught on that something was wrong. They always did.

'What's going on, you look stressed,' Harper said, placing a hand on his arm.

William shrugged. 'Traffic was a nightmare getting here, it took ages.'

Oscar gave him a dry look over Harper's shoulder. 'You live down the road. Out of the three of us, you're the one with no excuse to not make it,' he said.

'I know, I know I— I just couldn't find my tablets, and my knees give me havoc if I don't take them,' William said, scrambling for an excuse.

Harper rolled her eyes, her grey hair being tugged out of its bun and blowing around her face. She had always been the one to know when he was lying. Oscar could sometimes tell, but Harper had a sixth sense.

'Well, you're the one who called the family meeting together, so I don't understand why you would be late,' she said curtly. 'Besides,' she went on, 'it's not like you to ever be tardy.'

'I didn't *call a family meeting;* I just wanted to see everyone. I haven't seen your family for months, Oscar, and Harper – it feels like years since I saw you last.'

His brother and sister were saved from answering by the shrieking of their grandchildren as they ran up the pebbles, crossed the pathway and made their way up the grassy hill towards the beach hut.

'Uncle William! Uncle William!' they shouted over one another.

'Hey kids,' he said with a smile.

They reached him a little breathless, looking up from the ground through the wooden bannister. 'What have you got for us?'

'Kids!' Oscar scolded gently, but they ignored him with their palms outstretched towards William.

'Only if you say the magic word,' he said, reaching into his pocket.

'Please!' they all chorused.

Leaning over the balcony of the beach hut, William dropped a few sweets into their open hands and watched with a smile as they ran away back to the beach with their prizes, the promise of a sugar buzz just around the corner.

'You spoil them,' Harper said fondly.

'I don't have any grandchildren of my own, of course I'm going to spoil them,' William responded.

They sat in comfortable silence, all taking an occasional sip of tea and sighing softly. The wind continued to whip through the many rows of beach huts, causing William to turn his collar up against the breeze.

'Are you going to tell us why we are really here?' Harper asked finally.

William turned to look at them. Oscar shrugged.

'We only come to the beach hut for important occasions now. Harper's wedding was the last big event we spent here... what's going on, Bill?'

William couldn't meet their eyes. Instead he squinted out across the ocean. There had been many constants in his life, including his home here in Whitstable. It had never occurred to him to move from his childhood town, just as it had never occurred to him to do what he was about to. He had honestly thought he was going to die with the secret he had been carrying around for years.

'I'm gay,' he said finally with a whooshing breath.

There was silence. In that moment William played out a hundred different ways his siblings could react, each one worse than the last, but what they did took him completely by surprise.

They smiled.

'We know,' Harper said through gentle laugher.

'You do?' William's eyebrows shot up.

'Of course we did. We're your siblings, how could we not?'

Oscar said, calmly taking another sip of tea as Harper brushed the hair away from her face whilst continuing to watch him.

'Why didn't you say anything all these years?' William asked.

Oscar shrugged and placed his mug down carefully on the table beside him. He then locked eyes with William and became serious.

'Because it's your choice to tell us. If you weren't ready, that was fine,' he said. 'We loved you regardless.'

'But I always knew you had a thing for Rock Hudson,' Harper said, still chuckling.

'And to think I might have had a shot with him,' William joked, starting to see the funny side.

Oscar laughed and said, 'you watched Pillow Talk far too often, and I knew it wasn't for Doris Day.'

William settled down into his chair and let the last of the sun rays seep into his skin. He had been worried for nothing, he realised. They had grew up in a different time, where being different was a crime and sexuality was a straight line. He couldn't imagine ever being brave enough to admit who he really was.

'I'm proud of you, William,' Harper said, taking his hand.

'Me too,' Oscar piped up, 'but it wouldn't hurt you to dress a little better now, brother.'

William gave him a glare before smiling. The teasing he could withstand, in fact there was nothing he wanted more. Assurance that things would always be the same.

'Do you remember that time, when we were about sixteen? I always thought you had a crush on Fred Bartley, that boy who used to do the paper round on our street,' Harper said.

Oscar sat up a little straighter. 'Didn't he come to that party where Alice and I got together?' he asked. 'I think I remember him being there.'

They both looked over at William, as if he had the answers. William just shrugged.

'He was actually my first kiss,' he confessed.

His siblings both made noises of surprise and Harper

smacked his arm.

'I don't believe it! When? At that party?' she said.

'No, no – it was long after that. A few days before your wedding actually, we were both working at the paper mill in Chartham and it just happened after a shift one evening,' William said.

Oscar smiled in disbelief. 'I can't believe it. All this time, and you never told us… I'm not mad, I'm just – stunned,' he said, leaning back in his chair. 'Fred Bartley… he was surely out of your league,' he went on.

William looked around for something to throw at his brother but came up empty handed. Instead he flipped him the bird and in response Oscar laughed outright.

William watched the sun set, his family sat beside him and down playing on the beach, as a wide grin refused to fade from his face. Behind him the paper flying fish, the exact replica of the first fish that had been bought over forty years ago, was hanging from the beach hut pole and continued blowing in the breeze.

Unsafe Harbour

by Kim Miller

It was the first day since he joined the Merryweather that Ned hadn't felt cold and sick. An unpredictable March had included rain, wind and snow, all suffered to their fullest on board. Conditions at Ned's home in the sooty streets of east London were more consistent or, at least, less noticeable.

There had been brisk wind and weak sunshine on the day his Ma waved him up the gangplank, shouting to the skipper to look after him. The Captain nodded distractedly at her: there was no telling if he would take care of Ned or not.

Ned knew he would have to go away; his brother, Herbert, had gone two years ago – families couldn't give sustenance to members able to earn their own money. It broke his mother's heart all the same. His Pa said nothing but looked wretched; and there was little comfort on board for a boy who needed his Ma.

Their neighbour, Mrs Ardle, hadn't stopped talking about the Kaiser in the 18 months or so since war was declared, relishing speared-baby drawings in the newspapers, no story too wild to be gleefully passed on. Ned's exasperated Pa was only partially able to dispel the effects from his wife's mind: her skinny boy was no match for the barbarous Hun.

Ned had seen a Zeppelin in the early days of the war, everyone talked about it for weeks. Though terrifying, Zeppelins were glamorous and exciting to watch but you couldn't see U boats

– that was more sinister. Pa said U-boats wouldn't be interested in merchant ships and they wouldn't dare come into the Channel.

One of the old deck hands, Thomas, had shown some patience while he instructed the boy in the basics of life on board and Ned was grateful. The bane of Ned's life was nineteen-year-old Ernest: on his third voyage, no longer the youngest and most ignorant, Ernest enjoyed using his position to make Ned miserable and knock his confidence. The older hands ignored Ned for the most part and he preferred that to Ernest's low level, sniping bullying.

The day started sunny, full of spring, and later they anchored the schooner with its cargo of pipe clay at Margate Roads, along with a dozen or so other ships, ready to sail into the Channel with the next day's tide.

The mood of the harbour was lifted by the weather and people strolling along the front stopped to look at the ships at anchor. It was Ned's first time in an exotic location and he felt some pride in belonging to a vessel in the centre of it all.

On still water, with warm sun and lighter duties, the crew were relaxed, even laughing; cheerful voices carried from other ships adding to the Merryweather's easy atmosphere. As the sun lowered, the extracted molar of the tower at Reculver was silhouetted against the orange sky and they had their evening drop of rum – something Ned had taken to very well after the first surprising mouthful.

The post-rum tales of the other hands, Samuel, Joseph and John, were more than usually tall today. Competition was always fierce to have seen the worst storm, been in the worst wreck, had the nearest scrapes with death and narrowest misses from losing appendages. The scar across the top of John's bald head had been hit by a jib, scraped by a shark's fin and sliced by a dagger to Ned's knowledge. Samuel's finger had been lost to frost-bite in the North Atlantic, though Thomas, scornful, said he lost it on land to a bookie.

Ned was inspecting his painful, tired hands; raw skin,

aching knuckles, the backs cracked and open to every stinging substance. The light breeze increased and he surreptitiously spread his hands into its soothing coolness.

'Hello, we'll be glad of that wind in the morning,' said Samuel, implying insight, looking up at the rigging tapping the masts.

'Aye,' answered John, nodding with grave wisdom that added to the ever-present lead in Ned's stomach.

'It's a bit of wind, of course it's useful. Fools.' Thomas raised his eyes to heaven then winked at Ned.

It certainly appeared more like wind than breeze to Ned now and growing by the moment. Although weather didn't seem the same on board as on land, so maybe this wasn't unusual.

Joseph got up from his place on the deck boards and made his way to the hatch, stumbling as an unexpected gust hit the side of the ship sending fine spray over the crew.

'How much rum you had, there?' Samuel called out, hooting at his own joke.

'Wasn't ready for that,' called back Joseph.

'Call yourself a sea dog?' asked John, laughing.

'Not very often I shouldn't think,' answered Thomas wryly.

With the next big wave – every seventh one, they said – a bigger, heavier shower of spray covered them.

Samuel grunted a short laugh. 'Old Joe's got a point though, that's enough for me; I'm going below.'

'Aye, come on, we'll all go,' said Thomas to Ned and Ernest. 'I don't like the look of this. See that rain coming in?'

Ned struggled to get to his feet as the ship rocked in a now battering wind. Looking over the side, the aggressive roll of the waves was obvious, and the rain clouds further darkened a sky that had rapidly become looming.

'I ain't never seen a swifter change in weather than this,' observed John, soberly.

Thomas frowned at the horizon. His weathered face was further beaten by the wind and spray from the bigger, whiter waves that were now sent at them every moment by an angry gale.

'The wind has changed direction, that's no southerly, surely?' Ernest's limited experience could recognise the cold menace in this wind and his voice was tense, trying to hide his unease.

'Right enough, that's a north-westerly now,' said Thomas.

'I'm getting below.' Samuel shouted this time. 'Come on, you lot.'

Arms outstretched for balance and groping for fixed objects far out of reach, they made for the hatch. Leaning into a wind trying to carry them away, they made exhausting progress across a deck that sent them reeling and swaying.

Below, at the table, Samuel said, 'I don't know that I've ever seen a wind change like that. Swing round, like it did.'

'Nor me,' agreed Joseph.

'Nothing like,' John answered.

'It will stop soon though, won't it?' asked Ernest. He now looked every bit as scared as he felt and was secretly glad to have Ned beside him.

'Of course it will, lad,' said Joseph, standing behind him.

'Aye. Aye,' agreed Samuel.

'I think it's easing already,' said John. 'It was just a squall.'

They all agreed, though each of them could feel it getting stronger, hear the rigging slapping louder, and the small, dull thuds of the rain hitting the deck above them, a million spears thumping into the wood.

With a sudden violent lurch of the ship they were thrown from their stools. Joseph initially stayed upright, to have his feet taken away by Ernest's flying body and land rib cage first on the edge of the table. He caught a wheezing breath and clutched the ribs he knew were probably broken. The skin was removed from Samuel's lower leg as he skidded across the rough wooden floor.

Ned, Ernest and Thomas were on the floor, their weight pinning each other against the wall of the cabin; the others, heaving against the pitch of the vessel, hauled them to their feet.

Ned's eyes flicked continually to the underside of the deck, drawn by the din that fuelled his imagination to all kinds of destruction. No-one offered reassurance.

Something smashed against the mast, solid and heavy enough to reverberate through the ship.

'A full barrel's hit it, I reckon,' said Thomas to Ned's frightened face.

The waves that slammed and battered the schooner were now washing below deck through the hatch they'd been unable to close against the wind. Though not yet deep, the water sloshed from side to side in the rough sway, slopping into their faces, making them gasp with the cold, then choke on the salt water.

'We can't stay down here, it's only going to get deeper,' said Thomas.

'Aye, we might be better on deck,' shouted John, motioning upwards in the racket.

Thomas nodded.

The ship gave its most violent lurch yet and whipped round half a turn, tossing them across the cabin more pitilessly than before.

Even Thomas panicked now. 'We've broken anchor!' he screamed.

'The rocks!' Samuel screamed back, pulling himself up from the floor.

'God, no!' bellowed Joseph.

'Help us, God, help us,' pleaded Ernest.

'We need to get away from this damned water and see what's happening,' shouted Samuel gasping through another face-full of the invasive sea.

'Aye.' John pulled Ned, white, shivering, petrified, away from the bunk he clung to and pushed him through the rising water towards the hatch 'Now! Come on lad!'

With the ladder almost horizontal at times, they clawed their way step by step to the opening.

On deck the floor moved alarmingly, steep in front of them one moment then falling away like a cliff the next. They dragged themselves out of the hatch on their bellies, needles of freezing rain beating their heads and backs, the fight against the gale sapping their strength. Pulling themselves to the side of the ship, they were able to sit or lie with their backs to it. They saw chaotic shades of black and felt a force of nature that left them discarded and useless in its wake.

Thomas waited until the ship pitched away from them then allowed himself to slide down the wet deck. He grabbed the mast, crying out as his shoulder crashed into the hefty wood, but held on.

With the wind behind him pushing him into the mast, he pulled himself up to take in the scene.

Rain in his eyes restricted his view, stinging so he could look for only moments at a time. In those snapshots he saw they were not the only ship adrift.

The sea was rougher than he'd ever known; waves continually crashed over the ship and he could see other craft tossed and powerless, copies of their own plight. The wind was a hurricane now, he had no doubt; he'd never seen one but he'd heard tales of them. The noise was unrelenting, ships were lost in dips to reappear flung to the top of a ruthless swell. There was no chance of rescue and no question that their lives were in danger.

Police Constable Frank Chambers arrived head down leaning into the wind, at a lowering harbour: lashed by the elements, it was far from the place of refuge it was intended to be. He squinted at the scene; shadow ships bobbing madly on the sea like puppets on sticks.

There was light in the lifeboat station but there was no sign of urgency and he couldn't see either of their boats on the water.

'Willie!' Frank approached the station calling out to the lifeboat skipper. His voice was nothing in the wind and he walked closer before calling again. 'All right, Willie!'

Willie Epps turned and saw the PC. 'Hello, Frank. Where's

your helmet?'

'Long gone,' answered Frank, waving his arm in the direction of the town.

'How are things inland?' asked Willie, watching Frank tackle his skewed cape to rights.

'There's a lot of roof tiles comin' off and God knows what else flyin' through the air. There's lamp posts down. Some shop fronts in. The other lads are at the train station clearing the line but they'll be needed in the town before long, I should think.' Frank nodded seawards. 'Course, it's out there there's the real problems.'

'Yeah. Look at them ships out there, while we've got two boats sitting here. There's nothing we can do: we can't row against this.' Willie looked stricken.

'Course not. If I can't stay on my feet in this wind on land, how are you going to row against it in that sea?'

'You come a cropper, Frank?' asked Harry, a lifeboat man.

'Yup. Over by the clock tower.' Frank rubbed his elbow to demonstrate the veracity of his tale. 'Threw me whole body over, quick as anything. Bashed meself all down that side.' Frank dabbed at the side of his knee to further confirm his woes.

'Nasty, Frank, could have been bad, that,' commented crew member Joe.

'Small mercies, eh?' nodded Harry.

The constable looked round at the sombre faces. 'Try not to get too down about things, lads, you'll do your best, like always.'

'We'll be ready to go as soon as it drops,' said Willie.

Frank clapped a hand on Willie's shoulder. 'Good luck, lads. I'm going up to the train station, I'll be back later.'

'Mind how you go, Frank.'

Willie looked out to sea; he saw a vessel wildly out of control, being carried with every swell closer to the bow of a schooner.

'Jesus Christ! She's going to hit it!' Willie was compelled to watch, dreading to see a ship go down.

~~~

Ned had moved from the deck where he'd been thrown around and terrified. Sliding about, crashing into solid objects, and being crashed into by other crew members; he had had no idea of the force of one body hitting another. Everything was bruised, maybe broken, and he was cold beyond what he would have imagined he could endure.

He was hanging onto the rigging, arm wrapped around the tough, wet rope, torturing his flesh and his grip slipping continually. Thomas made his way over to him collecting a severe limp as a leg went from under him. He had a coil of rope in his hand. 'Tie yourself on, boy. Come on, I'll help.'

Ned couldn't hear but understood and allowed Thomas to fasten him to the rigging; it was painful and freezing but he wouldn't be in constant fear of being washed overboard. Thomas waved Ernest to come over, he tied him on, then himself aided by Samuel who had joined them.

The Captain and rest of the crew followed suit, making their way to other parts of the rigging and securing each other.

Out of nowhere the stern of another ship loomed over them, a hulking dark shape. The ship jolted and heaved, pitching more savagely than ever and a sound came that could be heard even above the raging wind. A terrifying sound, like the earth itself was tearing, as the stern of the other craft was run through by the Merryweather's bowsprit. The crew cried out, held their breath and screwed their eyes shut. A deep trough pulled away the rogue ship taking the bowsprit with it.

They lurched again, almost capsizing as they were violently released by the impaled vessel.

Their weight was now badly distributed and who knew what damage had been inflicted. The ship was borne relentlessly on the turmoil towards the jet-black, shadowy rocks.

'Don't worry, lads!' Thomas yelled to the two youngsters, though they had no hope of hearing him. 'We're tied on safe.'

Ned screamed in his head: 'What if we sink with us tied up?'

They couldn't see where they were or where they were going.

Heads were down, trying to keep the lacerating rain from their eyes, bodies hurting and faces sore, feeling flayed and raw.

Last to tie on, without assistance, Joseph's ropes were less secure: an arm came free and he hung on for his life, shouting soundlessly as the ship was hurled wildly around.

The collision with the rocks came with a smashing and jarring that dwarfed everything that had gone before. They were skewered on sharp jags, torn, lifted and plunged again on to the stone blades. Finally, they came to an uncertain halt, loosely poised on unyielding crags.

For hours the ship groaned, settling then tearing again on its rocky anchors as the wind continued its horrifying rage.

Ned no longer had the will to be afraid, the rain was easing a little at a time but there was no abating of the wind that thrashed his tender, ravaged body.

As promised, Frank Chambers returned to the lifeboat station to give and get information.

'All right, lads,' he greeted them.

'All right, Frank,' they limply chorused. Their morale was draining.

'How's things in town? Railway line OK?' Willie enquired.

'Not bad, all things considered. There doesn't seem to be much that can't be fixed, like I said; lamp-posts, windows, roof tiles. Not whole buildings and roofs, which wouldn't have surprised me earlier. Railway line's better than I thought too; trees are still bare, so they don't come down so easy.'

'Not so bad then.' Willie tried to be pleased at the news; he was really, just not enough to overcome his anxiety for the sailors in the harbour.

Frank had something to cheer up the beleaguered life saver. 'I called in to see Mary,' he told him.

Willie's eyebrows raised in enquiry. Mary, second wife, stepmother to his three girls, herself previously widowed, phlegmatically affectionate and recipient of his grateful, loving loyalty.

'I saw a light on so I gave a knock. They're all fine. She sent this.'

Frank held out a roughly wrapped small parcel that Willie opened to reveal two thick slices of bread stuck together with butter.

'I think it kept dry,' said Frank.

'It's fine Frank, I'll be glad of that. Thanks.' He fondly patted the rewrapped parcel and put it on a shelf.

I think we're going to be all right in town now – everyone's in and stayin' in. I'll tell the ambulances to stand by for when you get out there.'

Wish us luck, Frank.'

'Course. See you mate. See you lads.' Frank raised a hand to the crew and left.

Hours later, as morning came, the rain did cease and the wind eased enough for the lifeboat crew to launch their boats. In the daylight, three craft were clearly in greater need than the rest, listing badly, obviously damaged and close to sinking.

'We'll get them three first,' said Willie, pointing. 'Then the schooner on the rocks.' The crew had been up all night but found energy now they had purpose.

They rowed against the strong wind, standing still in the water much of the time, the wind icy in their faces, exhausted and freezing in minutes with many hours ahead of them.

On board the Merryweather, the shattered crew remained tied to the rigging. The ship was unstable on the rocks and the Captain had ordered them to stay put.

Thomas called out to Ernest. 'Are you all right, lad?'

'I'm fine.' Ernest's voice was sapped.

'What about you, Ned, lad.' Thomas checked the other youngster.

There was no answer.

'Ned! Ned! Are you going to answer me?'

'Yes.' Ned's reply was weak and he didn't lift his head. He had been shaking all over with cold but now he had stopped shivering. Ernest was relieved, it had upset him to see Ned shake; they'd all shivered but he didn't want to get like that.

They hardly spoke; odd words to let the others know how the lifeboat was getting on. Now their senses were less consumed by the conditions, their pains were more noticeable. Joseph's ribs were agony, every breath searing through him. Samuel and John were relieved the weather had calmed, but afraid more danger was to come from the rocks before the lifeboat got to them.

Ned feebly moved his hands, trying to get free from the ropes that had loosened a little.

'What you doin', boy?' asked Samuel, who saw him.

'I'm hungry,' said Ned. 'Need my dinner.'

'There'll be food soon enough when we're rescued. Don't you worry about that. It won't be long.' Samuel shook his head and muttered, 'Dinner?'

Ned continued to wriggle – it was ineffectual but was using up his tiny bit of strength.

'Stop struggling, lad,' said Thomas. 'It won't do no good.' He was exhausted himself, he didn't want to be dealing with a silly boy.

'Need shirt off.' Ned mumbled. 'Hot.'

'What?' asked Thomas.

'He wants to take his shirt off,' said Ernest.

'Heavens above! Leave your shirt alone. We'll be rescued soon.' Thomas was exasperated.

Ned's head lolled on his neck, and hung still as he murmured about his dinner and his mum.

'He's making me hungry,' whined Earnest.

'So hot,' murmured Ned.

The lifeboats, the arms and legs of the crews in burning pain, were on their way to the third listing craft.

Sorry sights had greeted them on the first two ships; the crews had been freezing cold, battered and afraid, beyond being pleased to see their rescuers. There were various injuries, cuts and bruises of course, some lacerations that would need attention, and broken bones; along with those showing signs of hypothermia, they would need the ambulances that waited on shore.

Willie and the crew were disbelieving – how were there not worse injuries? They'd been watching all night expecting the worst, appalling injuries and fatalities. They were growing optimistic, the carnage they thought they'd witnessed hadn't happened. They felt confident now to just send single boats to the remaining ships.

The hands of the Merryweather were quieter, with few commentaries on the lifeboat's progress. Ernest's fears had been realised as he and John began shaking badly. Ned was still and quiet now, asleep, thank goodness.

Finally, the Captain spoke. 'They're on their way, men. A quarter of an hour will see them with us.'

'A quarter hour, that's nothing, we'll be off here soon,' said Joseph.

The lifeboat arrived at the rocks that held the Merryweather, the crew spilled out and clambered across them to the wounded vessel.

Joseph freed his loose arm then untied the rest of his limbs. He forced his numb body across the treacherous deck, picked up a rope ladder and lowered it over the side.

The lifeboat men set about releasing the Merryweather crew from their self-applied shackles.

'We've got you now, lads,' said Willie making his way first to the Captain who waited for the rest of the crew to be released before he made for the ladder.

'Get these boys down first,' said Thomas as they approached to untie him.

'Right you are,' said Willie. He released Ernest and sent him to the lifeboat.

'I'll wait for Ned,' said Ernest, afraid to go on his own.

'Wake up, lad,' said Harry pulling the ropes away from the

young boy. 'Come on, you're safe now, you're getting off the ship.'

'Wake up, Ned. We're rescued,' said Ernest.

As the ropes came away, Ned slumped, caught by Harry, who laid him down. He smacked Ned's face and laid his own face on the boy's chest for signs of breathing. He shook him, gently at first, then more vigorously.

'Come on lad! Wakey, wakey.' Harry continued to shake and cajole Ned then sat back on his heels, drained and desolate.

'He's dead. I'm sorry. He's dead.'

The crews of both vessels stopped and looked at the dreadful tableau, the relief of one and the optimism of the other drained away.

Ernest was stricken. 'What? What? He can't be, he was talking about his dinner and all sorts. Ned! Ned! Come on, we're going.'

Sorry lad, he's gone.' Harry stood up and made his way to untie Thomas, whose head hung in exhausted misery at the news.

Ernest cried, sobbed. Thomas took him to the side of the ship and encouraged him on the treacherous climb down the ladder.

'How's he dead? There's nothing wrong with him,' blubbered Ernest.

Samuel joined them. 'The cold's killed him,' he said.

'No! No, he was hot. He said so, said he was hot. Kept saying it. Thomas!'

'Sorry lad, they're right.' Thomas guided him to the waiting boat.

The lifeboat crew carefully carried Ned's body across the rocks, defeated.

They laid him in the bottom of the lifeboat, covered his face with the corner of a tarpaulin and rowed to shore.

Although this is a work of fiction, on 28th March 1916 a sudden change in the weather brought a fierce storm to the Kent coast. In the harbour at Margate a dozen ships were 'disabled and driven ashore'. Despite the severity of the storm there was only one fatality; a fifteen year old boy on his first voyage, who died while tied to the rigging of his ship. He was buried in Margate in a grave occupied by another corpse. Ninety-two years later The Friends of Margate Cemetery marked his grave with a cross bearing his name: Walter Edward Lewis.

The Ultimate Slow Food

by Helen Howard

If you walk the Pilgrims' Way along the chalk downs of Kent you may be lucky enough to see the remains of a pilgrim's packed lunch. The story goes that as devotees made their way to Canterbury they carried snails in their pockets to break their fast. These are superior Roman snails with their big chalky shells, brought to this country 2,000 years ago to grace the table of our invaders. So it is fair to say that eating snails, and indeed farming snails, is part of our cultural heritage.

Kent is the place to come if you want to see Roman remains. Look for the remains of a Roman villa like the one at Lullingstone Castle and you're likely to find an ancient colony of pale-shelled snails. As any local gardener will tell you, Kent is a very good place for snails. It's the chalk, which molluscs need to make their shells grow. But you probably won't find Roman snails eating your precious seedlings, just the common garden snail.

Snails are eaten all over the world, not just in France, and especially during Lent. I hear stories every day about baskets of live snails being offered for sale in market places from Malta and Corsica to Singapore. In the UK they were particularly popular in monasteries, where the monks classified them as fish – wallfish – so they could be eaten on Fast days. Food historians have suggested that they only fell off the menu here at the Reformation when it became dangerous to do anything that could be seen as associated with Catholicism. But now they are back, with sales increasing year on year, not just to restaurants but to adventurous cooks everywhere. Indeed, Grow Your Own Food enthusiasts buy breeders and hatched eggs so they can add snails to their back garden farm.

When I was made redundant from a job that paid the mortgage but did little for my sanity, what was uppermost in my mind was that there had to be a better way of earning a living. As a child I had an aquarium of water snails on my window sill – no fish, just snails, and I found them fascinating. From time to time they laid their eggs in a blob of jelly on the glass that over the weeks slowly turned into miniscule perfectly formed transparent snails and crawled away.

Many years later, farming snails was an idea that grew from an internet search on food and farming. My garden is quite a good size, but it's not a smallholding, by any stretch of the imagination. As farm animals, edible snails have a lot going for them and one advantage is they don't take up much space. They are very accommodating creatures, quietly sleeping as they wait patiently for the next meal to arrive.

Starting any business involves a lot of outlay before you have income to pay for it. Many of the hundreds of small food businesses in Kent started at the kitchen table. Mine started in the spare bedroom because it was already warm and the space was just aching to be filled. Filling the room with snails also had the advantage of working wonderfully at keeping unwanted relatives away.

Finding out how to rear snails was no easy task and with so few snail farms in Britain ten years ago, it was quite a lonely furrow to plough. So it's been really great to encourage other people to take them on and now I have a growing band of other snail smallholders to talk to. I started by writing a booklet with some of the basics of small-scale snail rearing. But people kept on asking me where they could learn more so eventually I gave in and set up a one day course.

We mainly sell snails live and the main crop spends the summer living out of doors on fresh vegetables and fruit. They like to eat a wide range of vegetables and fruit. As well as the everyday green stuff provided by the cabbage family and windfall apples, from time to time mine have benefitted from the annual courgette glut and been treated to such delicacies as cherries, plums, mangoes, overripe figs and bean sprouts. But they like their fruit and vegetables peeled.

It's not exactly free-range farming because of the need to keep all those potential predators at bay – I refer to my patch as Alcatraz. Just about everything in creation seems to enjoy a snack of escargots au naturel: rats and hedgehogs, badgers, foxes, mice, shrews and that's before you get to thrushes, frogs and carnivorous beetle larvae. Did you know that one of the biggest threats to our protected Roman snail population is the carnivorous larvae of that other protected species: the glow worm, which is a beetle?

A lot of our snails go to conservation projects and that's what makes it so satisfying as a career. When the RSPB needed 200 baby snails a week right through the summer to hand feed baby birds on their captive breeding programme, I don't think there was anyone else who could supply them.

Because snail farming is still relatively unusual in the UK we have featured many times in the Press and TV from Taste of Britain to Countryfile and from the Alan Titchmarsh Show to Easter Eggs live. There's quite a demand from film companies for snails to film for advertisements so we offer a film package whereby they can hire the snails they need for a few days then return them, and I supply them with housing, food and care instructions. So our snails have become film stars and 'strutted their stuff' in front of many cameras. Who knows where the business will go next?

We've been eating seafood in the UK for centuries and snails have similar food value. Old fashioned seafood stalls have returned to beach resorts in Kent and you can see holiday-makers enjoying potted shrimps and fresh cockles. We even have restaurants that serve nothing but mussels. Snails don't taste of the sea; they taste like mushrooms, and if they are cooked properly they have a lovely soft texture. Go on try one. You know you want to!

Thornden Wood Trouble

by Mark Crawford

Deathly silent they sprinkled to the floor. The sun scattered through the ones that remained. The trees covered a wide area to the left of him; they went on, into the distance far, far out of his sight. They were a mixture of oak, ash, birch and hornbeam, with the occasional thorn bush that always snagged him as he passed through them along well-trodden paths. He didn't like this part of the wood. Even during the day it was murky and the light was dim. He disliked the uneasy silence that stirred nervousness and worry in him. It was slightly better at this time of the year as the leaves began to fall and more light was able to get in yet he knew that would in turn be leading to more gloomy days and colder nights. He was not looking forward to those days.

The other part of the forest was different. It was a clearing with smaller tress set out in straight lines surrounded by grass that was kept short by the other inhabitants. Although it was not dark or dim during the day, unlike other less favoured parts, he did not like visiting this part of the wood either. For this posed a problem. The youngling found it difficult to go anywhere in the woods, apart from his favourite place, his sanctuary. He was extremely worried and shy at seeing anything or being anywhere different. The slightest flutter of a wing or the scampering of a neighbour off to find food or returning made him tense and jittery.

He felt it more so at night. At night everything seemed so much more. The sounds were louder, the snaps were snappier, the crackles were cracklier, and the twit-a-woos more wooier. Night time for him was even more of a problem. For it was at night that everyone else of his variety insisted they go foraging. They would scuttle out of their warm, cosy, snugglyness and go out into the dark to find food. This he didn't mind because he loved food, but the cold, the dark and the scariness, he did mind that.

So there it was: this problem that made his days long and his nights even longer. Everyone else was busy busying themselves with daily and nightly business.

On this particular night it was stormy. There was no thunder or lightning, just cold (as usual) and especially windy. The wind howled around the trees, rustling through the long, thin branches, waving the thinner ones, making them look like they were alive. The wind blew more. Rain started to patter down, making it more miserable to go out. This wind made that unsettling blustery noise even though he was close to the ground. Even before he had made the effort to move out of the cosy abode, the wind was getting into the passages and penetrating into his snug, making him chilly. He snuggled down further with his nose into soft fur, hoping this would change the situation.

After a few moments it was no use. The need took over for his least favourite time of the night yet also his favourite time of the night. Being brave he moved out into the open, dreading the vision that would meet him. Dark everywhere, strange shapes and noises, wind whistling and rain rattling. In fact, it was much worse.

He hadn't heard what must have been a very loud creaking and crunching as the giant wooden arm had dropped to its resting place. The bulging extremities of the cumbersome bulk were indeed protruding rather awkwardly into his and others' entrances, exits and importantly his route to food. He looked up; silhouettes that were long scrawny fingers were towering above him sending worry and fear straight into his mind. He froze. To his left some hope, a small clear passage perhaps but it would be a squeeze. To his right a mangled maze of more scrawny fingers and the remnants of the large, prickly bushes that were once upright covering their homes. Below him just earth; he thought but only for a second about this option. No, not tonight, that would be too much effort. To the left it was.

Judgment of space was never a strong skill of his and this was being proved as his head was fitting nicely between the hard and very rough surface of the colossus. His kind were not blessed however with an aerodynamic shape, thus when his behind came to follow, it did not. This was not good. This was not how the quick outing into the night with the wind and the rain was meant to be. He had not even got to the finding food and eating the food part of the night. It wasn't meant to be going on for so long. Struggling turned to panic. Would he ever get enough of a grip on… the… dirt… to… push… himself… through? Last chance.

And then it happened. The sound went through him. It startled him so much that it went through his ears, collected inside his head and rushed along his whole body ending at his quivering small tail. It might have given him an incredible fright but it had been beneficial, the jolt had been such that it gave his back legs the speed and power to push him through the obstacle, and the light that covered the floor, only for a second, had given him some assistance in seeing where he would end up.

Now to work. The rain had become harsher in the fleeting moments and his fur was beginning to feel uncomfortable. The hunger, however, prevailed and so must he. Others were heading off to an area just beyond a small rise to his left that was covered by some undergrowth. Safety in numbers but the pickings would be less. What to do? Safety in numbers was his decision and he scrambled off.

When he arrived he regretted his decision. Clawed earth, half-eaten this and that and some deposits that follow after eating. Animals, he thought indignantly. Disgruntled, he noticed beyond this wreck of a scene some fresh undisturbed earth. Eagerly he scampered over to the tempting patch hoping that there were prizes to be discovered. Thankfully, this was to be true as when he dug there were many delicious, scrumptious trophies of delight. Mmm, mmm, mmm! They were wriggly but wonderful and oh so delightful. They were oh… the relief that he found them.

Just then a cracking thunderous racket came from all around, but he did not flinch; he barely noticed the booming blast for he was enjoying the sumptuous and delectable feast too much. He did, however, notice from the corner of his eye, as he was manoeuvring his bulk around to grab another tasty morsel, something that made him freeze. It was if his body had been paralysed by an invisible force that held him in his gorging position; the only moving being done was by the unfortunate meal he had between his teeth.

The image became ever so much clearer as he moved his vision towards the sight. It too was standing frozen still, its outline shining as the flash of light lit up the sky. The triangular shapes upon its head, the long legs at the front and rear and the bushy form that ended its body. The image struck fear and terror within him. What on earth was that? The wind, rain and storm were bad enough and now this to contend with, this was becoming a busy, busy night.

Something nevertheless happened that was quite unexpected. This unexpectedness took him by surprise, an instinct, a self-preserving action not of fear and worry that was the normal, but the opposite. Perhaps it was the overwhelming of the senses during this night that awoke something inside; the noises, the sights and not forgetting the juicy deliciousness of his bounty all came together to deflect affliction and now summoned strength, courage and defiance.

What came next, as it was felt, seen and heard, was most out of character. The charge began, forgotten was the next course on his food fest for he bounded through the forest, fully focussed on the chase. Out of his mouth came a screech that pierced the darkness only to be amplified when a bolt of lightning lit up the scene. The silhouette reacted too with speed but not with haste for it too had a boldness.

The claws he had always put to good use for foraging and building were now to be used for an entirely different purpose; the swipe was rapid but missed its target as the long face darted to the left. He gave immediate chase, gathering speed as he went, he let out another screech that this time was with more gusto and even more unexpected. The two had run down a well-trodden path worn away by the two-legged creatures that roamed this part of the wood. The trees had been cleared either side and the storm loomed over the chasing duo.

His mark quickly dashed to the right down a small incline into a large arena-like area. This was a part of the wood he had never been brave enough to venture to as there was too much evidence of the two legged creatures. It was hiding in such evidence now, within a large wooden structure made up of long branches too unnatural to be made by anything else. The stare was penetrating; he replied with an equally menacing stare. It was good cover but the urge took over him to approach. He did so unflinchingly toward the structure.

As he did so, the captive dashed from the wooden cage to the left; the speed was like lightning. However, his reactions took over him again, and not for the first time that night, left him surprised. As he was scampering, his thoughts momentarily made him aware of what he was doing. He was chasing after a creature although he was not fully aware of what it was, in the night, in the rain with a storm overhead, with lightning and loud thunder, and he was alone in a part of the wood that he would never normally go to, but he realised as he watched the furry tailed creature bound off into the woods up ahead of him, he was not scared, he was not worrying about the noises and the shapes that surrounded the woods. This was his home, his patch, his buffet that needed to be protected. There was nothing to fear for his newfound fearlessness would see to that. He would bravely go out and find that scrumptious food. He would build a new set and look after the others. He would brave the cold nights and not be afraid of any part of the wood. He would not be jittery from the sound of a snapping twig or from the rustling of leaves. He would defend this home; this leafy oasis of eggs, nuts, berries and worms; this wood was his paradise, his sanctuary. He would defend it with his might, his courage, his rather high-pitched screech and his earth-digging claws. He would look after his set and its inhabitants, for it was his duty now, his mission to protect; it was his charge to be a BADGER!

Puppy Love

by David Williamson

(A sparse stage. A table, chair, bucket and a wire framed single bed. Upon the table is a plastic cup and a small pile of books. She stands, runs her fingers around the edges of the table, sits on the chair and opens a book – Anna Karenina.)

'All happy families are alike; each unhappy family is unhappy in its own way.'

I'll give you that again. 'All happy families are alike; each unhappy family is unhappy in its own way.'

The opening lines of *Anna Karenina*. Tolstoy. I've picked up this book a hundred times, but never got past that first line because my mind would go off wandering; thinking about my own family; my Mum and Dad. My married life with Puppy. I love reading books. I love those book shops where you can sit in a comfortable chair and browse through thousands of different books – poetry, home decorating, photography books – and whilst I'm sat in one of those cosy armchairs I have freshly made coffee.

There's not many of those bookshops anymore though, but I like Waterstone's in Canterbury and when I'm in London I go to Foyle's hoping I might bump into J.K Rowling or Katie Price. Sometimes I take out my pen and pad and write a poem too. I'm quite good you know; I love the indulgence of words. At the moment I like 'Droplet', 'Turquoise', and 'Serendipity'. Do you like those? At one time I would have included 'Butterfly', but there are reasons now why I really hate that word.

Privacy and time to yourself is so important, even when you are in a relationship, don't you think? I used to love heading off to the Kent coast, Whitstable or the long beach at Deal, and sitting on the flinty pebbles in front of the beach huts and staring out to sea. I could sit there for hours with my pen and paper and my camera. I like taking photos of people passing by on the shoreline. If I was away for too long he would send me a text. 'Where are you?' he would say, 'I'm getting hungry.' That would mean he wanted me to come home and make him some dinner. Bless him; he would be lost without me.

I went to the Lake District last year for a weekend to get some 'Me time', and take some photographs of the stunning scenery. It was sad in a way. There were too many memories of Dad. We used to go up to the Lakes together for long weekends when I was in my teens. Dad's Nissan Micra with all our camping gear stuffed in the back. We left Mum at home; she hated anything to do with the outdoors. She liked her telly. Don't know how Mum and Dad got together, they were so different. Dad and I must have climbed every fell; well, it seemed like it at the time. He would tell me about the history of each valley and we would take photos of the flora and the beautiful views. He would tell me how the land was formed during the last ice age. Stuff like that. We would pitch out in our little tent in a field in the middle of nowhere, and on a morning we would fry up bacon and eggs on the calor gas cooker and we would be set up for the day.

It wasn't the same being in the Lakes on my own, without Dad. I cried a few times, thinking back to those happier times. After a couple of days on my own I couldn't wait to get back home, and to you-know-who, and give him a love poem I had written as a present. So that's a healthy thing to do, isn't it? Have some time to yourself, but then look forward to being together again.

I always made sure the tea breaks and lunchtimes at work were also entirely 'Me time' too. I refused to check the inbox or answer the phone. I'd tell my team 'Take the break girls, if you don't, they'll think we don't need it and they'll take it away from us. They would say, 'Yes boss, will do boss, we'll take the break boss.' They were a good bunch, were my girls, but there was one or two of them I didn't trust, they had an attitude like 'We know better. We've got our Chartered Institute of Personal Development certificates.' Anyhow, come appraisal time each year I soon sorted them out. I told them they must have been having trouble at home with their husbands and that was why they were not concentrating on their work. I would get them to agree that was the problem, and they were fine after they had admitted that's what it was. There's always a man at the root of most problems with women like that. Of course, there are lots of lovely men out there, the trick is finding the right one, isn't it? I thought I had chosen well when Puppy and I got married.

You can be living with someone and still get 'Me Time'. Like when we used to curl up on the sofa and watch TV together. I loved to put on my jim-jams and cosy socks and rest my feet over his knees whilst he was watching the football or playing on his Xbox. 'Me Time' is very important, but 'Us Time' is important too. With the busy lives we lead these days couples have to make time for each other or else the flame will just extinguish. Don't you think? So my advice, girls, if you want it that is, is to keep your marriage burning as best you can. It's far easier to keep an old fire burning than try start a damp pile of rotten wood. Anyhow, I've got plenty of 'Me Time' these days in this place.

The very first time it happened was on a table. We had both chosen it a few years back, just after we were married. It wasn't like this, though. This is a cheap looking table all right but ours was even cheaper. IKEA. We had to go to IKEA because he was too mean to spend that bit extra on anything decent. We'd waste fifty quid in petrol just travelling to the IKEA at Dartford and paying the toll, so we were already out of pocket just getting there. But that was him. He had no taste. As long as it looked 'modern' it didn't matter if it was made of MDF or poor-quality wood held together with a couple of screws; whatever was cheapest would suit him just fine. Although I must say that IKEA is great for art. The canvases they have there are lovely and much better value than those art galleries. Of course, money was no object to him if he wanted a new car, oh no, that was just fine, or a new games console or a night out in Maidstone with his friends.

I would come home from work and lay out two place mats, the ones his Aunty from Folkestone bought us with hunting scenes on them. They added a bit of class but I hate fox hunting. My Dad used to say 'They ought to do the same to them farmers and toffs as they do to the foxes and see how they like it.'

So for the eight years we were together, I would come home, lay two mats, two forks, two knives, and have a meal ready for when he came in. He insisted that I couldn't have candles in the house, which is a shame because candle light is so romantic. So because he was being mean, I insisted we always had to eat at the table, never with plates on our knees in front of the telly, although occasionally, as a special treat, I would let him take his tray into the front room if there was an important match he wanted to watch.

The first time I knew something was wrong, he was already home. I arrived back at the house one evening and he was laid out across the sofa watching children's cartoons.

'You're home early?'

'Yeah,' he grunted.

'Any reason?' He didn't reply.

I went into the kitchen and took off my coat and shouted again.

'So why are you home so early, Puppy?'

I called him 'Puppy' or 'Darling' in those days. He hated being called 'Puppy' but didn't mind 'Darling.' I called him Puppy because he had such a hairy back and he was soooo cute. He came into the kitchen in his socks and his belly hanging out over his track suit leggings. I can still smell those feet of his. He propped himself up against the doorway.

'This makes a nice change, what happened to my wittle Puppy-Wuppy today then?'

'Finished early,' he said, as he yawned and stretched out his arms.

'Finished early?'

'Yeah, what's the fuss? I finished early today so I came home – all right?'

He seemed just a little too laid back, yet on edge at the same time. Do you know what I mean? Edgy like. He didn't look me in the eye at first but when he did it was almost like a look of defiance, I'll always remember that. Anyway, I said to him, 'Couldn't you have started preparing the dinner rather than watching kid's cartoons? Just how long have you been home?'

He never cooked. Men don't, do they? Real men don't unless it's their job, but I always tried to get him interested. I bought him a Jamie Oliver cookbook last Christmas and he refused to even look at it.

'Not reading anything by that gay boy,' was his reply.

'He's not gay, he's got a wife and children and he's made millions from cooking, so don't be so silly.'

'Well, still not reading it.'

So I said to him, 'How would you ever feed yourself if I got run over by a bus?'

'There's only three buses a week round here,' he said flippantly. 'What's the chances, eh?'

'Well, what if I had leukaemia or breast cancer, or something like that, and I died?'

'I'd get a new wife' he said, trying to be a joker. He wouldn't marry again; he'd better not do. Who would have him anyway, eh? He knew what a good thing he had in me even if he wouldn't admit it, and especially with me now earning more than him he knew which side his bread was buttered. Besides, it was Dad's money that bought our lovely new executive house with its double garage and two bathrooms. He'd never have been able to buy anything upmarket like this at the price new houses go for round here. It was all in my name anyway. We would never save anything if we relied on him. He would squander every spare penny we had at the bookies given half a chance. The bookies, the soccer, the cars, the pint, the laugh with his buddies down the pub. Those are the things most men like, aren't they? I didn't mind that too much, just so long as he didn't start flirting with other women. That's when the rot starts to set in.

He went back into the front room to watch cartoons. I called out 'You haven't answered my question, how long have you been home?'

'Not long.'

'I wrote you a love poem at lunchtime.'

'Thanks,' he grunted.

'Thought I might go to Northumberland and take some photos of the coastline up there, why don't you come with me, we could have a romantic weekend together.'

'What's wrong with the Kent coastline? Get yourself down to Dover and the cliffs. Save on the petrol,' he called back. 'Anyway, who's paying for it?'

'Well, I will if you want. My special treat.'

'When?'

'Weekend after next.'

'Nah, Chelsea is playing Man U then.'

'Well you can watch it on the TV at the hotel we go to, can't you, silly?'

'It's alright babes, you go, I'll be fine here, I'll get some takeaways in.'

That was typical of him, always thinking of his stomach. But he still hadn't answered my question.

'So how long have you been home?'

'Give it a rest,' he shouts back, 'Does it matter?'

'Yes, of course it matters, how long?'

There was silence, so I shouted out again 'How long? How long?'

He came storming back into the kitchen and I pounded him on his chest with my fists, really hard. 'How long? 'How Long?'

I didn't get the chance to ask again, he just grabbed my arm like this, pushed it behind my back, and threw me face down on the table like this.

(She bends over the table.)

He had his full weight on me, forcing me down so that my chin was rubbing the table top. My breasts hurt with the pressure, and then he pulled my arm up behind my back so hard I thought he was going to dislocate it. I couldn't move. He leaned over me, pressing me down even harder and shouted in my ear 'Shut it now! Just fuckin' shut it!'

He let go and went back to watch his cartoons.

~~~

(She composes herself and stands up slowly.) I got up slowly like this – stunned, holding on to the edge of the table trying to keep my balance. I couldn't believe what he'd just done.

We didn't talk that night, or the following day. When we did, it was him who spoke first.

'Sorry babes,' he said apologetically, shrugging his shoulders a little. He told me his work was getting him down. That's understandable, he had really long hours sometimes with his lorry-driving job. He should have stayed in the Police Force, but he couldn't handle it, and this delivery job was only going to be for a short time; five years later he was still there and all his old workmates were now Detective Sergeants, or had good jobs working in IT and pulling in lots of money, and they all had children and we didn't, and that was pissing him off, so I forgave him.

He gave me a handkerchief with two entwined hearts and our initials embroidered on it. He had made it himself. He was good at embroidery, I'd shown him how to do it when we first started going out together and he's made some lovely pieces over the years. There are not many men who can pick up a needle and thread and embroider a primrose or a daffodil. It made such a contrast, that tiny little needle between those big chubby fingers of his. He had his faults, but it was those little things that I loved about him. He said I must never tell his friends he embroidered because they would take the piss.

So, he said he was sorry for hurting me. I could see in his puppy dog eyes he meant it. So I let him tie me up that night as a special treat. That's something he'd want every week if I gave in to him. You've got to ration men haven't you or they'll just take it for granted. You lose your value to them. Give them just enough to keep them loving you. My Dad was the same.

I went to Northumberland as planned and phoned him every day to see if he was okay.

'Stop worrying, I'm fine here, just enjoy yourself,' he said, so I did. But when I got into bed on my return something was different. For a start there was no groping, as you'd naturally expect when you haven't seen your hubby for a few days. I noticed something else, a smell. Perfume; but I thought nothing further about it. A few days later I came home from work a little earlier than usual. On the table there was a glass of milk. Now that's strange, the glass was half empty. *(She lifts the plastic cup from the table and inspects it.)*

Half a glass of milk. This wasn't here when I left that morning. But there was no sign of him. I began to chop an onion and cried. I wasn't upset, it was the onion. I peeled the potatoes and chipped them. We had chips with most meals. He liked chips. That doesn't mean to say we didn't eat healthily. I always made sure there were bananas in the house and I had the freezer stocked up with those frozen 'healthy options' meals, but give him more than a day or two without chips, well, he would get withdrawal symptoms and act like a baby.

'Where's me chips, Missus?' He would say, knowing it would wind me up.

'I wasn't put on God's earth just to make you chips for the likes of you.'

'Sure, but you're the Princess of chips if ever there was.' He was great with the witty one-liners.

(She walks around an imaginary cooker.) A week or so later I was in the kitchen. The hot oil was bubbling away in the pan on the cooker here as I put in the chips. I heard him at the door. He threw his bag down in the hallway and came up behind me, placing his big arms around my waist. He buried his face in my neck and began nibbling at my ears. Mmm, it felt lovely. He said he was tired after a long day's drive to Cardiff and was looking forward to a relaxing bath. As he made his way upstairs I called after him.

'You've not been home today then?'

'Home? I've been to Cardiff haven't I – why?'

'Oh, nothing.'

I heard him kick off his trainers as he sat on the bed. Whenever he took off those horrible trainers any room he was in would stink. He had dreadful feet, and the trainers made them smell even worse. You could retch at the smell of those feet. How can I explain it? A combination of malt vinegar… an old wet Labrador…and a piece of cheese you've had in the back of the fridge that's gone all sweaty. The more I nagged him to change his socks he would just laugh. Thanks be to God it was bath night. I heard him running his bath and he started to sing to himself. He liked those girl pop singers. He fancied that Taylor Swift. Don't know why, what's so special about her? Do you know what he used to do? He would go dancing round the room singing her song *Shake it Off*. Like this. *(She gyrates her hips and dances.)*

His favourite when he was having a bath was Kylie Minogue He reckoned that given the right place, and the right time, little Kylie and him could have been an item. Yeah, he should be so lucky. I must have been the only woman in the world that let her husband have a framed photo of a pop star on his bedside cabinet. You'd think Kylie and Taylor were part of the family the way he behaved. Anyway, it was harmless enough; it wasn't as if either of them would be knocking on the door any day soon asking him out on a date.

I took a good look at this glass of milk, half full. Who else could have been in the house? I wondered. There was only his mum who had a spare key, and she knows she's not allowed just to call by unexpected. So he must have been home. I felt a knot in my stomach, have you ever had that feeling? A tight knot that comes from nowhere and makes you feel like you've done something wrong, even though you haven't. Why had he denied being at home?

~~~

(She sits upon the wire frame bed.) That night we were laid in bed. Him on the right, me on the left as usual. His hand snaked its way under the duvet. Here we go again, we know what's coming next. I could feel his long finger nails running up the inside of my thigh. If I didn't cut his nails he would just let them grow, lazy bastard. Do you know something? Right up until us getting married his mum used to cut his nails for him. But I suppose I was okay with that, I had cut Dad's after me own Mum had passed away.

Anyhow, here came his groping hand again and those long finger nails slithering up between my legs, just as I was wanting to get to sleep. That's what men are like aren't they? No kissing, cuddling or pillow talk if they can get away with it. I would have liked a little more romance, but I loved him you see, and men have needs don't they? So if he wanted to get on with it then it was his right, I guess. I had made a wedding vow hadn't I? To love and obey, to honour with my body. Well that's a load of old shit that no one takes any notice of these days, not like in me Nan's day. Still, tell me one woman who doesn't let her husband do it every now and then just for a bit of peace and quiet? Best to get it over and done with than have to put up with all that petulant long-face sulking.

As his hand was like this… *(She places her hand in her lap)* …I asked him, 'Why did you lie to me Puppy?'

'Eh? What are you going on out about now?' he said grumpily. Then he quickly changed his tone. 'Come on, gorgeous, how about letting Puppy wag his tail a little?'

I told him I found the glass of milk. He immediately took his hand away.

'You wouldn't understand' he said.

'Why? Why wouldn't I understand?'

'Forget it,' he said, and rolled over.

'Are you ill?'

'No.'

'Things okay at work?'

'Fine.'

'Did you actually go to work today?'

'Yes, course I did.'

'Liar.'

'Shut up now,' he says, pulling the duvet over him.

Then I knew I had him. 'Liar, liar, you're a fuckin' liar...'

He rolled back over to me. His face was contorted like this. He was going mad. I called him a liar again and then he screams into my face, 'Shut your stupid bitch mouth! Shut your stupid bitch mouth!'

He knelt on top of me like this pinning my shoulders to the bed. His fat knees dug into my back and the palm of his fat hand rubbed hard against my face like this – pushing my nose to one side and my face deeper into the pillow – I could hardly breathe. He pressed harder and told me I was a bitch. I tried kicking back. Then he slapped me hard, really hard, several times.

'Shut it, okay? Just shut it!' he screamed. 'And stop writing me those fuckin' love poems!'

This was the same man who had promised to cherish me, to take care of me, to protect me and he couldn't even protect me from himself.

We should never have married. Hey, heard the one about the old couple who were a hundred years old? They go to the Solicitors and say they want to get divorced.

'A divorce?' says the Solicitor.

'Yeah, we've never really got on, you see.'

'But why have you waited so long?' he asks.

'Well, we thought we'd wait until the kids were dead.'

Do you get it? I know it's only a joke, but if you think about it there's a message there. They put up with each other for all those years trying to keep the damp wood burning when they could have been on fire with someone else.

~~~

I slept in the spare room that night. I cried and wished my Dad had been there to give him a good slapping and tell him to be nice to me. It was another woman, it was obvious, wasn't it? The bed sheets were never made the way I left them on a morning, never tucked in really tight at the sides. He was so careless, so bloody stupid. I even found two coffee cups just left on the work surface one day, still warm; one had lipstick on the rim. Then it clicked, when I was in Northumberland she must have been here. But I didn't say anything. I just boiled up inside.

In the weeks that followed I took a few long lunch breaks and drove home. I parked the car in the cul-de-sac opposite. The car couldn't be seen from our house, but looking through a gap in our neighbour's hedge I could see the front of our house easily. It was a new car, one I had wanted for a while, same as Jacqui Preston's next door, but mine was a better model. I knew Puppy fancied Jacqui. I could just tell by the way he talked to her sometimes when her husband Mike wasn't around. I'm sure he must have fancied Fionnuala Corrigan from across the road too because he used to go over and fix her car after her husband had left her. He admitted once he found her Irish accent sexy. I once interviewed her for a job. I bet she thought that because we were neighbours I would give her the job. I couldn't stand her, asking Puppy to do little odd-jobs for her all the time, so she had no chance. Anyway, it wasn't Fionnaula or Jacqui who I saw one lunchtime when his lorry pulled up outside the house. A little red mini cooper pulled up behind him and I saw the pair of them go into the house. It was usually a Tuesday or Thursday afternoon, but there was no real pattern to it, just when they were feeling horny, I guess.

I still slept with him. In fact our sex life was better than it had been in years. I'm sure he must have been confused because I didn't even ask him to shower first like I usually do. Why?

I'll tell you why. Because I wanted to get to know her. I would entice him to make love to me even though I knew he had only been with her a few hours before. He must have been knackered trying to keep two women satisfied at the same time, but he could hardly refuse could he? That would have given the game away. I could smell her. Like a hound smells a fox. I could smell her perfume and her body smell on every part of his fat, cheating body.

His eyes were no longer the eyes I knew. Gone were his doleful puppy eyes. He had snake eyes now. Yellow devil eyes. He still grunted his lies into my ear as he got excited, how he loved me, how I turned him on. He told me how sexy I was, how I always made him hard and how beautiful I was. But I knew he was really talking to her. *(She sits up.)* When he entered me, then so did she, they both did, didn't they? He still had her scent on him. They made a fool of me, I'm a lot of things but I'm not a fool. 'Don't ever be anyone's fool darlin',' that's what Dad used to say. Something needed to be done, right?

So, this is what happened. I left work one lunchtime, sped down the Thanet Way back home and parked the car in the cul-de-sac where I had a good view of our house. Our lovely house, on the lovely new estate, exclusive development, only been built three years. Ten past one, I saw them arrive. First the Mini Cooper. I could see her tapping away on her phone. A few minutes later his lorry arrives and they go into the house. I got my first close-up view of her. She was late teens I reckoned, nineteen at the most. Blonde, from a bottle of course, short skirt, pretty I suppose. As they walked up the path she preened herself like one of those stupid pop star girls he fancies, pushing back her long hair with her fingers as if she was in some video, trying to impress him, trying to act all sophisticated, looking all grown up. As if he cared whether she was grown up or not. Men like younger women, don't they? Men can talk a load of old bollocks and young girls will think they're talking sense. Stupid little bitch, why do girls like that go for older married men? What's the attraction? I never did. I loved my Dad, and although after Mum died he didn't have her to cuddle up with at night, I still didn't fancy him. Do you know what I mean?

I saw the bedroom curtains being pulled across. I lit my first cigarette in months. I stared at the beautiful flickering flame of the match as it burned and withered to charcoal. Then I walked slowly over to the house. I looked through the back window and quietly let myself in through the kitchen door at the side. I sat down, crossed my arms and legs, and looked around the kitchen. I couldn't hear anything. What were they doing? I stared at his flower embroideries in their frames on the kitchen wall. I thought of happier times as I looked up at the big canvas photo of our holiday at Disneyland in Florida, in all that lovely sunshine and blue sky and the two of us posing with Price Charming and Snow White. Now look at us. A damp, grey, afternoon in Faversham, Prince Charming upstairs with some little slag.

Of course everyone deserves a second chance. Maybe I should have gone up to the bedroom and said, 'Hey you, you little whore, get out of my house now! And you, you dirty snake, you're going to have to be extra nice to me for the next thirty years... and there'll no trips to IKEA anymore... and no more sweaty trainers... and no more chips with every meal AND from now there's going to be a new a set of rules which I'll pin to the cork board and if you break any of them you can go back to your Mum's and she'll have to cut your horrible long fingernails for you!'

It was still quiet. Maybe they were just cuddling. Maybe it was just a bit of petting they got up to, I could just about forgive that. As long as it wasn't love, well, maybe we might be able to sort it all out. Let's face it; I'm sure every man fancies himself with a different woman every now and again. I loved him, but sometimes, just sometimes, I would lie in bed at night thinking how it must feel to have a different man wrapping his arms around me, someone just a bit more, I don't know... refined, cultured and a lot less sweaty and hairy!

(She closes her eyes runs her hands down her arms and then across her body.) Mmm. That's it. Just soft, smooth flesh. Soft smooth flesh of a nice man. Now that feels so good. My first boyfriend, Liam, had a lovely slim, smooth body, you know. I was seventeen, he was nearly twenty! He seemed so grown up. Sensible and polite. He would come out with Dad and I when we went camping and hill walking. Dad wasn't too keen on me having boyfriends but he didn't mind Liam. He liked the love poems I wrote for him, not like mean old Puppy. We would snog for hours. Couldn't keep his hands off me. Then he went to University in Edinburgh, 400 miles away. Not long after he called me to say we'd have to stop seeing each other, he didn't have time with all his studying. Then I found out he had a girlfriend up there and that's when I torched his Mum and Dad's. No one was hurt. Just furniture, you know. Oh Liam, what a nice life we might have had together. He's a Doctor now. Married some Doctor-chasing nurse. Soon as they've walked a Doctor up the aisle do you ever find them nurses back on the wards emptying bed pans? No you don't.

But do you know what? I only think about Liam occasionally, that's all. I've found out on Google that he lives near Tonbridge these days. I know the GP surgery he works at, but I don't go calling him up and saying 'Hi Liam, remember me, fancy having an affair? I've changed, yes, I really have, all that angry teenage stuff is behind me now, Liam, and I know you used to think I was gorgeous, didn't you? There's no more fires, Liam. No more fires, and I promise you there's no need to worry about your wife, I won't say anything, she'll never ever find out, you can end it anytime you like, no strings, just a lot of fun to be had, your lovely soft flesh against mine, what do you say, Liam? Would you like to put your strong arms around me and hold me tight and cherish me and protect me?'

I could easily contact Liam. Arrange to meet one night after work. I'm sure he would be tempted. I'd tell him that I was now the Deputy Head of HR for the Borough Council. That would impress him. Yeah, that's right, HR, Liam, I've always been a people person, you know. I'd wear something sexy, a bit revealing. You know, show a bit of what you've got; flaunt it if you've got it, that's what I say; oh, I'd love to be a Doctor's wife.

But you just *don't* do those things once you've made a wedding vow, do you? You're not supposed to go cheating. Then I heard them at it. The bed creaking. So that was it, time to get on with what I'd planned. I closed the kitchen door really gently so they couldn't hear me and I went straight to the cooker. I put the chip pan on the hob and turned the gas it up to its highest setting. I reached for the smoke alarm on the wall and took out the batteries. Then I took off my shoes so as not to make a noise and paced the kitchen waiting for the pan to boil. I imagined what the newspaper headlines would read the next day.

20 YEARS ON:
'FAVERSHAM FIRESTARTER' ATTACKS
HUSBAND AND LOVER

She was a noisy little bitch. I could hear her muffled moans and squeals through the ceiling. He just grunted, so nothing new there. As the bed began to bang against the wall upstairs… *(She reaches for an imaginary chip pan.)* …the hot oil began to sizzle in the pan. Blue smoke was coming off it. I opened the kitchen door, made the sign of the cross, and lifted the heavy pan slowly up the stairs. Have you ever tried to carry a pan of boiling oil up the stairs without spilling it? It's not easy. Oh no, look, another drop spilled on my beautiful new carpet, it's going to take ages to get those fat stains out, now look, I've left a trail all the way up the stairs. It was still sizzling and crackling as I got nearer the bedroom door which was half open. He was laid down on our bed and the little whore was on top of my husband. She had her back to me. Her blonde hair swinging from side to side, making silly little squeals as he did it to her. He had his fat hands, with those long fingernails digging into her buttocks and caressing the sides of her hips. She had a tattoo of a butterfly on her bottom and he had a stupid smile on his face.

I stood there like this. The pan was getting heavy in my arms. I could have changed my mind. I suppose I never really intended to go through with it, but then she told him to push harder and faster and then ... and then I was transfixed by that little butterfly flying up and down on her backside. I didn't want to hurt the butterfly. The butterfly was innocent. I took a step back, I couldn't go through with it and edged back like this... but then he told her that he loved her. And that was it you see, that's when I snapped. He said he loved her, when he should have been loving me! I was his wife wasn't I?

I rushed into the room. He saw me, his eyes wide with shock. He immediately took his hands off her hips and tried to push her off. I lifted the pan high like this. The girl turned around and we locked eyes and she let out a scream – and whoosh! I threw the hot oil over him, and then whoosh! The rest over her. Burn little butterfly, burn cheating husband. I shouted out 'How much do you love your chips now Puppy dog? Burn!'

I stood back against the wall and watched as they wriggled in agony on the bed. The boiling oil hissed; their skin bubbled up like poppadums in hot pan, burning them to a crisp. I had done a really good job covering them all over, and the pair of them screamed out like lobsters in a pot. It was a great sight; they were frying alive, gasping for breath. Her butterfly just sizzled away. I dropped the pan, walked out of the house and left them to it. It was as simple as that. I drove down to the coast and sat on the flinty pebbles and stared out to sea. I didn't think about what I had just done. I thought about the time Puppy and I were in Disneyland. I thought about Liam's lovely smooth skin. I thought about camping in the Lakes with Dad.

It was beginning to get dark. Two police men came walking along the beach towards me. They said Puppy and the girl had been taken to hospital. I got in their police car. That was about a month ago. Now I'm in here.

She won't be stealing other women's husbands again with all her pretty looks gone. And him, well I don't know, I haven't seen him, why hasn't he come to see me? That's how good a husband he turned out to be. Won't even visit his own wife. If my Dad was still alive he'd get me out of here, that's for sure. He'd stand up for me, he'd get it all sorted.

They've sent a half a dozen different psychiatrists to check me out. They all come in here, tilt their heads to one side, talk re-a-lly, sl-ow-ly, and say 'Uh-mm, I see, yes, well, tell me about your teenage years, and those fires you started back then. Take your time, we're here to listen.' They try to look so concerned. One bitch said she could empathise with me.

'What? Empathise?' I said to her. 'Empathise?' 'When was the last time you poured boiling chip pan oil over your husband?' She said she never had, so I told her to stick her empathy up her fat arse.

Now, some people think I've gone mad, and some don't. They don't actually say 'Mad', oh no, they've got a 101 different words instead. *(Gesturing quotation marks)* Deep-rooted psychological, pyromaniac, paternalistic pap, psychosomatic ... and load of other piss sounding words beginning with the letter 'P'– blah, blah, blah, whatever.'

~~~

What's all the fuss anyway? All families go through bad patches. Remember those lines from *Anna Karenina*? 'All happy families are alike; each unhappy family is unhappy in its own way.' That's how Puppy and me were. We were just going through a bad patch, that's all. We don't need all this interference from Doctors and the Police. He got punished for what he did; he learned his lesson, and as soon as I'm out of here he'll be wagging his little puppy dog tail begging me to have me back again.

So, what do you think? I'm not mad. I'm not mad am I? Come on, I know you're listening; I know someone out there must be listening and watching me. I know you'll all be tut-tutting and rolling your eyes. But he deserved it, didn't he? You can see that, can't you? 'Don't let any man make a fool of you, darlin'.' That's what Dad always used to say to me; and he was right. Puppy *had* made a fool of me, hadn't he? So he deserved it, didn't he? Puppy deserved what he got; didn't he?

Well didn't he? *(Blackout)*

The Parkrun Spirit

by Lin White

I took a good hard look at myself in the mirror. It was not a pretty sight. Overweight, unfit, on the verge of depression – it was time I took control of my life.

'Why don't you take up running?' a friend suggested. 'You could try parkrun.'

'Parkrun? What's that?'

She explained that parkrun was an organised, timed run. At 9am every Saturday morning, at various locations all around the country – and in some other countries as well – people would gather and run 5 kilometres, just over 3 miles, and receive their times via an email a short time later.

Just a few days later I tried the parkrun experience myself. I stood by the kiosk at the top of Tankerton slopes in the cold wind, wearing cheap pair of trainers, a pair of jogging bottoms and loose teeshirt, with a sweatshirt doing its best to keep the worst of the chill from me. All around me were a whole host of people in high visibility running gear, shirts declaring their owner had taken part in various races, expensive shoes, high-tech watches and gadgets, and were busy chatting, stretching or doing both at once. I wondered what the hell I was doing there. Would I even manage the whole distance? I'd been out walking and jogging during the week, but still couldn't manage to run very far before needing to take a break.

'Let's get down to the start,' the call went out, and I followed everyone else down to the prom, feeling like an interloper. I hovered at the back of the crowd while warnings and notices were given, and then we were off!

For one heady moment I was in the middle of a pack of runners hurtling along the prom. I felt fantastic. I could do this! All around me were people of different shapes and sizes, and I was one of them. My feet ate up the ground in a steady rhythm, and the beach huts approached steadily.

Then my breath ran out.

I slowed to a walk, legs feeling like lead, watching the proper runners disappear into the distance. I could scarcely catch my breath in the icy wind coming off the sea, but I struggled gamely along after the fast-disappearing crowd of runners, forcing myself back into an unsightly run whenever I could.

Just after the sailing club, the route took a right turn up the slope, turned right again and headed back along the top of the slope, on the grass. I staggered up that mountain, gasping for breath, and gazed in despair at the last runner just disappearing past the café a few hundred metres further on. How in hell's name was I to stand a second lap of this course? We were only halfway round the first lap, and I was exhausted. What was the point? I was not a runner, and never would be. I was useless, in this as with everything else.

At that moment, I heard a voice. Glancing to the side, I saw a man sitting on the bench, watching us. He looked to be in his seventies, but with the lean build of a runner. He wore full running gear, blue shorts and a pale green top bearing the name of a local running club. His trainers looked as though they'd seen some distance. *Oh, great, yet another person who's fitter than me.* He smiled at me. 'You can do it,' he said. 'You're doing a fantastic job. That's the spirit.'

Buoyed up by his words, I increased my pace again – not that there was much difference between my walk and my jog – and pushed on towards that kiosk. All I had to do was get back there, and then I could slip away to the nearby car. I didn't know anyone here, I was only doing this for myself, and who would care or even notice if I dropped out after one lap?

But something strange happened as I plodded along on the grass. My breathing had eased a little, and I found my rhythm. I drove myself along by thinking of the problems at work. I was out of my depth, and under pressure from management. I was worried about my job, but lacked the courage to act. Anger and frustration worked its way through my feet, and when I reached the end of the first lap I found myself heading down the slope at the kiosk end of the course, heading away from the car again and back along the prom. The runners ahead of me were all out of sight by now, but I no longer cared. I was moving, and it felt good.

I looked for the old man as I staggered up the slope a second time, and there he was, watching. He gave me a thumbs-up as I went past, determined to run rather than walk, and grinned. 'That's the spirit,' he said again. 'You've got this. Fantastic. Just take small steps up the slope, and it will be easier. Same effort, not same speed.'

By the time I reached the finish line, most people had disappeared. Only a few remained, packing up the table, gathering in the markers for the finish funnel, and one solitary person with a scanner, who took my scruffy piece of paper and finish token with a smile, scanned them both with the portable scanner and handed my piece back with a 'well done.'

When I got home, I lay on the sofa, aching, sore, lungs burning, and did very little else for the rest of the weekend, but when I thought of parkrun, I had a sense of achievement, and decided that I would be back.

That week at work was hard. The new manager seemed determined to pile pressure after pressure on me, and while I did my best, it was exhausting. I just kept my head down and kept going. 'Little steps,' I reminded myself. 'Make the same effort, don't try to keep the same speed.' It seemed to work. The manager was satisfied and I got through the crisis.

~~~

I saw lots of runners the next few Saturdays, but not the man who had encouraged me that time. At least I was getting fitter. The rest of the pack would still disappear in the distance, but I could keep up with them for longer. I still struggled on the hill, but would always remember my friend's advice.

Then, one day, he was there again, sitting on his bench. He waved when he saw me, and I waved back, happy to see him.

On the second lap, he appeared beside me, keeping up easily. 'Don't let me hold you back,' I said, but he just smiled.

I told him I was thinking of entering a race, but wasn't sure whether I'd be fast enough.

'It doesn't matter,' he said. 'You don't have to be fast. You just have to do your best.'

He ran the last leg of the course with me, striding out easily as I huffed and puffed. I'd set out to beat my time, and it was a struggle. 'You know you can do this,' he said, as we approached the finish funnel. 'The only question is, how much do you want it?' He peeled away, leaving me on my own for the final few metres.

I focused on my breathing and my stride, and put all the effort I could into it, and crossed the line nearly ready to collapse, but jubilant at the time on my watch. The text message I received a couple of hours later confirmed it – a new personal best!

Work became tough again. A big job, and it required all my concentration. 'Don't think you can do it?' my boss asked.

I scowled, knowing that he wanted me to fail. 'I can do it,' I told him. And I knew the secret was that I had to actually want to do it. All my effort, and things were finally completed as they should be.

I started talking to people before parkrun on a Saturday morning. After all, we were all runners; there was always something to talk about. Sometimes, now, there were even people finishing behind me. I tried to stick around and encourage them across the finish line. I knew just how bad it had felt to be so far behind. I always looked out for my runner, but he was nowhere to be seen.

The race was tough, but when I struggled, I imagined my runner beside me, encouraging me, and somehow I managed to push myself to the end. The sense of achievement was massive, and the thought of that triumph gave me the strength to make the decision I knew had been coming for a while: I handed in my notice at work the next day. It was time to try something new.

It was my 50th run, the one that would earn me a special red shirt with 50 on it.. I'd only missed a couple of weeks in the year, and so this run was almost exactly a year after my first. I strode out confidently, wearing shorts and the race shirt I'd earned a few weeks before. That first run seemed a lifetime ago; I'd gone a long way since then, literally and figuratively. I'd quit my job, started a new business, lost weight and grown fitter, and felt a million times better. Parkrun, and the people I had met there, had played a huge part in that.

I was at the back of the pack again. But that was because I was doing a special job: parkrun had decided that runs should have a tail runner, to support those at the back. I wore an orange tabard, and I would run behind the rest, looking after those who for one reason or another formed the tail of the pack. I had a couple of people with me, and as they struggled along we chatted together. Going up the hill I encouraged them: 'Little steps. Don't try to take it too fast, just keep going and worry about speed later.' I was almost too engrossed in supporting them to check the bench, but as I looked across I saw him sitting there, giving me a big thumbs-up. 'That's the spirit!' I heard him say. But this time he wasn't wearing running gear; instead, he was wearing a suit and tie, and looked so formal that it seemed odd.

On our second lap, he wasn't there, but I noticed that the bench he usually sat on had flowers tied to each end. I was curious enough that I diverted across to his bench, to read the plaque on it.

'Paul Hendon, 1940-2015. Much loved and missed.' A card on one of the bunches of flowers read, 'Thinking of you on the second anniversary of your death.'

I shivered. Was it the cold wind or something else?

When I reached the finish, I asked about the bench, and the man it was dedicated to. 'Paul? Yeah. He was one of our first runners. He did a lot for local sport. He died of a heart attack, while out running. Must be a couple of years ago, I think.'

I looked on the web when I got home, and found a photo of this Paul Hendon. It was my runner, complete with the running gear, and the club shirt. He smiled at the camera, and was giving a thumbs-up. I read about the man who gave so much to the running community.

I saw him only once more; the next time I ran, I looked up at his bench and he was there. Back in running gear, looking younger than he had before, and smiling as he saw me looking at him. He gave his usual thumbs-up. 'That's the spirit,' he said.

I turned to my companion, and pointed him out. 'Who?' she asked.

I looked back at the bench, but it was empty. I smiled to myself, understanding at last. I thought about all I'd achieved over the past year, and the way he had challenged me just when I needed it. Just as parkrun itself had done.

'I guess you could say he's the parkrun spirit,' I said.

Love and Cyn

by James Dutch

People say that love finds you when you least expect it, so I guess it was the right time for me. Cyn was everything I could have hoped for, but never did, fearing failure. Elegant, caring, intelligent and graceful, but also funny, down-to-earth – and she was beautiful. Almost *too* beautiful. Not in a conventional, airbrushed way, but she emanated something unexplainable, unique.

I met her in *The Lane* in Deal, a cafe I started frequenting out of self-pity at first – it was where I'd proposed to Jackie. That question didn't get the response I wanted, but I think I loved her, so when she moved out of our tiny Canterbury flat and back to Scotland, I travelled back to *The Lane* once a week to see if I could still smell her perfume, or catch a glimpse of a memory that would bring her closer to me. The guy making the coffee only asked *where's your girlfriend today?* once – tears fell and I got that coffee on the house.

But that was nearly four years ago and, after a couple of dates that didn't work out, I settled into a routine that suited me just fine. I'd hit the road every weekday morning and get down to Deal for around 10am for coffee. I had found that after a suitable period of mourning my relationship with Jackie, all was not lost, and my writing output increased significantly. And *The Lane* had become *My Office*. I'd sit and flick through *The Independent*, reading the small articles and making a mental note of the bigger features I'd read later at home, before opening the laptop and churning out the words.

When the school holidays arrived, I would visit Deal less frequently, staying at home and working on new ideas; I preferred the solitude and sleepiness of the seaside out of season. As soon as the kids had all returned to school in September, I began the ritual again – I'd wake up, hit the road, and arrive at My Office around 10am, laptop and newspaper in my rucksack.

As soon as I opened the door that first day back after the summer, I knew something was different. I breathed in deeply, a habit I'd started when Jackie had left; at first it was a way to search for her – she wore that rich, tomato-soupy perfume by Jean-Paul Gaultier – but after a time it became part of the ritual of starting work. Just before I entered My Office, I took a deep breath of fresh sea air to clear my olfactory senses. Then I opened the door to smell the coffee.

As the warm air hit my nostrils I became immediately aware of a new scent. It was all over, under, and through the earthy, bitter, dark chocolate warmth of the coffee – a sweet bottom note of rich, caramel with a perfectly balanced top of fresh vanilla. The effect was mouthwatering, but the new smell also aroused something base and primitive deep within me. I shook my head, trying to clear the light-headedness which threatened to overcome me as I stepped over to the counter, and smiled at Mr Barista (I could never remember his name and still felt bad about crying on him).

'Morning, my friend.' The same old greeting; I guessed he couldn't remember my name either. 'The usual for you?'

I half-closed my eyes and sniffed the air again. 'What is that amazing smell?' I asked, ignoring his question.

He cocked his head in the direction of My Seat in the corner by the big chalkboard wall. 'It wafted in with her,' he whispered. I looked over, prepared to be annoyed that someone was sitting at my table. 'Beautiful scent for a beautiful woman.' He was right. She was the most beautiful woman I'd ever seen. Mr Barista leant over the counter and gently pushed my lower jaw back up to its proper place. 'Doesn't do to drool, my friend.' He smiled at me. 'Just wait until you see her face.'

I realised then that I was staring at the most beautiful back of someone's head I'd ever seen. Her short, dark red hair was in the sort of tousled mess it takes at least half an hour to perfect, leaving her slim, delicate neck and the lightly freckled skin of her shoulders visible above the wide neckline of a green jumper. I nodded at Mr Barista. 'Right,' I said absently. 'I'll take the usual then, please.'

He made my small Americano. 'This one's on the house,' he said as he passed me the drink. I took hold of the saucer, but he didn't let go. A glint came into his eye and he smiled mischievously. 'As long as you take a seat at your table.' The cup rattled slightly in the saucer as he released his grip; my hands were shaking.

'Thanks,' I said, my voice just a dry whisper. 'Right then.' Part of me thought, just pay the man and sit elsewhere. I mean, just what kind of schoolboy dare was this? But another part of me already knew, *you're falling into her, either way*. I walked slowly towards the red-haired woman, stopped and looked back. Mr Barista nodded encouragingly. Just a few more steps – enough time for me to realise that I wasn't in a movie, and that this approach just doesn't work in real life. I decided to back out before I made a complete fool of myself.

I placed my coffee on the table made for two, the table I'd used for one for at least four hours a day whenever I was here, and felt an unpleasant twang of surprise at my automaton actions. The woman looked up from her book, smiling, and her forest green eyes twinkled – and I mean they literally twinkled, as though they were reflecting the ancient light of a thousand bright stars. And then, a look of confusion crossed her face, breaking the fairytale magic, and she looked back at the empty chairs behind her, to Mr Barista, who started whistling innocently, and then back to me.

'Can I help you?' She asked. Her voice was as smooth as the caramel she smelled so sweetly of, and had a mellow, musical tone. It seemed to come from all around me, although her full, pink lips parted to speak. I looked into those deep green eyes and shrugged, saying nothing. My heart bounded in my chest, and I hoped I wouldn't start sweating. 'Are you all right?' She leant her head slightly to one side to regard me, narrowing her eyes. It was a simple movement, but one which made her look so unbelievably cute that I'm afraid to say I let out a small sigh. 'You don't look all right.' She shook her head ever so slightly. 'Sit down.' I sat.

'I usually sit here,' I blurted out. I felt I had to say something, and regretted immediately that I hadn't chosen my first words more wisely.

'Oh! I can move. I didn't know—'

'No, please don't move,' I said hurriedly. 'I just... Well, the thing is... It's just that I've never seen...' She looked at me as if I were a curious creature hatching from an egg. The words I used every day to earn a living, my tools, my language, failed me. I held a hand up in a gesture I hoped would gain me a few seconds' thinking time. I took a sip of coffee, and then spoke my simple heartfelt sentence slowly. 'You are the most beautiful

woman I have ever seen.' My cheeks immediately flushed hot.

She looked at me for a second without emotion, and then she laughed. It was a genuine laugh – it was a perfect laugh. And she wasn't laughing at me, just at what I'd said. I wanted to tell her – this is not a chat-up line, this is just me being honest – and then she stopped laughing and smiled. 'Thank you, that's very sweet.' She reached a hand across the table and placed it over mine. 'I'm Cynthia, and you are a very handsome man.'

I didn't take my laptop out of

my bag that day, nor did I read the newspaper. Cynthia and I talked over our coffees and then we walked side-by-side around to the sea-front and along the pier where we sat around the back of the restaurant, looking out to sea together. The sun was behind a haze of low cloud, the sea was calm, the gulls were quiet and I melted into her words. She talked about her passion for small, fluffy animals, bashfully mentioning that she ran a rescue centre for unwanted pets out of her house. I told her about my writing – the novel I'd been working on, the articles I'd written – taking care not to sound self aggrandising, by omitting names of well-known newspapers and journals in which I'd recently started being published.

We ended up back at Cyn's place, just down the road in Walmer – a large detached house just off the sea-front near the castle. I whistled, impressed. 'Nice place,' I said as my car crunched onto the gravel driveway.

Cyn smiled and looked slightly embarrassed. 'My dad's very generous. I'll show you around.' She took my hand and gave me a quick tour of the house. I'm not one for interiors, to be honest, but I could tell that this woman had good, expensive taste. She pointed up to a colourful, modern chandelier of colourful blown glass. 'I adore Chihuly,' she smiled.

'Wasn't he the hairy one from Star Wars?' I joked. Cyn laughed her wonderful laugh again, and I almost went weak at the knees. Still holding her hand, I pulled her gently toward me and put my other arm around her, gently tracing my fingers across the back of her neck. My pulse increased and my breathing became shallow and quick; I was so nervous I trembled. She gazed at me with those eyes and I felt her warm breath on my cheek before she turned her face ever so slightly and our lips touched.

When I woke two hours later, I kept my eyes closed. I knew if I opened them, I'd be back in my single bed in my small apartment overlooking the main road back in Canterbury. The thought of the A28 made my ears alert to the sounds of the constant traffic, but all I heard was the solitary cry of a gull. I stretched my leg out; I was alone, but whatever bed I was in, it was certainly bigger than my own. I began to think that maybe I hadn't just had the best dream of my life. My eyelids opened fast, my senses buzzing – she was real. I almost fell off the bed in my haste, and jumped into my clothes before making my way back downstairs, passing back under the ostentatious light fitting. I walked silently, any noise my footsteps made swallowed by the deep pile of the sumptuous carpet, and followed the voice I could hear coming from behind a closed door down the hall.

'...so I don't want you making your stupid animal noises, Jeremy.' It was her. The voice of an angel, only now with a slightly hard edge. I slowed my walk and crept to the door, leaning in so I could hear her better. 'That goes for all of you. When you see him, *be nice*,' she said, sounding like a strict school headmistress.

There was a whining, followed by a few seconds' silence before the door opened. I reached for the handle to make it seem like I'd just arrived and hadn't heard a thing. Cynthia looked at me questioningly at first, then saw my flustered look. 'Sleep well?' she asked. I nodded and she smiled. 'Feeling awkward?'

'I... a little, I suppose,' I admitted. 'I've never done anything like this before.'

She took my hand and kissed my cheek. 'A first time for everything,' she whispered; her warm breath in my ear sent shivers down my spine. 'And hopefully a second and third when you've woken up a bit.' Cynthia pulled me back through the door she'd just opened. 'My menagerie,' she announced as she took me into a large room containing several cages. In the first was one of those savage-looking dogs that seem to be a legal replacement for a deadly weapon; Cynthia opened the cage and stroked the dog's back – it seemed to cringe away from her touch, crouching so that its belly touched the floor. 'This is Jeremy,' she said. 'He can be a pest, but he knows who the boss is.' The dog couldn't take its wide eyes off Cyn. She now had her hand resting on Jeremy's flank and he was as still as stone.

'Jeremy?' It seemed an unlikely name. 'Where's he from?'

'Unwanted,' was all she said. She took her hand out of the cage and Jeremy finally took his eyes off her.

'How long have you had him here?' I asked. The dog looked at me, then crawled into the basket in the corner of the cage.

'Only a few months. He's still getting used to his new life, but he's a quick learner.' She sighed. 'It's so sad when no one wants you, isn't it Jeremy?' The dog buried his nose under the blanket.

'What other animals do you have?' I asked, looking at the other cages. 'They're all so quiet.' Each cage had a small mirror set close by. I was about to ask what they were for, but Cyn had already moved on.

She walked along to the next set of cages. 'Rats,' she said. 'I've been collecting these over the past eight years or so.' Three rats sat separately in corners of the cage. One, white, had its eyes closed. 'That's Greg,' she said, then pointed to another, white with brown splodges, who seemed to sway slightly. 'Liam's a daydreamer.'

'That one looks like a surly teenager,' I said as the third rat, black with a white eye-patch turned its back to us, stood on its back legs and faced the wall, crossing its front paws.

'Matthew? Yes, he's a tiresome little soul, but I couldn't bear to part with him.'

Matthew looked over his ratty shoulder, wrinkled his nose and hissed.

Cynthia showed me the rest of her rescued animals. A mouse called Jim, twin hamsters – Bill and Ben – and a venomous snake called Lee. And then she closed the door behind us as we exited the room and took me back upstairs to try out the king-sized bed again; afterwards we discussed when I should move in.

~~~

Over the following few months, my writing output dipped somewhat. Cyn would send me out to My Office every day, but convinced me to follow my dreams – *work on the novel, you have a great story in you,* she said. When I worried about not getting paid, she reminded me of her benevolent father. Cyn never did a paid day's work, just looked after her animals – *lost souls* she called them – and read books and made love to me. I can honestly say that most days felt as dream-like as that first afternoon when I woke up in the bed of an angel.

One mild evening in early March, six months after we'd first met, Cynthia came downstairs wrapped deliciously in just a slate grey towel, her skin pink and glistening, and told me that she had received a text message while she was in the bath. 'Daddy's coming to visit!'

'That's great,' I replied. 'When is he coming?' I'd wanted to meet the generous man who'd been indirectly funding my sweet new lifestyle for some time, but whenever I mentioned it, Cyn had said he was an extremely busy man.

'He's on his way now.'

'Now?' I wanted to make a good impression and felt that time to prepare would have been nice.

Cynthia nodded. 'I know it's short notice, but he's so busy and...' She paused and approached, putting a hand on my chest. 'Look, don't worry about Daddy; he'll love you as you are.' An unusual look of concern flickered across her face for a brief moment.

'What is it?'

Cyn sighed. 'Remember when you asked me why I was single? Well, it's to do with my dad – partly.'

All I could say was: 'Oh,' as handful of awful, awkward scenarios played through my head. Cyn stood there, looking stunning, and biting her bottom lip nervously. 'Why? What is it?'

'It's his job,' said Cyn.

'He's not a Tory MP, is he?'

'Well, it is government work at the moment,' she said shyly. 'But, it's more than that – it's also his way of life, his very existence you might say.'

'I'm not really following,' I said. 'Can you just tell me, in black and white?'

'He's the Devil.' She said this with a cute, albeit apologetic smile and a small shrug, as if she'd just told me that her dad constantly cracked rude jokes, or something equally innocuous.

'I'm sorry?'

'You know the Devil, right? Well, that's my Dad, and it kind of puts men off.'

'I'm not surprised,' I said, playing along. 'Still, better than being a Tory.'

'You won't let it put you off, will you? It's just that when people don't believe me or my Dad, well… I just can't stand it!' She stamped her foot on the luxurious carpet. 'It's the one thing that makes me mad and it's been the end of every relationship I've ever had.'

'You have my solemn promise,' I said taking her hands in mine. 'You have my heart. You have my soul. I love you.' And I meant it, every word, I really did. Whatever little joke she wanted to play on me, was absolutely fine. She smiled, showing her beautiful white teeth, and her deep green eyes sparkled, just like they always did before she led me to the bedroom. We began kissing and she let the towel fall to the floor – and then there was a knock at the door.

Cynthia gasped. 'It's him!' She laughed, snatched up her towel and ran up the stairs, calling back that I should let her father in while she got dressed. I took a few steps towards the door, rearranged my erection so that it wasn't too obvious, and then scuttled down the hall to greet Cynthia's father. As I opened the door, I had surreal visions of a huge, red man with a pointy black beard and two whacking great horns – but I was mistaken.

'I'm Stan. You must be Cedric, nice to meet you.' Cyn's father held out a hand and I shook it. It was limp and a little clammy. 'You look somewhat confused,' he said in a nasal, jobsworth tone of voice.

'I was expecting someone...'

'Bigger?' he guessed.

'Definitely. And redder, and more hoofy. With less of a pot-belly.' I felt shocked by my rudeness, and had no idea where it had come from. I put my hand quickly over my big mouth.

'Oops, good one,' he laughed, apparently not offended. 'Shall I come in?'

I nodded, stammering an apology, which he waved away. 'Where's Cynthia?'

'Just getting dressed upstairs,' I said. Stan nodded and clucked his tongue, and we stood awkwardly, smiling and raising our eyebrows in a ridiculously comic fashion. 'So, let me guess,' I asked. 'Accountant? You look like an accountant. Oh, sorry – I didn't mean...'

Stan half nods and I notice he has the same beautiful green eyes as his daughter. 'Taxation at the moment,' he said. 'Do you take an interest in the news?' Without waiting for a response, Stan continued. 'Budget day tomorrow – I've been extremely busy with it, hence my unusually relaxed attire this evening. Sometimes it does one good to throw off the shackles of the workaday week, don't you think?'

'Ah, yes, yes I suppose so.'

'Did Cyn tell you much about me, or our family?'

'She did, briefly, yes.' I laughed nervously. Stan waited, patiently, but obviously eager to know what had been said. He raised his eyebrows and waited for me to continue.

'Oh, just that you're the Devil.' I made stupid claw like hands and attempted a little monster-ish *Rarr* noise.

Stan exhaled and sat down in Cyn's favourite leather armchair. From a small bag, he produced a slim, unlabeled bottle. 'A drink, that's what we need.' He pointed to the drinks cabinet. 'Brandy glasses if she's got any.'

She didn't, so I brought two whiskey tumblers. Stan poured us both small measures, and we clinked glasses. I took a small sip – brandy isn't a drink of choice for me, but I felt awed by the sweetness of the deep gold liquid; something about it reminded me of the first time I kissed Cyn.

'Best drink on the planet,' said Stan, licking his lips.

'I've never tasted brandy like it.' I peered into the glass, marveling at the way the liquid swirled, almost too slowly.

'Not brandy,' Stan laughed. 'Something of my own concoction, just for special occasions.'

'Well, I'm honoured,' I said. 'But what occasion are we drinking to?'

'She told you.' Stan looked at me expectantly, but I must have looked confused. 'That I was the Devil?' he prompted.

I felt somewhat nervous, unsure of this strangely confident, pot-bellied little man. 'Yeah, but not one of her finest comedy moments, obviously.' When I laughed, the noise that came out sounded like a squirrel that had just been trodden on.

Stan shook his head, and smiled, raising his glass. 'To your good health, young man – and I hope you never upset my daughter. She's not as forgiving as me.' Snuggling back into the armchair, he stretched his short legs out. I noticed he was wearing tartan slippers – I could have sworn they were some kind of old-man loafer when he walked in. I looked back up and he was looking straight at me. 'My existence,' he said, 'is usually scoffed at, even by people who refer to themselves as *religious*.' He waved his hand dismissively. 'They say they love God and fear the Devil. Ha! It's *Him* they should be bloody fearing, not Me! I'm the one that's working hard balancing the books, making sure the wheels are greased.' Stan took another small sip of his drink. 'No, He lost all interest after his son took over.'

'You mean… Jesus?'

'Mmm, nice fellow. A real people person, but couldn't manage his way out of a paper bag.'

'I don't follow,' I said. I knew he wasn't lying to me, but

whether his perception of reality was aligned to mine, I didn't know.

'Jesus was a lovely man. He'd do anything for anyone, and that made him popular amongst the masses. But it also meant that his staff took advantage of his good nature. Long lunch breaks, sickies, disloyalty.' Stan counted the misdemeanors off on his fingers. 'I'd never allow that sort of low level, long term, disruptive behaviour to continue. It's no way to run a business.'

'Sorry,' I said. 'You know Jesus?'

'I knew him, yes.'

I nodded slowly. 'You'll excuse me if I don't actually believe a word of this, won't you? I mean – no offence, you seem like a lovely person, and I love your daughter, but—'

'You promised her your soul,' Stan interrupted. I must have looked confused, again. He sighed and then continued. 'Just before you let me in, you said "you have my heart, you have my soul".'

I scanned the room quickly for any evidence of a microphone that could have bugged the conversation. 'How did you know?'

'Do you love her?'

'Yes.' My mind wandered back to the moment just before Stan knocked on the door. 'We were about to have sex,' I said. Immediately, I clamped my hand across my mouth.

Stan rolled his eyes. 'Then you'll accept her for what she is, and who her father is. That's what it means to promise your soul.'

'I'm so sorry,' I said. It was the second time words had made their way from my brain to my mouth without permission since Stan turned up. 'I'm not sure why I said that.'

Stan leaned forward and patted me on the knee. 'Please don't worry, Cedric,' he said. 'Your mortal brain is probably a little frazzled by my presence.'

'You think highly of yourself,' I replied – again without thinking. Tiny pins and needles of embarrassment pricked my skin and my pulse rate increased. 'We had sex twice already before you came round.' I yelped and held both hands over my mouth.

Stan grimaced slightly then laughed. 'Now you know what can happen, the first thing you did was think of something else you shouldn't tell me. Classic!'

I kept my mouth firmly shut. My hands were shaking.

Stan saw the state I was in and tried to stop chortling. 'You're okay, son. Just try to clear your mind for a moment while I re-adjust.' He rubbed his hands together, closed his eyes and sat very still for a moment. A small hiccup of laughter escaped his lips, and he whispered 'sorry.' I assumed the apology was directed at me. 'There you go,' he said after a few seconds.

'What did you do?'

'I bent the rules. Go on, think of something I don't want to know about,' he nodded. Nothing came to mind, and he rolled his eyes at me again. 'You're not trying, Cedric.'

I envisaged a scenario involving myself and Cyn. It was hard work under the watchful eye of her father, and I felt myself redden – but no words came out of my mouth.

'Well, I guess that worked,' he said after eyeing my crimson cheeks.

'Are you some kind of magician, or hypnotist?' I asked, frustrated.

'Yes.'

I breathed a sigh of relief; the game was up. 'So you aren't the Devil? This is a prank.'

'No, I'm still the Devil.'

'But…'

Cynthia came back into the room. She was fully dressed, but looked a little nervous; wide eyed and smiling, showing her perfect white teeth. 'Hi Daddy,' she said. 'How's it going?'

'Hello petal, Ced and I were just discussing my job. He's a right non-believer, isn't he?'

Cyn nodded. 'Maybe I should have prepared him a little better,' she said, looking thoughtful. 'But I wasn't sure how to…'

'Ah, these modern times,' continued Stan. 'No one can truly believe anymore – I mean, when was the last time there was even a real miracle?'

Cynthia looked at the ceiling. 'Errr, I don't remember. Not in my lifetime, that's for sure.'

'Fourteen seventy-eight.'

'Really? No. That long ago?' She looked at me and raised her eyebrows in a *well, how about that* kind of way. I just shrugged.

'What one was that, Dad?'

'Oh, a minor miracle. Not even performed by a Saint.'

Cynthia tutted and shook her head. 'Huh, Saints! Always slacking off.'

'Hmm, I was telling Cedric about that earlier... But no, this one was performed by a young boy, seven years old – with a little help of course.' Stan leaned forward in his chair, lowering his voice. 'The boy and his younger sister had been foraging for duck eggs around a pond. She fell in, floundered for a few seconds and was pulled under by the weight of her wet clothes. He couldn't swim, and there was no one within screaming distance. He began clawing at the surface of the pond, but every time he thrashed away some of the brown stagnant water, it replaced itself. Simple physics, really.'

'I remember this story.' Cynthia sat on the broad arm of the chair I was in and put her arm around my shoulder. 'This is why I love my Dad so much. Go on, Dad, tell the rest of the story.'

Stan smiled sadly, held his daughter's hand briefly and continued. 'I was passing, by pure chance, and saw what was happening. The boy was frantic, wailing, half in the water, but not daring to follow, lest the same fate befall him as his sister. And he started calling for God to help him...' Stan shook his head. 'Nothing happened, of course. Why would *He* help? So, I stopped time; I whispered into the boy's ear '*move the water, dig her out*,' and he began scooping again with his hands. But now, the water did not replace itself when the boy moved it, and he dug down until he reached his sister's foot, and dragged her out of the pond by her tiny, dirty ankle.' Stan stopped talking and took a deep breath, letting it out slowly.

I found myself with tears in my eyes. Part of me knew how ridiculous this was, but something in his nasal, monotone voice had enchanted me, I felt like I was there, watching the event unfold. 'What happened to the girl?' I whispered.

'She was drowned.' Stan sat back in his chair.

I felt anger build inside me, and spluttered: 'But I thought…'

Stan held up a hand and continued. 'I whispered into the boy's ear again – *put your hands on her heart*. He did this gently and with so much sorrow. His beautiful little sister had drowned in his care, and he would have sold his soul to the devil to bring her back.'

'You took his soul?' I clenched my fists and tears traced wet lines down my cheeks. 'She was already dead, and you took his soul, too?'

Stan nods. 'Yes, she was dead. But—'

I put my hands over my eyes. My heart felt wrenched like never before. 'You took his soul,' I sobbed, unaware of where all this emotion was coming from.

Cynthia stroked my hair gently. 'Let Dad finish the story.'

I nodded, sniffed and wiped my eyes with my sleeve. 'Fine.'

'I pushed down sharply on the boy's shoulders, several times, until the girl spewed half the filthy pond from her lungs and started coughing and breathing again.'

'You saved her life?'

Stan nodded, still smiling sadly. 'The boy did, really. I never touched her.'

I took a moment to regain my composure and brushed Cynthia's hand away from my shoulder. This joke had run its course and she should have known better. 'Right,' I said, my throat aching from trying not to cry too much. 'Just suppose you are the Devil – and I'm not saying you are—'

'Why should I *save* lives if I'm the Devil?'

I shrugged. 'Well that wouldn't be your job, would it?'

Cyn turned to look at me, and asked: 'Do you know what

the Devil is?' Her tone was challenging, and she was wearing a frown.

'I don't know,' I felt tired of this game. 'I always thought he was evil. Like a fallen angel or something.'

Stan looked pleased. He thrust his index finger towards the sky. 'Exactly! A fallen Angel. Emphasis on the word Angel, if you please.' He paused. 'You still look confused, son.'

'What are you talking about?' I hadn't been to church since I was a child, but knew enough Bible to know how the Devil behaved. 'Why are you going around saving people's lives?' I continued, my voice rising. 'Why did you fall?' I stopped yelling. Cynthia looked hurt, and Stan looked weary.

'It's a long, long story,' he began quietly. 'How can I put it in mortal words? Imagine you are employed, forever, by one person. But you start to question the way that person runs the company, you believe that person does not have the best interests of his customers in his heart – he rules by fear, he allows a powerful few to oppress many, over half of his customers are considered not as valuable or as intelligent because of their gender or colour. Wars are fought and people die daily, needlessly, in his name. How would you feel about working for that person?'

I shrugged. 'I wouldn't like it at all – I'd leave.'

'Say you can't leave.'

'Then I'd go above the boss,' I fired back.

'There's no one above the boss, at least no one you can contact.'

'Then I'd expose him,' I replied. 'I'd tell people the truth about him. People would turn against him.'

'People love him, and those who don't – well, they're powerless to convince his admirers otherwise.'

I glanced at Cyn, she was looking at me to behave a certain way now, I could tell. She wanted me to show my true colours, prove I'd never give up on a cause. 'Then I'd try to change things myself, from inside the company.'

'Yes?' Stan sat forward, his face serious.

'Try to convince the boss that his way isn't right. Or maybe just do things my own way and hope he doesn't notice.'

Stan nodded. 'Exactly,' he said quietly. 'But what happens to such an employee? One who doesn't toe the party line, stands up to injustice? One who *is* noticed? Oh, and don't forget, this employee's contract is permanent – he can't be dismissed.'

'They get given the worst jobs, they get a disciplinary,' I said. 'But what has this got to do with you?'

'It's how I fell from grace. I still don't like how things are managed – or *not* managed, but I still have to do my job, to organize and balance.'

'Putting things into balance doesn't sound like the Devil's work.'

'You know,' said Cyn coldly. 'Dad wasn't always known as the Devil.' She had moved, without my noticing to sit next to her father. They were both looking at me.

'I have many names,' Stan said. 'Satan was one of them. I dropped the first 'a' for my current earthly name.' He smiled at his joke. 'I used to be called Lucifer, did you know that?' I nodded. 'Do you know what it means?' he asked. I shrugged and shook my head. '*Bringer of Light!*' He sat back and sighed. 'Still, that was before the fall; a different job title. Now I provide balance.'

'Balance doesn't sound evil,' I said. I wanted to argue against this foolishness, to put an end to the joke.

'Just bad publicity, that's all. I'm the black sheep, remember.' He tapped the side of his head. 'Anyway, evil is part of balance. It's the only way you humans appreciate light – when the darkness ensues.'

'So you're saying that there are terrorist attacks that kill people just so that we can appreciate the beauty of a flower?' I asked, incredulous.

'Yes and No,' replied Stan. 'And it's never as complicated as you humans would like to think, or as simple. One man's terrorist is another man's freedom fighter. One people's occupying army is another people's peacekeeping mission. A lot of it depends on your circumstances, your perspective.'

'Can't God just stop it?'

'People have free will—'

'Oh, yes,' I interrupted. 'I've heard that argument before. God gave people free will and then he doesn't have to take the blame for their actions. It's an old and nebulous argument.'

Stan smiled patiently. 'Do you believe people *should* have free will?'

'Well, yes, but God should have…'

'God should have what? Said *you have free will, now here's a list of things you shouldn't do?* No, the two don't work together.' He looked thoughtful for a moment. 'The Ten Commandments were supposed to be helpful, but God doesn't understand people.' Stan paused to take another sip of the sweet nectar. 'Anyway, God didn't give people free will, Cedric. I did. You know the story of Adam and Eve? The Serpent?' Stan pointed to himself and nodded. 'Showing Eve the tree of knowledge, and then everyone being thrown out of the Garden of Eden? Obviously, it's analogous, a way of showing people what happened without going into all the admin and bureaucracy. Heavenly Politics for Dummies, that's what the Bible is.'

'And that's why…'

'I fell, yes. God's little game led to consciousness evolving. It was very exciting for us all, we saw these little humans worshipping the sun, the moon, the stars; working with the rhythms of nature – the trees and rivers and seas, but they didn't know *Him*. And God is flawed and powerful, and prone to bouts of jealousy; he wanted these new creatures to love him best of all now they knew what love was. So, he pushed himself into their thoughts and made them grateful for all he had provided.'

'I suppose it's nice to be appreciated,' I said weakly.

'If he'd wanted something to worship him, he should have got a puppy!' There was a distorted growl just audible under the righteous whine of Stan's voice that gave me goose bumps. Cynthia must have seen the look on my face, and she just about managed to suppress a smirk. Stan rubbed his forehead and continued. 'Anyway, after that, the damage was done. God was pissed off, and I was to blame. He threw chaos at the world, and said – *sort that lot out*. I think he did feel *some* remorse later, what with his half-hearted attempt at helping me realign things, but like I said, Jesus was too nice to be able to effect a change.'

I was too freaked out to argue anymore, part of me wanted to laugh at this superbly executed prank, but a voice in the back of my head told me: *You'd better believe it...* A loud silence dominated for a while until I could no longer stand it. 'They say he'll come back. Is that true?' I asked, my voice a hoarse whisper.

'Jesus?' Stan seemed surprised by my question. 'He's been back several times. His last attempt saw him locked in an institution for most of that lifetime.' Stan leaned forward wagging his finger. 'No matter how religious a person says he is, tell him you're the son of God and he'll laugh in your face or lock you up.' Stan reclined in his chair and laced his fingers over his belly. 'I told him, I said: "Jesus, what you need to do is get into politics. You don't even need to mention your Dad, just use a bit of that extra oomph you can produce and make yourself prime minister, or president – one of the big ones, like China or Russia or the US." But he won't do it – says the people will come to him of their own accord, bless him. Such a nice bloke – he really bought into free will, even though it made his Dad so grumpy.'

Now that Stan's voice wasn't so scary, my rational mind kicked back into gear. 'I'm sorry,' I said. 'This is a really great joke, and you've prepared really well. But if you were the devil, I'd be terrified, and I'm not.'

'Myth!' Stan snorted, then he sighed. 'The human mind is a remarkable thing, really. You spend so much time worrying and being scared about what the future might hold, that you miss the real things occurring right under your nose.' My confusion must have shown on my face because Stan rolled his eyes and continued. 'I don't need to be Satan to sense how disappointed Cyn is right now, and I think that you can see it too. Your reaction to me will determine the rest of your life, and for that, you have my sympathy.'

'You're not the Devil,' I said simply, then looking at Cyn, 'I'm sorry – I know what I said earlier, but—'

Stan turned to look at Cynthia. 'Were you thinking this one was the one, love?'

Cyn raised an eyebrow, nodded and said: 'Yeah,' a half-smile playing on her perfect lips.

'It can't happen if he won't believe,' he said, lowering his voice.

'I know,' Cyn sighed. 'I thought he was better than this, but maybe he's just another mortal animal.'

'Why are you talking about me like that?' I demanded.

'It's a serious business,' said Stan. 'If a mortal pledges his soul in love to someone with angelic blood, they have a decision to make. Either the angel shares their immortality, or they share their lover's mortality.' I opened my mouth to speak, but nothing eloquent was available. Stan held a hand up. 'Not as simple a choice as it sounds. Immortality is not like in fiction. There are important things to think about – what if you fall out of love?' Stan asked. I opened my mouth again, but Stan continued. 'It happens. I'm a single Dad, you know. Cynthia's mother and I loved each other very much once, but one night she flipped and threw a pickled onion at me.'

'Oh, Poor Dad,' said Cynthia sadly.

'A pickled onion?' I couldn't help laughing. It was not the correct response.

Cyn and her father looked at me like I'd just slapped their grandmother. 'I love pickled onions, Cedric,' said Stan seriously. 'Well, I used to. I'd crunch my way through a jar every Friday night with my fish and chip supper in front of Corrie. One night she just thrust her hand into the jar, and let fly with a fistful of tiny silverskins. It turns out that was just the tip of the iceberg. She had grown to dislike me. My commitment to my work, my voice, my toenails… We made The Choice together – and that decision can't be changed. Now she'll spend forever alone, a pitiful existence for one who should have been mortal.' Stan shook his head. 'I never knew it all bothered Brenda so much, but then, I'd given her the same gift I gave you – I'd tuned out of her thoughts.'

'Dad's not used to subtle cues; most people just spill their secrets.' Cyn looked at me then her father, and I remembered my verbal slips from earlier. 'Oh, Ced!' she said, disappointed. 'You didn't tell him anything, did you?'

'No! I… Yes, sorry.' I shrugged.

'He couldn't help it, sweetheart.' Stan patted Cyn's arm. 'I wish I'd given him the gift as soon as he walked in.'

'I wish you'd take it away!' Cyn said quickly. 'It'd be interesting to see what he really thinks right now.'

Stan made a noise of agreement and clicked his fingers.

It was too much. I didn't even believe in God, and yet here I was, having a conversation with a man who thought he was the devil. 'You're nuts,' I said. Stan's eyebrows shot up in a comedic fashion. 'Really, bloody bonkers,' I continued. 'Both of you.'

Stan chortled and slapped his thigh. 'Well, there you go!'

Cyn stood up, hands on hips. 'How dare you insult my father?'

'And you, don't forget,' I reminded her. 'Seriously, you're either joking – in which case, you can't possibly be offended. Or, you're simply cracked if you think your dad is the Devil.'

Cyn prodded me in the chest 'You *know* he is.'

'No, he's not, Cyn. He's a tax man with a paunch.'

Cynthia stepped up to me, her beautiful face taking on the appearance of perfectly sculpted marble. 'We're finished, Cedric,' she whispered. 'You'll never find another woman like me.' And I knew it was the truth. The most beautiful woman I'd ever known walked away from me and stood by her father's side.

'Well, this is somewhat awkward,' said Stan. 'I must ask you to keep my secret, Cedric. Can you do that?'

'It's a fiction, you strange little man! And I will write it into a wonderful story.' I'm afraid to say, I said this out of spite, although I could see the situation making a neat little comedy. I was angry with them, but just as angry with myself; somewhere between my heart and my guts, a worm of realisation began to squirm.

Cyn wiped her eyes and let out a cold laugh. 'Have you ever heard the phrase truth is stranger than fiction?'

I didn't answer. Cyn's usually green sparkling eyes were dark, her pupils entirely dilated. Black clouds of grief began gathering.

'Well, I'm beat,' said Stan. He thumped the arms of the chair lightly and rocked his portly frame forwards to help him stand. 'Lovely to meet you Cedric, and sorry we disagreed.' He held out a hand for me to shake. I simply looked at him, and a laugh – or maybe it was a sob – made its way from my chest. 'You'll be all right dealing with him?' Stan asked Cyn. He kissed her on the cheek and headed to the door. I thought about reminding him to change out of his slippers, but upon checking, saw that he had his loafers on.

I laid my head back on the sofa and closed my eyes.

When I awoke, Cyn was looking at me. She seemed really close up. I blinked, but it was as though I was wearing someone else's eyes. It was the worst hangover of my life.

'Hello cutie,' she said. She seemed out of all proportion, out of focus and somehow like I was viewing her through a fish-eye lens, and her voice was deep and slow, and loud.

I wanted to tell her to go away, that I'd pack my things and leave in my own time. I tried to say her name, but my throat felt tight and nothing came out. My tongue swirled as I attempted to lubricate my mouth, but my teeth were all wrong and too long at the front. It felt like my brain was stuffed into a skull that was two sizes too small; I cursed her stupid father's sweetly lethal home-brew. I rubbed my eyes to adjust my blurry vision; the backs of my hands felt all scratchy. I looked again at Cyn and realised there was a crisscross of fine metal between us; my fuzzy mind began working on this as I tried to rouse myself from the stupor I was in. Snippets of the previous evening flashed through my mind.

'You promised me your soul, Cedric,' her deep honeyed voice continued. 'You can't break that promise, and Daddy has revealed his secret. So now you'll have to stay here with me.'

I looked around me – I was in the large room housing the caged animals. I couldn't believe that she'd lock me up here like an unwanted animal with her rescued pets, just to prove a point. I tried to yell out – *you can't keep me here* – but my voice was a mere squeak. I put a hand to my throat to see if my glands were swollen, and caught a handful of fur instead. I clutched and pulled at it, but it was stuck to my skin. I grabbed it fiercely to tear it off, but only succeeded in drawing blood with my nails. I looked at my hands and my skin crawled – my hand appeared narrow, padded and had four long, clawed toes.

Cyn laughed and I looked up to see her holding up a small picture in front of me – it was of a dark eyed, white and brown guinea pig. I looked from the picture to Cyn, and the rodent in the picture moved too. I jumped back, startled, and the image copied my movement. With my heart drumming in my chest at a pace I wouldn't have thought possible, my bowels constricted and I defecated onto the wood shavings I was scuttling around on. I realised that this was not a nightmare I would ever be awakening from; this was happening, and I was now just another of Cyn's unwanted dumb animals staring into a mirror at my own small, black, beady eyes.

I raced around the cage, gripping the bars, trying to wrench them apart, gnawing at them until I tasted blood in my mouth. I tried to reach the cage door, but it was too high and had a padlock securing it.

'Now, now,' said Cyn as stroked a finger down one of the bars. 'It might seem a little odd at first, but you'll get used to it.' I dived at her finger, just nipping her flesh, but she didn't bleed. She picked up the cage and shook it violently. When she put my wire prison back down again, all I could see were flashing lights, and all I could hear was the rapid pounding of my heart in my ears. Cyn left the animal room, slamming the door behind her, and as my senses cleared, from somewhere nearby I heard Jeremy's pitiful whine.

Zoo Life

by Kerry Mayo

Here in Kent we have both Port Lympne and Howletts Wildlife Parks.

Feeling Horny

Sweet Savanna, here he comes, arse first – charming! My eyesight might be poor but even I can see he barely fits in that crate.

Please! Let him be better than the others! The last one didn't speak a word of English, just kept saying his name over and over. And the one before that was so old his knees had more wrinkles than an elephant's and his horn wasn't sharp enough to spear a mango, if you know what I mean.

But this one! He's so fat they've taken the sides off the crate to get him out. Look at that belly – it almost drags in the mud. He must be nearly two tonnes. What do they take me for?

If we were on the African plains all he'd see is the dust kicked up by my fleeing hooves. As it is I'm stuck in this measly paddock and expected to breed with any old dinosaur they can find. Well, this lady has standards. Why can't they find me a mate with high tight flanks, a smooth rich hide, and a horn that looks like it could actually do some damage?

He's out and they've retreated to the other side of the fence, watching. There's quite a crowd gathered too – they must have told the whole world that Kali was going to get some. What do they think I'm going to do? Trot over there and lift my tail in front of everyone? There's more chance of a gazelle getting a full-body wash from a lion's tongue.

It's quiet now and the moon is shining off his hefty girth over by the feed bins. What a noise he's making! And he has done nothing but eat since he arrived. At least he's staying away from me.

From sun-up to sunset I ignore him. Some days he ventures closer than others but downwind he smells like a hippo's behind so I always know when he's advancing. We don't speak but the keepers have plenty to say. I hear them talking over by the shelter – what a disaster, how the whole programme is in jeopardy. As if *I'm* responsible for the future of the species! At least give me someone who'll improve the gene pool, not eat it.

Finally they talk about sending him home. The crate reappears but he doesn't fit. A new one is made; he is going tomorrow.

It is a full moon tonight. How many is that since he came? I don't remember. I'm giddy under the stars. I felt like this just after Frankfurt went home. I trot around the paddock feeling light and cheerful. I don't care that he's watching but – hey! – stop sniffing at my dung pile.

I must be feeling good that he's going home tomorrow.

Maybe I could be a little friendlier on his last night. Maybe I'll just trot round once more and see if, this time, he follows.

Pride of Britain

Yaoworrooah! Thank Engai there's finally some sun shining down on my back. Makes it so much easier to sleep. Although it also brings out the yappy creatures and their strange cubs.

Look at this pride – the male is hairier than that follicly-enriched baboon opposite although he's showing just about as much of his arse crack. Turn around, I don't want to stare at where your tail should be. And the female! With hair brighter than a cub's new mane, and cheeks as red as the setting

Serengeti sun. But she's flabby, which would not be good for my sleek flanks. As for the cubs, two males that need a good paw round the ear, and I can't tell what sex the one screaming and tied into the rolling cage is. Won't somebody give it a gazelle leg or something to shut it up?

They've gone, at last, but more are coming all the time. Look at these two – so old they couldn't outrun a three-legged cheetah. Move along, nothing to see here, I will not perform like those deranged Marmosets I can hear chattering and fighting from sun up to sun down.

Ah, delivery service has arrived. How dull. If I were back on the plains the females would bring me a giraffe neck for breakfast – a delightful delicacy – and impala for dinner. Afterwards, I'd get a hippo's wagtail to clean my teeth before sniffing him down as a palate cleanser.

Maybe they've brought a small antelope, or at least something I can chase. These old bones need a workout but maybe just an aged zebra for now. No, just a leg. How can I chase a leg?

Perhaps this afternoon I'll try one of these ungainly bipeds. They think I am trapped but I could get out of here if I wanted to. Their decaying food and low fences won't keep me if I choose to go. That vine covering the fencing just gives more grip and as for the lip at the top, well… I am a cat after all.

The leg is waiting. So are the irritating primates, with one arm stretched up, little box in their paws, like an upside-down flamingo with about the same colour on their hide.

Look at them go mad for me walking down my ramp. That's right, little creatures. I am here. Don't crowd in so. You want to see my teeth more closely? How about feeling my hot moist breath on the back of your neck? You think this is as close as I'll get, through a flimsy fence and a thin bit of window?

Mmm, horse. Not something I had back home but okay occasionally. I don't choose to be watched today so I'll drag this into the undergrowth and eat it there.

There, there, you screeching parrots. You wail for your loss.

But don't worry, and take my advice – keep moving, go see

the tapirs and the reeboks and the other dreary animals, but keep watch for me over your shoulder.

Maybe I'll pay you a visit this afternoon.

The Train Wyfe

by R.J. Dearden

06:10 Wendell shivered, staring at the bend in the railway tracks. His thousand-yard stare dared the train to come. Or not come. He missed snuggling against Susan, cocooned together under a thick duvet, enveloped in the dawn gloom. He wondered if their daughter, Patricia, had snuck into the indent he'd left in the mattress, elbows and feet fighting for space. He longed to be homeward bound, to be on holiday, to be anywhere except Platform 1, Whitstable station, London bound. *Damn February mornings!* The tannoy irked him and his companion travellers, jokey, smudgy faced commuters, haunted him. *God, what makes them so happy?* Maybe there was a secret ingredient in the Blueprint coffee they sipped through plastic lids, though he knew if he tried the caffeine elixir it would send him into a tail-spin all day. For he was a tea man and there was no pretending otherwise.

The thing was this: Wendell Fydel had a specific set of skills... IT skills. God, he was technical. Mind numbingly technical. Awe inspiringly and jaw-droppingly so. Automation. Virtualisation. Tasks, sequences, routines, slave bots, all hosted on platforms in a cloud far, far away. Pity the man or woman at a party foolish enough to ask what Wendell did. Not a mistake anybody made twice. Even the other consultants at work glazed over when Wendell began talking about his day. They used to joke he had a propeller on his head. But these skills had recently become an expensive luxury when an accountancy scandal had caused the company to hit lean times. Suddenly the pipeline of system transformations evaporated and they callously hired Wendell out to the highest bidder. His new assignment, a two-year project for an investment bank – think of an Austro-Hungarian-sounding name, secondary references to precious metals – demanded he present himself to the office, 08:30 to 18:30. Every day! Cursed presentee-ism! He could do his job from home, from a café... from the moon! Anywhere but in a windowless City basement.

Within the blink of an eye, Wendell had plonked himself down in a carriage he couldn't remember arriving in. He caught his reflection in the window. Blond hair, side parting, blue eyes, freckles on his nose. He carried ten kilos more than he liked. His fellow travellers began working, and licking the creamy latte from the coffee cups. Some watched films and documentaries, others played Candy Crush. But Wendell forced himself to stay awake, at least until Faversham. The train's electric whir threatened to drag his consciousness deep underwater but sleep he must resist if he was to maintain his perfect circadian routine. By Sittingbourne he had dropped his mobile onto the table and sweet slumber spirited him away.

The feeling of being watched stirred him, penetrating his wakeless dream. Two dragon-green eyes were studying him, before they darted away again and he was sucked back into kiptopia. The guard woke him at Cannon Street and he staggered, more tired than before, to the basement office he decided to call 'The Cell.'

The next day, Wendell stamped his feet and against the biting air and reviewed the same scene again. Was it still yesterday and he hadn't even done his day's work? Or was it today and it was all to be done? If he blinked hard enough, would it be tomorrow?

Dragon eyes woke him up at Gillingham.

'Dropped your mobile,' she said, handing it back. 'Again.'

'Are we London or Ramsgate bound?' he muttered, disorientated and struggling to focus on the woman's face, his eyes darting to the luggage rack to check his bag was still there.

'London, honey. New to the grind?' her voice lilted.

'Do I look so green?'

She was a peroxide blonde, shoulder length hair, clean complexion, perhaps an hourglass figure more suited to the 1940s than the twenty-teenies. Five foot tall, shiny black heels and smooth legs. She flashed a dazzling white smile. 'Poor you. You need taking care. What sort of name did your mum give you?'

'Mum was Italian. Mysteriously called me Wendell. Surname is Fydel. Fydel's with a "Y" not an "I". It's a common mistake. Wendell, well as it sounds. It means someone who –'

'Italiano? Well…mi chiamo Gloria. Gloria Nolan, spelt as it spells, Mr Fydel. Don't worry, I'll look after you. If you're lucky I might even be your train wyfe. But let's spell it with a "Y" not an "I". Now, Wendell. You look exhausted, you may power nap for fifteen minutes but no more, or you'll oversleep and wreck your circadian clock.'

'I knew it.'

Next day she got on at Faversham, large carpet bag in hand, and by the time the train left the station, she was offering him a steaming drink in a flowery porcelain cup, saucer and all. He accepted, sipping what turned out to be deeply satisfying cup of tea.

'Tastes better from bone china, temperature thing,' she said. 'Nothing else will do. These are charity shop so I won't cry if you chip it.'

'My, my,' he smiled, 'what a good train-wyfe you may prove to be.'

'We ain't hitched yet, Mr Fydel. I'll let you know if you pass the audition. Croissant? Freshly baked. Always had a sneaking fondness for the almond variety. Here, put this napkin around your neck or you'll cover yourself in crumbs!'

~~~

Every day became a feast. Teapot, flask of hot water, milk, croissants. Or Danish pastries, sometimes freshly baked bread rolls, marmalade and salty butter. Cold days brought forth bacon or sausage sandwiches.

'Got yourself a keeper there, mate,' a fellow commuter told him at Rochester. 'Most important meal of the day.'

'Well, me last husband died unexpectedly, so got to keep this one well fed,' Gloria replied. 'He was more husbad than husband!'

'Train Husband,' Wendell corrected, his mouth stuffed full of pain au chocolat.

'Hush dear, don't speak with your mouth full. You've got crumbs on your shirt.'

She always found his homeward bound train, even though she got on at London Bridge. Five days out of five. He had tried slipping away from the office early but there she was. He tried leaving late. Same result. One day he sat in the front carriage not the habitual middle. He got a proper telling off that day. Best to forget the day he went from Blackfriars to St Pancras and then came back on the High Speed... but he still got rumbled.

'Are you tracking me?' Wendell asked.

'A good wyfe knows where her husband is at all times. We have a spiritual connection.'

'Ah,' he muttered, thinking he would restore factory defaults to his mobile that weekend.

On bitter or rainy days there was hot chocolate. 'The mistake people make with hot choccie is thinking it always needs to be made with milk. Cocoa's packed with magnesium. Hot water and a drop of milk,' she explained, 'is smoother and better.'

'Delicious,' he agreed.

Soup when the wind chill bit. Party pastries and prosecco on Fridays.

Gloria was not naturally beautiful, though Wendell found

a radiance spilled out from her that made her face prettier on second, perhaps third glance. He spoke about his wife, a planned visit to Jo-Jo's for her birthday, about their little girl Patricia. She talked about her husband, Stephen, stay-at-home dad, and their eight-year-old son, James. She was a senior marketing manager at a media company. She found his job fascinating, asking him to explain intricate network topology. More and more they found themselves laughing, finishing each other's sentences and ignoring the frustrated glances of fellow passengers trying to sleep. He saw a young guy pretending to vomit one day.

On Sunday evening, his wife Susan poked him in the ribs. 'Piling the pounds on, Wendy. Got something you want to confess? Are you grazing in the day? Are you a chocoholic?'

'Don't call me Wendy,' he snapped.

'How does Mr Porky sound?' Susan shot back. 'El Chubbo? Monsieur Belly?'

'Well... actually,' he stammered. 'There is this thing. Silly really. Been meaning to talk about it for a while. The thing is ... uhm... well, here goes nothing.' He spilled the beans about Gloria Nolan.

Susan greeted his news with five long minutes of silence, before pulling long black hair into a pony tail. 'Wyfe with a "Y" you say? With a shitting "Y?" You've got to be kidding me. Little train-wyfey makes you tea and breakfast every day? Every day?'

'Erm. Yes, that's the rub. Sometimes there are snacks for the way home.'

'Well la-di-da to Wendy and Gloriana,' Susan shot back. 'Hip-hip-hooray. Cheers to the happy locomotive couple. Well, I couldn't be happier.'

'Err... you don't sound happy. Are you sure you're ok with it? God, I've been terribly worried. You know I love you and Tricia. Gloria... well she just makes something I loathe tolerable. The Bank is extending me, too. Talk of me doing managing their European techies. The office are offering a pay-rise if I accept. Gloria says—'

'Wendy, I don't care what whatshername says,' Susan shrilled, face white. 'You listen, you listen good! Trousers stay belted up. Zips at full mast. No rummaging in her dirty knickers. Not so much as a Christmas peck on the cheek. For I, your lawful wife, am a jealous woman! But if it means I don't have to make you breakfast or lunch any more, I'm going to let it slide for now. But remember, I can be a harridan bitch and will make the rest of your life a misery—'

'Yes, boss.'

'Now come here, your real wife has something to give you no train-wyfey could ever match.'

The next day Wendell overslept, and was running forty minutes late. He scrambled onto the St Pancras train, his stomach growling all the way to town.

Gloria was furious for the home trip. 'Bad train hubby! Bad train hubby. HUSBAD!'

'I overslept,' he said.

'You could have texted me. I had bagels with cream cheese and bacon.'

'I don't have your number,' he complained.

'Nonsense. It's there under T,' she said grabbing his phone and scrolling through the numbers. 'We did this on the second date!'

'How do you know my number?' he demanded. 'How?'

'Really, Wendell, you are a most frustrating simpleton today. It's Susan's birthday. You told me about your marvellous meal at Jo-Jo's and I just took a wild guess. Me and Michael went there the following week. We gorged on those potatoes bravas. Don't let it happen again! Or there will be consequences.'

'Really, Gloria. You take this train-wyfe thing way too seriously,' he snapped.

'I shall go elsewhere,' she said, voice small, packing her large bag away.

'Oooh err. Trouble in paradise,' a man in a suit, parallel to them commented, rubbing his hands together.

She didn't move but stared at the passing countryside.

'I'm sorry,' he apologised.

'Here take this,' she sniffed finally, reaching into a deep bag and producing a cushion. 'I suppose all couples argue. Let's vow we will never fall out again.'

'Yes, promise,' Wendell said, his eyes like lead. 'Best friends, best friends...'

'Never never break friends,' she joined in.

The musky smell of Gloria's perfume on the pillow enveloped him. His last thought before dropping off to sleep was that he thought her husband's name was Stephen. Not Michael. But he forgot by the time he awoke.

'Thanks train-wyfe,' he said.

'It's a small thing for my hubby,' she cooed.

Summer rolled round and the mornings became easier. Gloria enquired what time Wendell would be finishing most evenings and she began meeting him outside his office. The conversations stayed light and airy.

'When are you taking your summer leave?' she asked.

'Last two weeks of August,' he replied. 'Susan's booked Sardinia. Why?'

'Well it makes sense for me and Steve to take our leave the same time. I wouldn't want to leave you for two weeks. I might come back and you'd have met another train-wyfe.'

'As if. Does Stephen know about me?'

'Of course,' she giggled. 'Who do you think makes the sour dough bread?'

Autumn came around and they swapped photos. Stephen looked very handsome, lean, six packed, chiselled jaw. Wendell felt a stab of jealousy at his toned physique. James looked so mature, already starting at Queen Elizabeth's Grammar School. Gloria commented how beautiful Susan looked and her eyes misted at the sight of Patricia sitting on Wendell's shoulders.

'What a beautiful family you have.'

'You too. Not that I'm much of a critic, but Stephen could be a male model. I need to hit the gym again.'

'Yes, gorge, isn't he? But don't you worry, a train-husband needs insulating against the cold.'

'Can I borrow this photo to show Susan?' he asked, thinking it might stop some of the sarcastic sniping she'd been making recently.

'No,' Gloria snapped. 'That would be… too much.'

'Ah, okay,' Wendell sniffed. 'You could just Whatsapp it to me.'

'No!'

Gloria loved delays. Thrilled at the extra time they got together. Signalling delays at Swanley meant they got another hour talking. Leaves on the line left them stranded at Meopham for forty minutes. A broken-down train at Strood took an age to clear. Wendell fretted about being late but Gloria couldn't care less. As part of the deal, he kept Susan up to date with his train marriage. She brought up the topic when their friends came around for dinner and laughter split their sides. Wendell felt guilty but he laughed hard too. It had become pretty comedic. He told them what had happened the day a young woman had joined their table and tried to join in the conversation.

'Well, what happened, Wendy?' his friends had asked.

'She couldn't take the cue,' he had said. 'Then mysteriously sporting a black eye the following day, sat by herself after that.'

'You don't think?' the friends asked, slack jawed.

'No coincidence,' Wendell said.

'Remind me to upgrade the security on the rabbit's cage,' Susan joked.

November rains made the mornings hard again. 'You look like you're coming down with a cold, Mr Fydel.'

'No, I'm fine.'

But he wasn't fine and the next day he ached all over and

his nose was running. He was freezing cold, shivering. Gloria touched his forehead with a concerned look.

'You're burning up. Here, drink this,' she said producing a large cup of thick soup. He sipped it as the train sped through the countryside. Delicious, deep and velvety. He could make out chicken. Dumplings. His body warmed up, from his toes to his forehead.

'Secret recipe,' she smiled, flashing white teeth. 'For my charming prince.'

'Gloria, that's a tonic. If I wasn't married, I'd marry you.'

'Don't be soppy,' she blushed, eyes burning bright.

December icy rain wreaked havoc with the lines, freezing the rails and causing cancellations. Most of the regulars went home, giving up.

'Do you think it will be a white Christmas?' Gloria asked. 'Imagine if the sea froze like those photos you see about in The Old Neptune. Imagine that?'

'No, it never snows in December. Susan and I were just down at the Neppy last Sunday.'

'Coincidence,' she muttered.

A much-reduced service was all that was on offer, and the train crawled into Victoria. Then the snow tumbled from the sky, settling thick and fast on the icy cold ground. But Wendell, blissfully unaware in his basement office, beavered away until he got his marching orders from Susan and left, arriving in a snow-globe-like world. Heading up the stairs to the station entrance, a thin man, an over-sized suit nearly sent him reeling. The man's bobbed up and down, his eyes bossed and darting.

'Hey there! Careful,' Wendell complained.

'She must have left,' the man muttered, skittering down the steps, still babbling. 'Missed my chance!'

Nutter! Wendell thought skidding into the near empty station. Gloria pounced on him from nowhere, arms enveloping him.

'Hurray! Glad you could make it! There's only one train left. It leaves in two minutes. Quick. Chop chop!'

'Were you hiding?' he asked.

She laughed nervously as they slid along the train platform, holding each other up, and staggered into an empty carriage. Her eyes gleamed and they collapsed onto the seat laughing. The train pulled away and they watched with wonder as the blizzard covered the windows, transforming the countryside into a foreign landscape. After ten minutes, Wendell noticed that he was still holding her hand. He gently let go.

The train inched along, stopping dozens of times. Gloria had produced a hip flask of calvados and they sat sipping it, in silence. A nasal announcement startled them both.

'We regret to announce that this train will terminate at Rochester due to snow drifts on the line. As you can see the inclement weather means we can't guarantee your safety.'

'I know a lovely warm B&B in Rochester, not far from the station.'

'Well …'

'I'll give them a call right now.' She rang on the mobile. 'Do you have any spare rooms? Yes. Only one room left. Is it twin or double? Double. We'll take it. The name? Mr and Mrs Nolan.'

Wendell coughed.

'Well, I could hardly say Mr Fydel and Miss Nolan, could I? Look, isn't it magical? I love the snow.'

'But a double—'

'Relax Mr Fydel,' she mocked. 'It'll be two singles we can pull apart… if that's what you want,' she winked, apple brandy on her breath.

They checked into the B&B, Gloria's voice loud and sing-songy as she inspected the room. 'It'll do.'

They found a small Italian restaurant that was still open. Wendell's phone had no signal, so he used an old red phone-box, the stink of stale smoke making him dizzy. He called home. Susan grabbed the phone on the first ring.

'The train terminated at Rochester. The snow is terrible. I'm stopping at a B&B.'

'What? I can't hear you!' Susan said.

'Snow bad. At Rochester. Stopping in B&B. Having meal. Some Italian.'

'Is that little bitch with you?' Susan asked.

'What?' Wendell asked, though he had heard clearly.

'Be very care—' Susan said, the line suddenly cutting dead. He tried calling again but the line rang out.

When he returned to the restaurant, Gloria was placing orders for food. She smiled as she caught his eye. 'My husband will have the Palermo steak and I'll have the seabass. My treat.'

She giggled, humming the tune to 'Let it Snow.' Hiccupping, she poured him a large glass of Valpolicella. He noticed the top two buttons of her shirt were undone, her bra a lacy purple. She beamed, cheeks flushed, topping his glass up repeatedly through the meal. She ordered cognacs after the panna cotta. 'Maybe we'll sleep like babies tonight,' she winked. 'Feels like a chilly night, whatever will we do to keep warm?'

Then suddenly her face dropped and she spoke in the tiniest of voices. 'Isn't that your Susan?'

Wendell stood up breathing a sigh of relief, despite the laser eyes from his wife, car keys swinging like nunchucks in her hand, snow speckling her hair. She joined them at table. 'Fun's over, kids. Grab your shit. Home-time. Patricia's with a sitter.'

'That's marvellous,' Gloria said. 'How very brave of you to venture out in this blizzard, sweetie,' she said, downing Wendell's cognac.

'If I was brave, I'd have stayed at home, sweetie,' Susan muttered.

They kept it friendly afterwards but Wendell made sure he avoided touching Gloria again. That night, the lights had been off at Gloria's house and she had stepped gingerly through the snow to the door by herself, waiting for Susan to skid away before putting her key in the latch.

Things started awkwardly but then spring came and the months started racing by.

'Me, Michael and James are going to Cyprus,' she breezed.

'Stephen?' Wendell queried.

'Yes,' she continued, not missing a beat. 'Me, Stephen and James are off to Cyprus. Or Crete.'

Weekends sped by too quickly. Gloria showed glossy photos of their holiday adventures. 'The sea was so clean,' she said. 'Warm like bath water.'

Little by little, he noticed she'd started sleeping more in the mornings so he began using the time to scan his emails and work on designs. The pot of tea made its last and final appearance one Tuesday and then after that, it was thermos, then shop-bought. One day she passed out on Wendell's shoulder and he stopped working altogether. Her head fell onto his chest. He didn't wake her, as a peace had descended on her. He knew Susan would not approve as it violated their agreement but he put an arm around her and dozed off himself, hearing a satisfied murmur. When he awoke she was stirring. She moved her head and for a second looked at him with the same eyes he had seen on the snowy day. But the moment passed, and she dug him in the ribs for letting her sleep so deeply.

'My circadian clock!'

The next few weeks, she stopped bringing croissants and it was Wendell who provided refreshments. Her face had become pale grey, the sparkle snuffed out.

On Friday, she got on and gave him a wan smile. As the train pulled away, her skin visibly yellowed and a sheen of sweat broke out on her forehead. For some reason or other, Wendell remembered a summer job as a hospital porter and shuddered, recalling a day when he'd had to wheel a motorbiker down from Intensive Care for a scan. The poor man been crushed by a lorry on the M20 and was being kept alive until the doctors had decided which organs could be salvaged. The man had given off a weird sickly smell.

'Wendell, please help. I'm not feeling too well. Please… oh my God…'

He sprung up, struggling to find the guard as he bumped and banged against the other passengers. By the time they got back, Gloria was convulsing. The guard called ahead for medical assistance and the train made an unscheduled stop at St Mary's Cray and medical staff met them on the platform. For once the delay was their fault. After receiving oxygen, Gloria recovered enough to speak privately with the medical team. Wendell watched transfixed as they wheeled the gurney to the ambulance and then, freed from indecision, sprinted after them.

'Are you her husband?' they asked.

'Train…Oh dammit. Yes. Yes I am.'

'Hop in, there's room.'

He held her hand all the way to the A&E, dreading being back in a hospital. She perked up when they got closer. Wendell called work and rescheduled things.

'I suppose I could be your Ambulance-Husband for at least for one day.'

'Perfect. I knew you were a keeper,' she whispered. 'My guardian angel.'

There were tests and private conversations. Gloria wept. She refused to be kept in overnight, picking her things up and booking a taxi to her terraced house in Faversham.

'Sorry babe, you can't come in,' she said. 'Would tarnish the relationship. Think I'm going to take a leave of absence. I don't know how Michael will take it.'

'Stephen,' he corrected sotto voce.

The next day, Gloria wasn't on the train. Nor the following day. Nor a week later. He called Susan and told her he was going to go around and check on Gloria after work.

'I'll do it,' she said, surprising him.

'No, really,' he said. 'I should do it.' Though he was secretly relieved, imagining her giving off a weird smell. *Some train husband I turned out to be!*

That evening Susan met him at the station, the car parked on the cobbles by Choochoo's Day Nursery. He gave her a hug and a kiss, his eyes drawn to a child's painting of someone floating in the sky next to a yellow sun. He clambered into the passenger seat on the car, wiped out.

'Did you see Gloria today?' he asked, finally.

'Yes, I did, love. Look. No easy way to say this. I'm sorry, I really am. But you won't be seeing her again. Not ever. She's dying. She stopped chemo. Wendy… she's got days. Days.'

'What?' Wendell asked. 'Is this some sort of joke? Why did she refuse treatment?'

'I don't know. She hasn't even been at work the past four months. She's been taking the ride up to London and then whiling the time away until you come home.'

'What about Stephen? What about James? How are they going to cope?'

'Wendy, you fool! There is no Stephen. No James. It's all been a big lie. She made it all up. Those photos were off the web.'

'No!' Wendell snapped, but he'd always been able to recognise the smack of truth, especially when it walloped him on the nose. Ouch! The photos he'd seen of Stephen and James had been too slick. Too professional. So obviously photo-shopped. *Hindsight, what a wonderful thing!*

Gloria Nolan died the following Friday at The Pilgrims Hospice in Canterbury. He'd taken a day off work and they'd spent Wednesday chatting and reliving the old times before she'd fallen asleep.

'Not sure how Mike will take it,' she muttered. 'He always was the jealous type.'

'Stephen,' Wendell corrected her, before remembering the fiction.

When the will was read, Wendell Fydel was sole beneficiary. Susan helped organise the funeral – a quick service at

Our Lady Immaculate, followed by internment at Whitstable Cemetery. Apart from some obvious regulars who'd mistaken the funeral for 10 o'clock mass, there was only one person at the funeral dressed in black. A rakish man, in an ill-fitting suit with a head that bobbed left and right. The tears streamed down his face during Father Kevin's eulogy until he caught Wendell's eye and his eyes narrowed.

After the mass, the man bounded out of the church, Wendell haring after him. Northwood Road. He'd seen him somewhere before.

'What are you doing?' Susan called after him, stopping to speak to the undertaker.

Wendell scurried towards Kingsdown Park. He caught up with the griever at the park, grabbing his shoulder and making him spin around.

'Who the hell are you?' Wendell barked at the man. *Cannon Street, the snowy day,* he remembered.

'Michael Smithson,' the man stammered.

'Michael,' Wendell chewed the word over. Her lover? 'Michael. Were you her… boyfriend?'

'Hardly old fellow,' Michael scoffed. 'Chance would have been a fine thing. Gloria was my work wyfe. Wyfe with a "Y" is what she always said. She made the daily toil tolerable. I didn't know about you at first but I sensed there was someone else.' He reached into his pocket, yanking out a crumbled letter which he threw at Wendell.

The letter tumbled to the pavement, and Wendell bent down, picking it up, smelling musky perfume.

The words 'love him' leapt off the page.

He glanced up, suddenly mesmerised by the sight of the metal gun barrel protruding from Michael's hand.

A gun jammed in the face looks bigger than I ever imagined, Wendell thought to himself. *Huge. Metally. Is that a stupid thing to think at a moment like this?*

It was.

'You weren't worthy,' Michael sobbed. 'You weren't!'

'There, there,' Wendell soothed.

'She gave her everything for you,' Michael continued. 'Everything!'

'I know. The thing is—' Wendell began,

Three bangs from the gun finished the sentence.

Deep Sea Diver

by Nick Hayes

The deep sea diver helmet seemed to gaze back at Charlie Tyler. Unblinking at the front was a perfectly circular port hole eye. Jewel-like rivets fixed the eye in place within an enormous bronze-hued bulb of steel. It was smooth, polished by the work of the sea, yet battle scarred: the tell-tale tracks of a Kraken throwing its tentacles around a doomed Victorian diver, the toothy gouges from a frantic shark attack in tropical waters and a mottled stain when the ship wreck collapsed around the original owner.

The boy gazed into the eye... so he went in and tried it on...

It was tough at school away from this newly acquired booty. The Seaside Academy was a mixed bag of anything from torture to torment. Heads down the toilets was as likely as being wedgied in assembly. Teachers were either entering or recovering from nervous breakdowns. Students were either literally or metaphorically crashing their cars into the establishment.

With the helmet on, Charlie could adventure to faraway lands and harvest gold from the secluded sea bed. While it stayed under the bed, he had no defence against playground bullies.

Charlie could only sit in the toilet cubicle and read the words scrawled across the door. His own name figured twice.

'Tyler is gay.' 'Tie up Tyler and kick his ****** nuts off!'

The asylum of the cubicle made him feel calm. However, the words made him catch his breath. He was an adventurer but not a fighter. And he wanted to keep his nuts!

Already missing maths, the time ticked by and into French. His teacher would be missing him – maybe a student would be sent to track him down. His hands were clammy. He wiped them on his shirt front. The shirt was already stained. He'd whipped it out the dirty washing basket before his mum could see. She was too busy on the phone to Gary anyway. Charlie was just like a passed-over status update these days. No comments or likes. Just a few desperate words, a cry of help into the abyss and overlooked.

The sounds of a visitor startled Charlie from his daydreams.

'Tyler, are you in there? Ya Pouff!' It was Form Captain, Rick. He whacked the cubicle door with his palms.

'Come on out, gay boy. Allez allez allez!' He snorted at his own joke. The palms turned to boot soles as the door rattled. Charlie rattled inside.

'Ya dozy, ******!' I'm going back to class. Get moving, ya prick.' The Form Captain departed and Charlie blew out his cheeks.

With the coast now clear, he unlocked the cubicle, crept out the toilet and off to sanctuary. There was no way he could go to French. Not with Rick and the Berserkers there. With those three together his arse was grass. His nuts were toast!

Rather it was the library where he sought sanctuary. Mrs Whyte, always pleased of customers, smiled as he peered in through the glass panel of the entrance door.

'Come in, sunshine, Come in lovely. Oh, Charlie look at your shirt front, darling. Mum not well again?'

Charlie smiled. 'Just busy with Gary s'all.' He felt a pang in his heart.

'She loves you best, darling. Go and find some books, luvvie.'

He walked a much practised walk to the fiction aisle and the Hardy Boys books and then the Nancy Drew mysteries.

His father had given him a stack years ago – long before the Big Split. Today he just ran his fingers over the spines. All multicoloured and neatly arranged. He ran his fingers over the ten or so spines for comfort. He even had a quick look at one gaudy cover and let himself fall into it.

But today he was bound for non-fiction. ' D-day, Danger, Dartmouth, Devon... Diving!'

He angled the book out at 45 degrees to scan the cover. He slid out the 'Diving' one and carried it under his arm to the desk. Jacques Cousteau was pictured on the front. Charlie felt calmer. He smiled over to Mrs Whyte.

'Got to read this for a project, Miss. Forgot my note but ask Mr Vendee. '

'S'alright, luvvie. You know you're always welcome here.'

He sat and flicked the pages. The passages about scuba and free diving didn't interest him. He went to the introduction – the origins of diving. Diving beneath. Diving deep. Diving down.

His heart quickened at the sketches and diagrams. Men lined up on ancient ships in orderly rows for the photographer. In the centre was the diver – the Hero of the Underseas. The bulb helmet was clasped to his chest like a cosmonaut preparing for lift off!

Charlie thought about his secret beneath his bed. He thought about the Deep Sea Divers of yesteryear. He thought about The Berserkers. He closed his eyes and mumbled to himself. He turned to the front cover.

'Please help me, Jacques. Please!'

But today he wasn't in luck. He was sunk.

'You boy! To the office! NOW!' It was Monsieur Vendee.

The wind was blowing in the wrong direction at Charlie's school. Vendee was a cruel man – he had no time for excuses and no time for Charlie. The detention was actioned and Charlie found himself after school in Lab One, watching the minutes tick by.

Two other students were waiting for the hands to move around so they could escape this stifling silence. One face was all too familiar to Charlie. One of the feared Berserkers, Timothy (his forgotten first name) Drew sat somewhere behind him after chewing up a pencil and spitting out the remains in the face of a year seven girl. Charlie thought that he could still smell the remnants of pencil that Drew had chewed.

The boy in front of him was new. Unlike Drew and Charlie, the new boy did not sit uncomfortably. He did not scribble nonsense on his A4 sheet about the school's code of conduct. He was upright and assured and reading his book. Behind him, Charlie could not see the boy's face or hear his words as he occasionally read aloud in his hushed, whispery voice.

Charlie wished he had brought his book from Mrs Whyte's library but Rick had been too quick in setting off the alarm to bring Vendee to the library then to bring him here. He'd left the book on the desk – it'd be OK. He'd go there on Monday and fetch it. He was missing the pictures most of all. He'd read most of the book already – the pictures were what beguiled him. He closed his eyes and saw the master, Jacques Cousteau, propped on the boat somewhere in the sunny Pacific, getting ready to dive.

'I'll be back, Jacques,' he thought. 'I'll be back Jacques and that's a fact.' He grinned to himself.

For now it was just two other naughty boys and the scribbles on the A4 sheet. Plus, of course, Mr Ramsey at the front of the lab – 'Rambling Ramsey.' But this Friday he was marking his year nine exam papers so had not spoken a word to them for the whole duration. Charlie was in fear of getting his own exam paper back. His mind drifted to warmer seas...

The hour passed uneventfully and the boys shuffled to the exit. Charlie's eyes followed the new boy as he put the book back in his bag.

'What's that?' he asked as the boy zipped the bag tight and slung it upon his shoulder.

The boy nervously tossed his head and ran his long fingers

through his fringe. 'Just my book, mate. Gotta go now.' He turned to go and Drew pushed past them both.

'Outtaway!' he barked and as the pair was pushed aside, Mr Ramsey barked too.

'Get outahere, gents! You Tyler, you can go and learn some bloody Chemistry!'

And as those angry words echoed in Lab One, the two boys headed home together.

As it turned out, both boys lived in the same estate of houses. They ambled wearily together and spoke to each other about their weekend plans.

Ziggy was the new boy's name. Ziggy Campion. He knew that he sounded like a character from a Roald Dahl adventure. His parents were big Bowie fans, of course. Now, as his family had moved to the suburbs, he found himself about to start his exam years in a new school.

Ziggy was new in town and Charlie was alone at his school with the Berserkers berserking him at least once a week. Charlie and Ziggy both sensed they could be life buoys to bind together.

'So see you Monday?' ventured Charlie.

'Yeh, yeh, Monday's good.' The two boys started to unpair and go their separate ways.

Just as the new boy broke off to go right he stopped in his tracks.

'Do you want to see Tarantino?'

'Tarantino? What the hell is that?'

'Come on, Charlie. Come with me and I'll introduce you.'

Tarantino and Ziggy were unlikely partners. The former was a blue and white Siamese fighting fish. Like Ziggy, he was brightly flamboyant and fascinating. Unlike Ziggy he was prowling his watery world with a restless menace. He was alone in the tank but for the plastic shipwreck and the aquatic plants.

Charlie looked into the tank and gasped. 'He's a beauty.'

Ziggy proudly put his nose to the glass.

'Yep – beauty all right.' The new boy handed Charlie a whiffy cylinder. 'Go on feed 'im.'

Charlie took the cylinder and sprinkled the fishy glitter on the surface of the water. He'd had some fish years ago and remembered the way to spread the food across the water. Tarantino was in fish heaven – he hungrily hoovered up the fish food.

'Better go now,' Charlie said gathering up his sack and onto his back. 'See you Monday.'

'See you Monday, Charlie.'

Charlie smiled. 'See you... Ziggy.'

'Zig.'

'Zig?'

'Zig.'

'See you Monday, Zig.'

In the library at lunchtime, Ziggy and Charlie were having a ball. Mrs Whyte had helped them out and they had a mountain of books between them on the study table. There was no tyranny of silence in this library. Not at lunch. The sounds of laughter and chat and joy rebounded from the walls and through the aisles of books.

Mrs Whyte brought around biscuits and some squash but this had to be drunk in the social space by the entrance. She didn't mind the crumbs – she could clean up later – but she wouldn't have her books ruined by any drink spillages!

The Diving book lay open between them and they took turns to flick open a double page and revel in the pictures and the facts.

'Forty fathoms!'

'The Kraken of course!'

'The Victorian outer space!'

'Journey into darkness!'

They were like tiny tots in a sweet shop. Safe from the Berserkers they whiled away an hour, surreptitiously eating their sandwiches and filling their minds with stories and facts. They gorged on the books and their imaginations glowed from the fantastical feast.

When it was time to go – the pair had separate year nine classes – Charlie caught his friend by the arm.

'Do you want to come around my house tonight? I'd love you to come.'

He forced out the words. He rarely had anyone home – not since his disastrous thirteenth birthday party. Who would have thought his Dad would have turned up? Stinking and shouting. He'd not had anyone else since. But Ziggy was different.

'OK, then. See you at four.'

'Yeh, four. See you there. Mum'll cook chips.'

'Great. See you, Charlie-Boy.'

The boys departed and Charlie's mind went to the treasure beneath his bed

Charlie Tyson only lived a few streets away from Ziggy in Sheerness. They both lived in similar terraced streets – Ziggy with his parents, fish and baby. Charlie with his mother and brother and sometimes Gary, his 'step-dad.' His father only ever appeared at Big Days since the Big Split. He missed the idea of him but not the real thing. He loved his mum and she loved him back. She loved Gary too – more than she loved ironing, that was sure.

Charlie opened the door before Ziggy could knock. 'Come in. Come in!' he hurriedly instructed his new friend.

'Lovely to see you, Zig,' his mother said from the corridor. 'Chips in thirty mins, alright!'

Both boys nodded then sped upstairs. On the way up the cry of 'Quiet!' echoed from behind the closed door off the landing.

'I'm studying, mate!' cried his older brother, Jamie.

'Simmer down!' replied Charlie. 'Keep your hair on!'

Inside Charlie's room the boys sat the books and the games between them. Ziggy was still new to town and needed this friend. They both loved nature and the sea and this was a perfect bonding moment.

While they swapped nautical facts and zoological details, Charlie's thoughts slipped to the treasure beneath the bed. It was an elevated bed – a cabin bed – with a space underneath for storage. Hoards of clothes and random stuff covered the space completely. The deep sea diver helmet was safely stored in the corner beneath where his head would lie on the pillow. Only he knew what he had. Only he knew what lay beneath. Only he knew what lurked under the blankets and inside the box.

That was until now...

'Zig, can I show you something?'

'Erm? Not another mammal model – you're mad, Charlie-Boy!'

'No – this is even better than Airfix whales! It's—'

'Chips up, boys!' came the cry from below and off they went. The moment was lost.

Time passed and Charlie found himself becoming a familiar face in Ziggy's home. While sea adventures had always fascinated Charlie they were more than fascinating to Ziggy. A week later, in Ziggy's bedroom, he had relics from the sea displayed all across the window sill.

Standing up proudly, with Charlie sitting in awe on the bed, Ziggy took his friend through the different pieces: the jaws of a sea serpent, a fragile claw from a Crabzilla, some scrimshaw on a sperm whale's tooth, an intricate ivory coloured badge, some Mermaid's hair in a bottle and a musket ball from Blackbeard's gun.

Ziggy reached across and placed a tiny object on Charlie's chest.

'This whale badge – look after it for me.' Charlie held it in his palm and nodded. It was the shape of an ocean leviathan fashioned from the smallest shard of narwhal's horn.

Secreting it away he murmured, 'This is just amazing.' He

thought again about the secret plunder beneath his own bed. The boys had not been together back at his place since that first night. This latest trip sealed it though. He would show Ziggy but he just had to find the right time.

Downstairs the cry of 'Dinner!' summoned the pair.

There were no chips here. The dishes laid out were all exotic and colourful. Ziggy's mother, Zoe, dished up cous cous and chick peas with pepper, sweet chilli sauce and falafel. His father, Martin, cooed over the meal and squeezed his baby daughter's cheeks.

'You're so peachy, darling girl.' The baby girl squealed.

Charlie felt a wave of sadness. This life was not his life.

'What do you like then, Charlie?' Martin asked.

'Same as Zig, Mr Campion. Sea and animals and stuff. '

'Lovely to be near the sea. Been in London too long.'

Mr Campion had found a new job near Sheerness. The Campions were renting in the town while finding the right place.

'What you do?' asked Charlie.

'Look after these pesky kids,' he answered and fed his daughter some crushed pulses. 'Don't I, Amber?' He paused to wipe her face then continued. 'The prison, Charlie. I work at one of the prisons.' His kind smile ended that avenue. 'I love the sea and its stories – beautiful but dangerous, clear but opaque, warm but frozen, near but far...'

'Is that a poem?' asked Charlie.

'That's the Truth. Sometimes the Truth feels like a poem.'

The family ate as Charlie pondered over the secrets in his own bedroom.

Over the summer months the boys spent days and days together. Ziggy was introduced to the 'Sheerness scene' and Charlie revelled in the role of tour guide. Their time was mostly spent in the tacky arcades playing out of date and state of the art machines to earn tokens and the respect of their peers.

They came across the Berserkers a few times. Rick cornered them after one morning of success in the arcades. Flanked by Drew and the other member – Robbie Shufflebottom – the trio pushed the diminutive pair into a corner demanding their winnings of a clutch of tokens.

While Charlie shrank back and quivered Ziggy had no such fears.

'You get off – ya Ber- jerkers! And you Shufflebottom – you go away and get yourself a proper name!' With that he landed his right knee squarely in Drew's groin and he and Charlie scarpered.

Free from the fear of the gang Charlie and Ziggy explored the locale over the long, sunny holidays. Bike riding to Harty, beach combing along the coast, prison van spotting in Eastchurch. The best adventures were twilight or night time escapades.

During one twilight jaunt the boys walked out on the mudflats and into the fog. In seconds they had lost their bearings and no longer knew which way was home. Disorientated but elated they span themselves around and fell onto their knees in the mud. 'Omigod. Omigod. What now?'

Ziggy screamed. 'Omigod, mud monsters!' With that he took his hands full of mud and splatted them 'Tango-style' on the sides of Charlie's face. He ran off and his friend stumbled after. The race continued but they had no care which way they went – back to shore or out to sea.

One night they sat at the end of Sheerness jetty watching out for fish or fishermen. Ziggy dared Charlie to dive in fully clothed.

'No fear, mister.' Charlie had grown to love this time with Ziggy but he feared Ziggy's wildness at times.

'Just me then,' he chirped. And with that he swung his legs over the bars and dropped over the edge.

'Jesus, Zig – what are you doing?'

But Ziggy was fine. He had seen a shelf on the other side of the bars and stood on it safely, ducking low to give the illusion of diving into the murky, swirling waters.

'You bloody shit, Zig.' Charlie was shaken and inspired in equal measure. He didn't want the summer to end.

Days after this jape, Charlie thought hard about bringing out the diving helmet. The more the days passed, then the more difficult it became. Ziggy (and his family) had shared it all. From the glorious collection in his room to the insides of their fridge and larder. How could he keep his secret from Ziggy now without seeming a fraud?

Mermaids turned out to be the distraction from this worry. The bottle of Mermaid's hair had bewitched Ziggy when he was first given the treasure The long, fair strands caught his sense of magic and wonder and even though his rational self suspected they were fake he cherished them most out of all his nautical plunder.

One warm summer night, Ziggy described the Great Adventure – to see the mermaids in the deep waters of the Estuary. More precisely to see them in the wreck of the boat off the Sheerness coast – the SS Montgomery.

A few miles off the coast it had broken its back on a sand bank and had been left to rot with its volatile explosive cargo. Everyone knew if it went up then the town went with it! Ziggy just thought that added to the drama.

'But mermaids, Zig? Charlie implored. 'Really?'

Ziggy warmed to his project. 'And if not then maybe giant eels – Conger Monsters. 'Let's all do the conger!" With that he grabbed Charlie by the waist and walked him off in Conga-style.

'Too far out – too far out!' Charlie giggled at his own joke. 'It's too crazy and we've no boat anyway!'

Ziggy tutted and grinned. 'I'll get a boat – you get some diving gear.'

Charlie prickled. How did he know?

'Get some snorkels and wet suits. Hire them on the high street.'

Charlie relaxed. 'OK. Maybe – let's see.'

'You gotta week. Next Monday we dive – dive – DIVE!'
Ziggy fell to the floor and rolled on the grass. Charlie fell next
to him and they rolled down the hill together.

In his head, Charlie knew that there was no such thing as
Mermaids. But he hadn't any faith in finding any friends until
Ziggy turned up. Anything was possible.

Anything except getting diving gear and a boat, it seemed.
He'd told himself that he wouldn't share his secret yet – the
time still wasn't right. Meanwhile, two fourteen-year-old boys
could not hire a vessel. Even with the help of older brother
Jamie!

Regardless, Project Mermaid was set to continue! Both boys
had stolen out after bedtime and met up by the Corner House
at midnight. Each carried a rucksack with provisions. The
nearest they got to the diving gear were two sets of masks and
flippers.

'Can we do this?' mumbled Charlie looking at the meagre
equipment spread on the grass at his feet.

'Anything else?'

Charlie thought about the diving helmet he'd left behind.

'Mmm? Anything else? No boat? No dinghy? '

Charlie guiltily shook his head. 'Nothing.'

'Well we'll just have to nick one, then!'

Dragging the wooden dinghy from its dry dock on the pebbles
proved to be easier than either boy thought. The chains 'locking
it' in place had slipped apart easily and the dinghy contents
were minimal so they had plenty of room to row. In the bluey
darkness the boys pulled hard to drag the vessel free then push
towards the high tide mark and the gathering waves.

'The Little Oyster,' Ziggy gasped between shoves.

'Hmm?'

'Look – the name there.' On the side of the wooden boat
was the name. 'Let's go diving for pearls and mermaids in the
Little Oyster.'

Midnight plus two and the darkness had engulfed the sea. Navigating from lights either side of the channel, the pair shoved off into the inky blackness. The wind was low. The tide was high. The moon was smiling amongst its celestial chums and the air was cool but not cold. Summer's heat lingered just a little.

Each boy had an oar and together they pulled with all their might towards their own date with destiny.

It was always a long shot to reach the wreck. In quick time the boys knew their course was not in their own hands but in the hands of the tide and the swirls of currents in the Estuary. Their arms had tired quickly but their spirits remained high. Accepting their failure to reach the wreck, they slid the oars on board and allowed themselves to drift.

'OK?' asked Ziggy.

'OK,' said Charlie. This was Mad. This was Dangerous. But with Ziggy beside him Mad and Dangerous were OK. 'OK,' he repeated. 'So let's eat.'

The pair unpacked and shared their packed lunch goodies. Sandwiches with peanut butter, Marmite and jam. A Tupperware pot of coloured rice. A pasty, pork pie and bharji. Some crisps and fruit. Crackers.

'Crackers!' said Charlie.

'Crackers!' said Ziggy. The boys collapsed into fits.

The night had grown colder and the boys felt a little cooler after eating. Their thoughts went to rescue and retribution. They were 'in the shit' for this.

'Light's up in an hour,' insisted Ziggy. He checked the time on his phone.

'Shall we ring?'

'Not yet, Charlie-Farley. Let's look for Mermaids first. '

'Of course.'

So they did. The two boys pushed their faces overboard into the darkest waters and scouted for girls through their face masks. Beautiful girls with long, blonde hair and full, uncovered breasts. Girls with tails like nautical demi-gods and wet through from salty waves.

They looked and they looked and as the clock ticked on the more they saw.

'That one – she's lovely!'

'Hair like strands from the sun!'

'That one – what boobies! Amazing!'

'I think I am losing it. Feels like I'll need new pants, mate! Phwooar!'

The pair giggled and grabbed at each other. Drifting on the tide they were lost and didn't want to be found.

A thread of sun pierced the clouds – dawn was breaking. In the epiphany of light, under the joy of creation – the pair hunted for Mermaids. Then before either could stop themselves the boys kissed. One kiss. Then silence.

The wreck trip was the final time Charley was ever to see his friend. The coast guard rescue was the smallest of the dramas they had to face.

Ziggy immediately went off sick from school and through the grapevine Charlie learned that he was off to another school. His father had a new posting somewhere in Devon. Presented with the choice of Sheerness or Devon, Charlie could understand why they would go.

Alone again, Charlie fell into the hands of Rick, Robbie and Drew. His toilet times grew longer and his times in lessons grew shorter. Even Mrs Whyte and Jacques Cousteau could not save him.

The winter arrived and one walk home saw the scores settled.

'Ain't got your friend now.'

'Come 'ere queer!'

In seconds he was battered and torn. His whale badge was ripped from its place on his shirt. It was tossed into the gutter and through the grate.

The walk home was long. Gary and his mother were out for a pub supper when he arrived. Brother Jamie was on his computer.

'I'm sorry, Zig,' he whispered. 'Sorry I lost your badge.'

He sat at his desk and put his arms on either side to steady himself. He picked up a book on Oceans from the floor. It was one of Ziggy's – he had borrowed it a long time ago.

As he opened it he saw some scribbling on the inside cover. A poem had been written in the preface entitled – The Power of Whales. The handwriting was surely Ziggy's. He'd signed and dated it the day before the kiss.

The Power of Whales.
Darker than black
Colder than icebergs
Blind eyes are
The only ones to see
In the trenches of the deep.

Everything has come to
Rest on the sea bed in
Pieces. Salt and currents
Eat away at polish, colour,
Wooden accessories and all.

Impossible to fathom any path
To lead out of such a
Blackened wilderness. Moments
Of movement as shadowy
Transparent scavengers scuttle over shingle.

Navigation fails to make
Any headway amongst the
Devastated debris. A beacon
In the night flashes
For a second like the dome of St Pauls.

The arch of a giant
Whale shows itself above

The waves. The froth fizzes
In the air and sunshine dapples
Upon its massive bodywork.

The children ride its back
They speak in hushed prayers
We all surf
In the wake
To the sunlit
Breaking of the waves.

'The sunlit breaking of the waves?' echoed Charlie.

His head span to decipher the labyrinthine language.

'One thing I know, Ziggy,' he said. 'You've gone, Ziggy. You have swum out of my life and I am washed up here. I don't want to live like this.'

Winter's embrace put off any adventures to the coast for Charlie. He bunkered up in his bedroom and read his books. He had a few of Ziggy's which he read and re-read with relish.

The picture of the Victorian deep sea diver still bewitched him. The label underneath listed the names.

Jack Travis – diver. Percival Allbury – owner of the vessel. Jim Collins – winchman. Zachariah Smith – cabin boy.

The diver, Travis, stood centre stage. His kit was in a neat pile at his feet. His body was bare chested. His smile was difficult to read. He had one arm around Jim, the winchman, and another around Allbury.

The passage below read 'From the Persian expedition for the Holy Scimitar. Crew members before the final dive. After this picture was taken John Travis died in the tentacles of a giant squid or Kraken as he searched for the Scimitar. Percival went on to fund other trips but the holy relic was never found. Zachariah Smith went on to be a diver herself for Allbury.'

Charley looked harder into the eyes of the boy – the youthful face full of spirit and excitement looked familiar but it couldn't be. Could it?

Maybe there was a way he could find Ziggy again...

As the weather calmed so it was the day of Charlie's dive. He'd gone beneath the bed and found the treasure he was looking for. It slid nicely into the giant canvas bag from last year's county show. He would dive deep today. Off the jetty like Ziggy had done. But this time he would splash into the waters below. And there would be An End to it.

At the jetty he waited for a quiet moment. This was the point. He had the equipment now – he just needed the courage.

Helmet check. Air Flow check. Rope lead check. Life leads check. Survival check. Glove, boots, joints check. With no-one to be seen he edged himself to the brink.

Then.

Off.

He.

Jumped.

On the far side of the jetty, Mr Ramsey had been walking his dog – he screeched as the boy jumped.

'Noooo!' He loosed the dog and dived into the freezing waters.

Under the sea the mermaids held Charlie to their bosoms. The mermen held him to their chests. Charlie floated in their arms – bobbing in an airy pocket of love. He was home here.

Back on the beach Mr Ramsey had dragged the boy back. Frantically he was giving him the kiss of life. He thumped the boy's chest. He thumped again and felt the crack of his ribs.

'Breathe. Breathe. Breathe, damn you!' Charlie was drifting off.

Somewhere else Charlie took off the deep sea helmet and smiled at the light. The light was Ziggy and it smiled back. Charlie dived into an abyss of love. The deep sea diver floated and sank. Spiralled and swam. Whispered and sang. And his heart sang too!

Among the pebbles and flotsam and jetsam Mr Ramsey

yelped like the dog he had been walking. He howled at the sun, at the clouds, at the stars. He screamed as the boy still lay limp in his care. His arms scooped him to his chest and he started to sob – huge, shuddery sobs.

And as his body juddered and his mind dismantled into fragments the little boy gave a little cough.

'Breathe. For God's sake. Breathe.' The cough gave way to a choking splutter then a vomit of water. The boy moved to sit up in the arms of his teacher.

A hint of pink now pebbled his cheeks. It was going to be alright.

Both their hearts sang.

And Ziggy and the mermaids sang too.

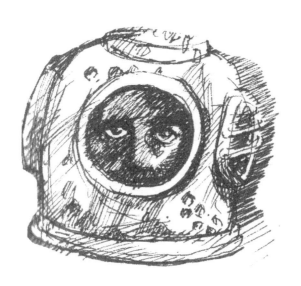

The Memory of a Dance Without Dancing

by John Wilkins

My older brother David and I were going through Mum's stuff. All that was left to do was to go back to her house in Chatham, in a quiet street behind where the Invicta ballroom had been. Apparently, some very famous acts had played there, back in the early sixties. Now the street, like her house, seemed as if the life had left it. It was a month after Mum's funeral and David had called me to arrange clearing her house. I had been dreading it.

'Sue, are you ready to sort out her house?' were the first words I heard that day when I picked up my mobile phone. I was looking out of the kitchen window, at the garden. Julia, my mother, came into my thoughts everyday now – more often it seemed than when she was alive. Being out in the garden would only make me think of her trying to turn me into a gardener, when I first moved into my house. I lived on Bluebell Hill along a narrow road in a house looking out over the North downs. It was very different to where Mum's house was in Chatham.

'Oh David, don't wait for me to be ready – I've got to face it soon. Why don't you just tell me when you can make it down here? Then you can stay over, and we can spend a couple of days to make sure the place is ready to hand over to the estate agent,' I suggested.

He didn't answer straight away, he never did. It always felt like he was waiting for me to unburden myself somehow. When he spoke, he confirmed a couple of days the following week would suit him.

I needed that much time to prepare myself to face going back into that house. As it turned out, it was David who was going to have so much more to face up to than me, after the discovery we made going through her things.

The day came and David turned up on time with his estate car, as planned. I opened the door and let him in, while I dashed about grabbing housework gloves and black plastic binliners. I didn't know what we would find upstairs in Mum's house – I hadn't been up there for years. I couldn't remember the last time Mum had talked about her friend from the agency coming around to give the place a good spring clean either.

David laughed at me when he saw the expression on my face. 'Don't worry, I doubt we'll find anything to surprise us. She hardly lived a life of wild abandon, did she?' he added.

The wildest thing I could remember about her was the laughter that erupted and rippled through Wednesday afternoons with her best friend Pam, as I returned home from school. I could hear her and Pam, laughing together in the kitchen, from down the street. I was never allowed to know what they were laughing about. Pam always said, 'You wouldn't believe us if we told you!' Then the pair of them would start laughing again.

David drove us to the house and unlocked the front door. As it opened, I flinched at the memory of how I had found Mum lying dead in the hallway – with a stillness that told me immediately she was gone. As the door opened I looked down the hall, but there was no one, only a sense of absence. An open window rattled remotely from behind a closed door, upstairs. The air in there wasn't stale, the house was just vacant, not open.

David put his hand on my shoulder. 'Come on, Sue, we'll begin upstairs – in her bedroom.'

'You're right – we will never get it finished if you let me just go off into a trance,' I said as I followed him upstairs. The door to her room was closed but not locked. David entered the room, with me peeking over his shoulder. It was just as I expected, neat and tidy. There was even a book on the bedside table with a bookmark sticking out of it. She was always a reader, and I wanted to turn the book over to see what the last book she probably ever read was. The bed was made, and a breeze blew the net curtains as David pulled down a couple of suitcases from the top of the wardrobe at the other end of the room. He passed them to me one after another.

Neither case was locked so I opened them straight away. We were disappointed not to find any faded envelopes tied together with ribbon, recording some secret romance that she had enjoyed in her life. We hadn't seen much romance between our parents as we grew up – it just looked like a strong friendship. Any passion there may have been had slipped away from them, until there was nothing left but a sense of duty to each other. David chattered away, suggesting the clothes went to the charity shops in the high street, as he passed the plain dresses and lilac cardigans across for me to fold.

I still thought we were going to find out some special secret about her life, from some clue concealed in that room. I felt that I might learn something more about her. Perhaps it was normal to grieve like this when you lose your mother.

Dad had been gone over ten years, but although I missed him it was no longer painful to regret that he was no longer there, in my life. Dad wasn't so close with David. It seemed more like a kind of strength that he gave to David: *'I'm there if you need me for anything, or to explain what you have to deal with, growing up, understanding'*.

I was folding the clothes to fill up all the space in the first suitcase for the charity shop run, when David found the shoe box. 'I wonder what she's kept hidden away in this, right at the back of the wardrobe,' David said quietly. I turned around to see a shoe box – there was a label on the front, with the illustration of a lady's dancing shoe from a time when my mum would have been in her mid-twenties. It was about the time she started seeing my Dad, I guessed.

David passed me the box. Looking back on it, that was the moment when I held the truth about him in my hands.

'This looks like it's a fashion item from back in the day,' David said, lightly mocking the label on the side of the box. There was the title *Electra* at the top of the label and underneath was an illustration of a lady's dancing shoe, with the slogan 'to dance in every moment' below it.

I carefully took the lid off the box and found, partly wrapped in faded pink tissue paper, a pair of the most beautiful shoes I had ever seen. They were a deep blue that showed some signs of fading, probably caused by age. I couldn't stop myself from taking one shoe out of the box. I saw straight away they had never been worn – there wasn't a mark on the sole of the one I held. A piece of paper fell out of the shoe and David caught it.

'This might tell us something,' he said passing it to me. I couldn't make out much, apart from the heading *Fine Times* and that it was a receipt from that boutique where Pam, mum's friend, had been the manager once. I handed the receipt back to David.

'Sorry, I can only make out the words *Fine Times*,' I said as he took the receipt carefully and examined it, almost forensically.

'I think it's a birthday present she bought for herself – the date on the receipt is her birthday.' Then he stopped, and looked at me – we both knew when her birthday was. We didn't know anybody who could have afforded to pay the price for the shoes that he read out from the receipt.

He read it out slowly as if that would tell us who bought my Mum the shoes. I wanted to believe in some romantic explanation for the gift of the shoes.

'Pam used to manage that boutique, and she was at the funeral,' I said. 'She said then, if I ever wanted to talk about

Mum, who had been her best mate since they were at school together, I could give her a ring and we could go for coffee and have a chat.'

I went out of the bedroom to fetch the house phone from downstairs – Pam's number would be in the memory. As I ran back up the stairs with the phone, I remembered again how Mum and Pam had sat in the kitchen. Both were smoking probably. When I returned to the bedroom, I found David sitting on the bed looking at the shoes as if they might start talking, telling their story…

He took the phone from me and then seemed to change his mind and handed it back to me. 'You talk to Pam, Sue. It will sound better coming from you. Just remember to offer her all the tea and cake she wants in exchange for the full story about the shoes.'

I found the number in the hand set's memory and dialled. David reached over and pressed the speaker button on the handset. He probably thought it would save me from repeating what Pam might say. The phone rang out as we both sat on the bed waiting. *Time is different when you're waiting for an answer*, I thought. I was about to give up on getting a reply when I heard Pam's voice questioning on the line. 'Who is this?'

Mum's number must have come up on her phone screen. 'It's Sue, Julia's daughter, my brother and I are at the house, getting the house cleared. Do you think you could meet up with us for coffee and cake – we've found a box with an unworn pair of blue dancing shoes…' Pam interrupted me quickly as if she knew exactly how to respond.

'Ah, yes right, I'll meet you both tomorrow then, in the *Blue Rose* tea rooms opposite the burger bar, which used to be the *Fine Times* boutique in my day. Say about three. I'll bring all you need to know with me. That's what your mum told me she wanted. See you tomorrow then, bye,' and she was gone. David and I looked at each other, sensing that there might be a mystery about to unfold regarding Mum's past after all.

We carried on that afternoon, emptying out bedside cabinets and dressing table drawers, but there was no other mysterious window to peek through and get a glimpse of Mum's past. We imagined enough about the history of the blue shoes to keep us curious all afternoon. By early evening, we decided to go back home to mine with a big bottle of red wine and some pizza. That night we sat on the Downs watching the stars, wondering what tomorrow might bring. Somehow, we hoped to numb the sadness we felt at the goodbye we were giving Mum's life in the emptied house. Her past seemed to be waiting for the right time for us to discover it.

Pam looked after herself very well. She dressed classically but her hair and makeup were very modern. She could pass for a woman ten years younger if you didn't look too closely. She was already seated with a coffee and a large slice of gateau untouched on a plate in front of her, when my brother and I arrived at the *Blue Rose* tea rooms. She welcomed us both, and caught the eye of the waitress expertly as we sat down. Two large cappuccinos arrived promptly on the table in front of us. As we greeted Pam, she put her hand deeply into the Gucci handbag wedged down the side of her chair. After the waitress had gone, with our orders for cake, Pam smiled quickly before turning her attention fully to David. She had two envelopes in her hand by then. I could see a white one which had Mum's handwriting on, and a blue one which was definitely older. It had something written on it but it was quite faint.

'David, when you have read both of these notes, promise me you will forgive her.' He looked at Pam as if he would forgive his mother anything and had always done so. Mum had certainly forgiven him for every wrong he had committed (intentionally or unintentionally) since I could remember, as the very jealous younger sister.

Pam continued to hold the envelopes in her hand as if she was about to present a prize.

'All you need to know is in these two envelopes,' she said

with a smile, as if she wanted him to remember exactly the moment she gave him this message. I looked at him. I could almost hear his curiosity overwhelming his impatience, to find out what was in the two envelopes.

'You *do* look *so* like your father,' she said and after a brief sigh, she gave both the envelopes to David.

Recognising Mum's handwriting on the white envelope, he ripped it open first.

'It's from Mum,' he said as his eyes scanned the note taken from the envelope. Then he read it a second time as if he was translating it carefully from another language. He made me feel he couldn't believe what he had translated. Then he spoke, reading out some of the words on the paper in front of him. 'Put yourself in my shoes,' he said a couple of times, then put the note down on the table. I moved the cream cake out of the way.

He looked at me, and said, 'Mum says, Dad wasn't my real dad and that I was the result of a one night stand with a guy in a band, after a concert she went to with *her*,' and he glanced over at Pam. Then he leaned closer to me. 'Your Dad stood by her, and promised to bring me up as his because he loved her,' he said in a quiet voice, almost as if he was confessing a sin about his own life, which he was in a way.

My face went numb – that's the first thing that happens to me when I go into shock. I don't know what I was expecting but it wasn't that.

'Open the other envelope now, David,' Pam said, breaking through the ice that held David and me still. He couldn't rip it open quick enough. He took from the envelope a folded sheet of notepaper. He read from the notepaper aloud straight away. This is what I heard my half-brother read:

Julia
I woke up and you were gone. I didn't buy it when you said you couldn't dance to our music because of your shoes. So I've bought you the best pair of dancing shoes from Pam's

boutique – then you can think of us every time you dance.
With love from me to you
John Lennon

Sea Wall

by Carole Mandeville

The body lay in the bottom of a small blue sailing dingy drifting within sight of Whitstable Harbour, a turquoise waterproof jacket just visible above the boat's edge. A tall white sail flapped lazily against the boat's mast, untethered. In the distance the Isle of Sheppey merged into the sea and sky in a haze of early sunshine that was already lifting puffs of mist from the harbour path. The tide was coming in with the boat.

Stephen sat on the sea wall watching the fishermen steer their boats round the end of the harbour and unload their catch, the sound of their chugging engines punctured by the screech of dozens of following gulls. A couple of the men were slicing and gutting their catch and throwing blue-red fish entrails into the dirty harbour water, where the gulls swooped and fought their way to it, grabbing pieces and launching themselves heavily back into the air.

The scene reminded Stephen of the vultures he'd seen in the African savannah tearing at the carcasses of Dama Gazelles and antelopes, and sometimes, too many times, of elephants that had been killed for their tusks. He thought back to the impossible task he'd been hired to do there, to save the elephants of Uganda in the face of what had seemed at first to be local corruption, and maybe manageable, but which he later learnt was an international market. He couldn't remember at which point he'd started to lose heart, but he thought it was probably after three years into his five-year contract. He'd had some sort of breakdown, he knew that now, but it was only when he got back to England that he had realised how close to the edge he had been.

He remembered standing next to the body of a female elephant whose tusks had been sheared off and whose body had been ripped open by the lion he'd disturbed. In her womb was the perfectly formed foetus of her baby, almost to term, with its trunk tucked neatly into a circle close to its mouth and its legs looking ready to run. Everything looked so alive apart from its greyed-out eyes, stilled with a non-seeing film. He felt as if he had no point, that he didn't know what he was doing there any more, what he was doing with his life. The elephant had grown her baby for near enough twenty-two months and he'd had all that time to protect her and he hadn't been able to.

He stood with his head bowed over her body, his rifle slack in his arms, and felt the tears slow-running down his face. And when he finally looked up he saw the vultures floating on the heat of the day, waiting. Nothing goes to waste. He loved that about being here, no waste, none that is except the ivory, the vanity of it, the nonsense of it. He felt he was wasting his life on a useless pursuit to satisfy his own vanity, that he, Stephen Bowes, could help save the African elephant, that his ambition was as empty as the desire to own a piece of carved ivory. He had laughed then until he was roaring, his head screaming at the sky and the vultures. Then he raised his gun and put the barrel to his neck. His driver, Bahemuka, had gently taken it away.

'If you're dead you won't even have the chance to save her brother,' he said, nodding at the rest of the family standing off in the bush.

They'd gone back to the Land Rover and watched as the herd came and stood round the carcass, touching her, feeling her with their trunks. He asked Bahemuka to drive back to the camp. He didn't want the chance to save anything any more; he felt like a meaningless fraud.

~~~

He looked up and caught sight of the boat being pulled in by the tide. The waves were catching it sideways, tipping it gently towards the beach with each one. He wondered if it had loosened its anchor. It looked as if it there might be someone in it and yet it seemed adrift. He got up to have a closer look and jumped down from the wall and walked along the footpath towards the beach.

He'd come back to Whitstable because he'd loved it as a child. They'd come down all the way from Birmingham for holidays here. He wished he'd asked his parents why here when it was so far to come. How did they know about Whitstable? He wondered if his sisters knew. But he didn't want to see them, he knew that. They'd just be asking him what he was going to do with his life now, what did he intend to save now. He didn't think he could deal with their curiosity or tell them he didn't know if he was going to be able to save himself.

Ahead he could see the sailing boats collected on the foreshore in front of the sailing club, their masts tipped this way and that as they'd come to rest on the beach. Sometimes, when the wind was blowing off the sea, the rope tackle on the masts would clink and chink like tubular wind chimes. At night Stephen could hear them now and again from his small fisherman's cottage further along the beach. More than anything they took him back to the past, to his mum and dad curled up on a tiny sofa together and he and the girls playing ludo on the kitchen table, or arguing over whose turn it was to play on the electric organ which they'd found unexpectedly in the cottage. It made him think, too, of fish and chips eaten on the beach in the late afternoons after spending the day swimming in the shallow, flat summer sea, the water warmed as the tide came in over the shingle and sand, and afterwards looking for lucky pebbles with holes in them, and shells he could take home for his collection. He should have taken one of the pebbles to Africa. He didn't think he could eat anything now that had lived. That was something he'd changed since he got back. He couldn't bring himself to eat meat or fish of any sort. It just brought back all the pictures of dead animals he'd seen waiting to crowd into his consciousness and he found it unbearable.

He passed the Oyster House and the empty benches on the beach and started walking over the shingle towards the water. He remembered this was where they used to play cricket. He remembered his dad yelling 'Run! Run Stephen!' and he'd run between the groynes, his feet slipping off pebbles, stabbed by shingle, fiery with pain, running as if his life depended on it. He wondered what his dad would have said to him now that he had run away from Africa and all that he had believed he had wanted to do with his life, to be part of an environmental army, to mitigate climate change, to save the endangered animals. He felt a crushing sense of failure.

The boat had caught in an eddying tide and was turning this

way and that. Stephen saw now that there was someone in it lying in the bottom. The wind was getting up and he saw that it might smash into the end of the groyne. He started to run towards it.

'Hey! Hey! Your boat's in danger of hitting the groyne!' he shouted.

The body didn't move. He pulled off his trainers and went into the water. He was quickly out of his depth and the cold hit him like an electric shock, sapping the strength from his arms. He gasped for breath then began a laboured crawl towards the boat. It seemed to be much further away than it had looked from the beach and he began to slow. He felt the drag of his clothes trying to pull him back, the ebb of the tide strengthening with every wave, until the lack of oxygen in his brain made his head light, as if he was somehow flying, not swimming. When he looked up at the sky he saw vultures high up, circling, waiting. He knew they were waiting for him, not just for the elephant and her calf but for him too, for his life. He gasped again, trying to put more strength in his arms until he reached out and grasped for the edge of the boat. He pulled himself up and saw that there was a young boy in a turquoise waterproof curled awkwardly into the bottom of the boat. He had a large gash across the back of his head and there was blood on the mast where he must have fallen. The water was colouring pink in the bottom of the boat. Stephen clambered in and checked the boy's pulse. He was still alive.

Stephen tore the sleeve off his shirt to stem the blood, then put his ear to the boy's chest to listen to his breathing.

He glanced up at the horizon and heard Bahemuka.

'If you're dead, you won't even have the chance to save her brother,' he'd said.

Then he turned the boat towards the shore.

Down from London

by Joanne Bartley

We loved theatre to give us a new perspective on life, meaningful art, and friends visiting for supper. We'd drink wine and stay up late planning the future. We longed for a life away from the capital.

'We can get an en suite!'

Sam moved closer so he could share my laptop screen.

'Can I see the floor plan?' he asked.

He slid an arm around me, then clicked on the photo slideshow.

'It has an ugly frontage,' he said.

'But an en suite!' I pointed out. 'Just think of all the reading time on the train.'

'Maybe we'll join the yacht club?' he said.

'Life is all about walks on the beach and seagulls!' I smiled.

We were thirty-something lovers planning a new life. We checked Whitstable restaurants on TripAdvisor, explored quiet streets, and chatted about house viewings as we ate seafood. We were as close as could be when we dreamed of a seaside future.

'Will you miss London?' Sam asked.

'Not at all,' I said. 'We'll shop at the greengrocer instead of Waitrose. We'll watch films instead of going to the theatre. Our sort of people are here, I know we'll make friends.'

'And we'll get an en suite,' Sam smiled.

'Maybe a utility room!'

We bought a Victorian terrace in the conservation area. The seaside commute was easy, but the morning train to London became busier as the town grew popular. Our friends mostly became parents. They struggled to find babysitters, we pitied them but never offered help. Sam and I decided children were a mistake, we liked our tidy house and our freedom.

'Did you hear they might be opening a Waitrose?'

'Good news for house prices. Guess how much next door sold for?'

Sam was looking at his favourite property listings website.

'We can get two bedrooms and a study.'

'Can I see?'

Sam showed me a map of the countryside; he was looking at a property not far from Challock.

'It's the middle of nowhere,' I said.

'No neighbours, country air...'

'And we get a utility room!' I said.

'Think how much we'll see each other if we work from home...'

'Maybe we'll join the parish council?'

'Life is all about cows and blackberry jam!' he said.

We were forty-something dreamers enjoying life for just the two of us. We bought walking boots, ate pub lunches, and chatted about whether to grow a vegetable plot. We were as close as could be as we dreamed of installing an Aga.

'Will you miss Whitstable?' Sam asked.

'Not at all,' I smiled. 'We'll shop online instead of at the greengrocers. We'll get Netflix instead of watching art house films. It'll be just us two and we can relax.'

We bought a seventeenth-century cottage that needed renovation. Our days were filled with Farrow and Ball paint charts and extension plans. The nearby church was busy with christenings, weddings, and funerals. People parked in our lane, and when we complained to the vicar he told us about the importance of faith. We pitied the people who sought the meaning of life in Sunday morning hymns. We bought a 'no parking' sign and a gate to prevent trespassers on the drive.

'The estate in the village got planning approval,' Sam frowned.

'The school will be good for house prices.'

'We can get a conservatory if we move.'

Sam was looking at houses in Folkestone.

'Show me the Street View,' I said. 'It looks pretty busy.'

'We get a choice of takeaways, pubs with cheap beer…'

'And a conservatory!' I grinned. 'We can start that online business.'

'Maybe we can join the Conservative Club?' he said.

'Life is all about penny arcades and walks on the prom!'

We were fifty-something entrepreneurs with start-up dreams. We researched the coastal enterprise zone, ate fish and chips and chatted about business finance. We were as close as could be as we dreamed of a wealthy future.

'What will you miss about the cottage?' Sam asked.

'Not a thing,' I smiled. 'We can find bargains in charity shops instead of Amazon. We'll work on the business instead of wasting time with Netflix. Just think how amazing it will be to make a million!'

We bought a Georgian townhouse with four floors and views of the harbour. Our days were filled with negotiations and software briefs. A homeless old drunk sometimes slept in our front yard but the council did nothing. He made the wrong choices so we had no sympathy. We were relieved when he died, but worried that others would take his place.

'They're planning a new seafront development.'

'Do you remember when the only shopping was Poundland?'

'We could get outbuildings and land…'

Sam showed me a website about French property. There were villages with names I could barely pronounce.

'A whole new country,' Sam grinned.

'Vineyards and restaurants!'

'We can get a swimming pool.'

'We could sell the business.'

'Maybe we'll join the boules team?'

'Life is all about the vie dans la joie!'

We were sixty-something expats heading for retirement. We filled the car boot with hypermarket wine, we enjoyed prix fixe menu and chatted about our swimming pool options. We were as close as could be as we dreamed of life without work.

'Will you miss anything about town?' Sam asked.

'Not a thing,' I smiled. 'We'll shop in French markets instead of Tesco. We'll relax instead of working. Just think how amazing it will be to just be together.'

We bought a farmhouse with outbuildings and four acres. We got up when we pleased and ate long lunches. Sam's illness was a blow, and we didn't go out much when he was tired. I handled the medical insurance and did my best to make myself understood in the chemists. We took each day as it came.

'It's a plot made for two.'

'Can I see the location?'

'It's expensive,' Sam said.

'But it looks lovely,' I said. 'You never wanted to end up in a crematorium.'

'Will you visit me?' he asked.

'Of course,' I told him. 'Life is all about the memories.'

'Is it?' he said.

We were old folks sharing the pain of the end. We sat in hospitals, debated drugs that didn't work, and chatted about our youth. We'd never been closer than in those long-lost days of our past.

'Will you miss me?' Sam asked.

'Of course,' I said. 'I have no life but you.'

'We have a nice house with land,' Sam smiled. 'I like to think of you enjoying it when I'm gone.'

Sam passed away one night. The house felt cold and empty. I spent days wondering what to put on his headstone. In the end I put just his name and dates. There was no one to bury me when I was gone. I had no family or friends, no faith to give me hope. I had nothing to keep me busy, and no one in my community noticed I was there.

The house was worth half a million pounds, but where would I move?

I remembered our first small flat in the days before ensuites and a swimming pool.

I logged in to my favourite property website and typed 'London'. Our old place had to be worth at least two million. We should never have sold it and moved to Kent. Life was downhill from London to a lonely life in a foreign land.

Life was about theatre that gave a new perspective on life, meaningful art, and friends visiting for supper.

We'd drink wine and stay up late planning the future.

The Book Man

by James Dutch

The war had all but faded into a distant memory, as mighty events so often do in the minds of the young, and father had sent me to the tobacconist for his *pleasure*; as a reward for fighting for King and Country, he had been turned into an addict. At six years of age, I could barely see over the polished, dark wood counter to see the moustachioed man peering back at me, one bushy eyebrow raised. I handed over the coins, and the tobacconist handed me a small cloth pouch which I carefully stowed in my coat pocket before making my way home. When I arrived at the house, quietly through the back door, father was sitting at the kitchen table, shirt sleeves rolled half-way up his arms, reading the newspaper. Without taking his eyes from the print, he reached out with one arm, his hand palm-up as if to say *give*.

I was truly in awe of my father; a tall, broad shouldered man with sinewy muscles that visibly tightened like corded rope under tension every time he moved. He'd worked at the docks in London's East End since he was twelve, and we were lucky that after the war he managed to secure regular work there again. I cannot say that I loved my father; his presence only ever demanded silence from me and my mother, his own brooding silence unyielding. So rather I feared him, and remained humble and obedient, a well-trained pup.

I reached into my pocket gently pulling the pouch – any lost leaf was noticed – and felt a small and sudden pang of fear as something snagged on it. I looked over at my mother as my father, still not raising his eyes to acknowledge his only son, snapped his fingers impatiently. Mother, washing up at the sink, dried her hands on her apron and came to me, her brow knit in concern. She pulled my hand from my pocket and reached in. Our eyes met, and I saw her look of concern change to one of mild surprise. She took the pouch from my pocket and along with it a small, leather-bound book. Now she was confused; why would I have a book? Where did it come from? I knew her questions; they were mine, too. I followed her glance back down at the book, then to my father who had now stopped reading and was glaring at us both.

'What is it?' he growled.

'A book,' my mother answered, her voice barely a whisper.

'I can see that,' he snapped back angrily, making us both flinch. 'Why's he got it?'

'I...' Mother had no answer. She turned to me. 'Where did you get this?'

I also had no answer, but I knew that I was in trouble. I wanted to talk, but under my father's muting look could not even manage a shrug.

Father snatched the book from mother's grasp, looked at the spine, then flicked through it before turning to the first page. He held the book so that I could see the hand-written name. 'William Sullivan,' he said placing the book down on the table. 'This book belongs to the tobacconist.' He rolled up the newspaper, stood and smacked me around the head several times. 'And you steal it from him?' He dropped the newspaper and began taking off his leather belt.

'Tom, please!' Mother shrieked as she put herself between her enraged husband and crying son. 'It's not his fault,' she continued. 'He's probably just like me, remember? Before?'

'Then I'll beat it out of him like I did you.'

'No!'

'Yes! I'll not put up with thievery from me own son.'

He pushed my mother aside as I trembled, unaware of what was happening, or why I'd prompted such a response and the world went out of focus before pain and darkness descended.

That is where it began – my curious relationship with books – and for a time, where it stopped. I awoke, sore and light headed, to discover that the book had been returned and that I had been taken away from London and my father. I breathed in, and the air tasted different; not so heavy. I noticed too, that the usual boiling hubbub of our street in Stepney was no longer present. As she stroked my hair, Mother told me how as a child she would bring home all manner of trinkets, ornaments and cutlery without ever knowing where they'd come from – but never a book, she said thoughtfully. Her voice was strong and clear, and rang in my head like a crystal bell. I'd never heard her speak like that before, and looking back, I realise how cowed and subdued she must have been by my father's fierce temper.

'I was always being called Little Maggie Magpie for taking shiny things,' she said, smiling. 'But I never did it, you know. They always just... turned up in my pocket or in my bag. They sent me away when I was thirteen. They said I was mad; a kleptomaniac. And because I never admitted it, they locked me up. When they finally let me out, it carried on just as before.' She paused to sigh. 'Until I met your father. When he saw what happened, he... Well, you know how he reacts. But don't worry,' she continued, seeing what must've been a look of horror on my face. 'We'll never go back to him.'

And we never did.

For months, I was scared that another book would turn up, but it never happened. After a while, I forgot about it and I lived happily with Mother in our new home in Canterbury, surrounded by lush greenery and new friends, some of whom had also moved away from the smog-choked capital – and it seemed as though I was on a permanent holiday and my memories of that time are filled with sun and love and laughter.

I met Betty when I was twenty-four years old; she swept me off my feet, quite literally, and left me sitting in the shallows of the Stour when she accidentally knocked me from my bicycle.

Well, I was smitten and we courted for some months before I plucked up the courage to ask her to marry me. Well, in those days, we were more likely to marry young, start a family…

It still burns me up inside, even after all these years, that we never had the chance to start a family. My beautiful Betty died suddenly after we'd been married for less than a year. It's a story I do not wish to tell here, having lived it over and again in private many times; suffice to say that the grief was profound and it sucked me under, out of life and into dark places.

For a long time I could not communicate, barely ate or washed, and did not particularly care if I carried on living. I had recurring nightmares in which my father was continuing to punish me through Betty's death and where I, as a young child, was trying to reach Betty, but being held down by the weight of so many books tumbling on top of me.

Mother helped me through the darkness and, despite her own advancing years and declining health, stood me back up again; I am and always have been grateful for that – for I realised that Betty had loved life, and would not want me to waste mine.

But something had changed inside me; I could not say what it was, but it was definite. Upon returning from my first trip out of the house, I felt something bump against my hip as I took my coat off. The coat felt slightly heavier than it should; clearly something was in my pocket. I dipped my hand in, and flinched back as I felt the unmistakable firm softness of the closed pages of a paperback. I almost dropped the coat and swung round violently, expecting to see my father standing there behind me; but no, I was safe from him.

The book was by Agatha Christie, that much I remember, but I couldn't bear to hold it in my hand and tossed it onto the floor by the coat stand. Mother was in the kitchen preparing lunch and was taken aback by my colour.

'You look like you've seen a ghost,' she said reactively, clearly without thinking. 'I'm sorry…'

'No, it's…' I shook my head. 'Remember when you told me about the shiny things that would turn up in your pockets?'

She nodded, knowingly. 'What was it?'

'A book.'

Now she shook her head. 'I never had books. Always useless trinkets that got me into trouble. Where is it?'

I showed mother the book lying on the floor and she scooped it up and turned the pages. It was brand new. Mother asked what shops I'd been to and said she'd return it tomorrow to the Woolworths on St Georges street as that's where it would most likely have come from.

After that, it happened regularly; if I went into a shop that sold books, a library or even people's homes, I'd return with a book. For a long time, I couldn't bear to look at them, and the thought of my father's malevolence made me weak. But then one day, *A Brave New World* fell out of my bag and I thought to myself, *yes – it is about time you were brave*, and so I read it. And it didn't hurt one bit – I'll even admit to enjoying it.

Many years went by. Mother passed away peacefully, and I myself grew old, continuing to bear my unbidden, papery loads. I had more books than I could ever possibly read, but had grown to love the look, feel and smell of them – and they kept me company; I was in a state of comfortable stasis.

Things began to change though, as time moved on and technology advanced – one day I walked out of WHSmiths on the high street and a shrill beeping noise stopped me in my tracks underneath the brown and orange signage. The alarming noise turned out to be an alarm; a security alarm. A young man with a terrible complexion and greasy hair walked stiffly towards me, a serious look on his dreary face.

'Excuse me sir, can I check in your bag?'

I knew then what had happened and played along, feeling

rather bad for the blushing employee. 'Of course you can...' I squinted at the name badge. 'Terry.' I handed him my bag.

He immediately pulled out a cellophane-sealed copy of a monthly magazine about coin collecting. It had a set of replica roman coins as a free gift.

'Umm, do you have a receipt for this, sir?'

'I am afraid not, Terry,' I said, doing my best to look confused. 'Please forgive an old man, I'll gladly come and pay now.'

It was the first magazine I'd ever purchased in my life – at sixty-eight years of age. Terry said not to worry, these things happen and have a nice day. The magazine as it turned out, was a rip-roaring bore, but I felt bound to read it.

As shop security began to tighten up, books were security tagged, security guards watched you like hawks and before long, cameras glared unblinkingly, and I became known as *The Book Man*. You know the one – the one who steals the books.

I came before the local magistrate many times before eventually being given a custodial sentence, but by then, I was glad of it. No books – heaven! I had a young lady barrister provided by the courts to defend me, she was very new to it and extremely keen, having only recently passed her exams. She said she sensed that I was sincere in my belief that I hadn't stolen the books, and that she wanted my mental health to be considered. Well, I just told her I'm too old to be playing games and that if I knew how or why it happened I'd show her, but that I couldn't. She looked thoughtful, pursing her lips and tapping her pen on the table.

'Okay,' she nodded. 'Let's assume that this is some weird…' she searched for the right word. 'Magical event.'

I rolled my eyes and then chuckled. 'Magic!'

'Well if we had proof—' she began.

'Miss Andrews.' I held my hand up to stop her. 'I'll still have my dignity, whatever happens.'

It didn't stop her though. During our next meeting, she took a minute or two fussing over her things. She took her papers and legal books and put them on the table opposite her large bag which she placed over the other side of the room, and then rummaged some more in her briefcase, before excusing herself for several minutes.

Unbeknownst to me, she had set up a hidden recording device. The video evidence she showed in court was of me pacing thoughtfully (*shuffling around* would be more accurate but it sounds rather demeaning) across the room. At one point in the clip, as I pass by the pile of papers, a fuzz of distortion flits across the screen, obscuring the picture for a second. Then, as I continue my pacing, you can clearly see a small notebook in the back pocket of my trousers where before there was none.

'As you can see, this is clear evidence that my client has no control over the events that have led him to be here. Instead of a serial book thief, we have an elderly gentleman who is a victim of… rather unusual circumstance.'

The red-faced judge glared over his glasses at Miss Andrews, then looked at me. I shrugged. How could I possibly explain? The judge discounted the evidence and I was imprisoned for six months, although it was likely that I'd be released in as many weeks.

I missed my books as soon as I arrived at Standford Hill prison on Sheppey. I found it curious as I thought I'd be glad of the distance from the copious amounts of reading material I'd acquired over the years. And yet there I was, itching to feel the soft, light texture of the page under my fingertips. I had to wait almost a week to get to the library; when the day came, I shivered with excitement as I headed there along the prison corridor as quickly as I could. I opened the door and walked in – it was shockingly sparse, and I resolved immediately to donate all but one bookcase of my own books to their depleted shelves when I returned home.

'Good morning!' I said cheerily to the scrawny, tattooed man lounging on a chair with his feet up on a desk.

The unshaven man looked up at me with his beady eyes and wrinkled his nose. 'Are you that one what nicks books?'

I shrugged and began talking: 'Well, I was convicted for—'

The man sat bolt upright. 'Well you can bloody well bugger off. You ain't getting none of my books, mate, I'll tell ya...' There was more to his rant, and the fellow really knew how to swear, but those details are unimportant – I could well understand his reaction, given our surroundings and the company we were forced to keep.

I closed the door behind me as I left and shuffled dejectedly back to my whitewashed cell. I laid down on the starchy, regulation blue sheets of my bunk and stared at the ceiling feeling rather sorry for myself until a realisation dawned upon me. I had been to a library, and in close proximity to... I felt a lilt of hope, moved my hand slowly to my side and smiled, as one does upon meeting an old friend, as my fingers met with a familiar feeling – a rectangle of bound paper in my pocket.

About Writers of Whitstable

by Joanne Bartley

Writing is hard, a bit like a marathon but inside your head. To get something finished takes endurance (not looking at Facebook), mental strength (writing even when you're not writing well) and hard work (turning bad lines into good ones.)

If you keep going, eventually you get to the finish line. But there no tape to break and no medal won, you just have words; a big pile of them, with no sense of whether anyone might want to read them. So you rearrange them all and wonder if they're any better. But you still don't know.

That's why I started Writers of Whitstable.

Part of me didn't want to know whether what I'd written was good or bad, but another part of me knew I had to find out. A few others felt the same and we met in the Horsebridge Centre to give it a try.

It wasn't a great start. Nobody took the lead and it was a shambles. At the next meeting only two people turned up, but they were nice people. At the next meeting somebody rewrote a new member's story. Another disaster.

But somehow we kept going. We moved to the Marine Hotel. We read each other's stories before meetings and tried to make sure feedback was honest but kind. One day I noticed I'd stopped being nervous about the meetings, and realised that lots of people, supportive and enthusiastic people, were creating new work every month. What's more, I'd written half a novel!

Then it got too successful. With so many people coming each month we split into two groups, one group for novels and one for short stories, and we now meet twice a month.

We produced our first short story collection, Beyond the Beach Huts, in 2016. All stories were set in Whitstable. We enjoyed writing for a purpose and getting published so we've done it again, this time widening our theme to include the whole of Kent.

So here you'll find work from both experienced and novice writers, various styles, but all with the same enthusiasm both for writing and for our county – all created by people who took an important step in finding an audience.

There are too many people to thank for helping to make Writers of Whitstable a success. Lin, our editor, is one of them, as well as all those who helped someone else get the best from their work. Also, our thanks to the Marine Hotel who put up with us and allow us to re arrange their furniture.

Lastly, if you have any interest in writing, check **writersofwhitstable.co.uk** for details of our group – we might just have room for another chair. One thing's for sure, we all understand that writing is hard, and scary, but also terrific fun, especially when you have a group of writer friends to share its ups and downs. I hope our enthusiasm comes through in the pages of this anthology.

Introducing the Authors

Joanne Bartley

Jo studied Screenwriting for Film & TV at Bournemouth University, and her screenwriting career involved projects with Incubator Films, Visage Productions and the BBC. Paying the bills as a full time screenwriter didn't work out so Jo embarked on a creative career in the poker industry, then last year changed direction to coordinate an education campaign group. She is a self confessed 'story structure nerd' so created StoryPlanner.com to offer tools for planning novels. She is currently writing a dystopian novel about a digital future where coders are the privileged elite and unproductive citizens are eliminated. In her free time she likes to drink coffee by the gallon, play Exploding Kittens with her kids, and make Freedom of Information requests for obscure stats.

Mark Crawford

Mark has been writing short stories seriously for only a year yet his head has been filled with ideas and thoughts since childhood. It is only recently and with the generous assistance of Writers of Whitstable that his ideas have grown into short stories and a burgeoning novel. Preferring to write stories for children to young adults he has drawn on family historical events for his novel set in World War Two and his own childish imagination when writing about his children's characters. His wife and two children are his rocks and inspiration to continue his writing.

R.J. Dearden

R J Dearden is the published author of the super exciting time manipulatory yarn, "The Realignment Case." He was a contributor to the "Behind the Beach Huts" anthology and scraped the 2017 entry into the anthology by the skin of his teeth, having started the first draft in 2010. He is married with two young boys called Rory and Finlay. After George R R Martin, R J Dearden is currently recognised as the slowest writer on the planet. His next novel is due just before the rapture... probably.

James Dutch

When an idea plants itself inside his head, James lets it germinate and grow roots in his imagination for days, weeks, months, even years. These thoughts usually end up as the background to a story – the untold histories of characters that are all important to an author, enabling a truthful fiction to emerge.

James has written short stories, poetry, and novel-length pieces over a twenty-two year period, but has only published his work since becoming part of the Writers of Whitstable group. There are plans to continue publishing his work; a novel, maybe three, and short stories as and when inspiration strikes.

James lives in Canterbury with his equally creative partner, wonderful son and a fickle grey cat.

Jeffrey George

Eternal optimism for tomorrow, brave laughter at cruel misfortune, unreserved excitement in new relationships? Or are the best days behind us, setbacks inevitable and a date something to be feared? Whichever, life is an enigma, love an ephemeral intoxication and work a necessary drudge, at least for most. That's Jeffrey's starting point for stories of success and failure, endings and new beginnings, and love and loss. He is soon to release his first novel in this genre, *Falling Asleep at the Wheel*.

He has also studied the modern espionage world, researched terrorism and counter-terrorism strategies and met with UK military surveillance technicians for Europe and the Middle East, CIA security directors, and members of US Air Force One. Exploring the underlying human and sociological issues, he is now writing spy novels under the name Jeff Cook, and will shortly publish *Storm Shadow*, the first of a series featuring MI6 field agent Nikki Steel.

Nick Hayes

Nick Hayes has been teaching in local secondary schools for nearly 20 years but still has plenty to learn. He has been writing since he was able to hold a pen and his handwriting remains largely unchanged since his first effort – Sugar in Space (aged five and three quarters).

When he emerges from beneath his marking he enjoys writing poetry and short stories but doesn't think he has the stamina just yet for a novel although he harbours dreams of being the next teacher turned author like David Almond and Phillip Pullman.

In an alternative universe he wrote The Great Gatsby, the poems of Edward Thomas and all the strips from Peanuts. In this world he largely spends time with his family and two recently acquired cats. Any excess energy he spends on tending his long term illness – an obsession for Aston Villa.

Writers of Whitstable have been instrumental in encouraging him from thinking about doing more writing to actually doing more writing. He has come to agree with John Cheever – 'I can't write without a reader. It's precisely like a kiss—you can't do it alone.'

Helen Howard

Helen began to think about becoming an author one day at the tender age of nine, when she won a story competition at primary school. The story she wrote was about two girls who ran away from home but returned when the food ran out, and the prize was half a dozen eggs.

As an adult she tried her hand first, unsuccessfully, at short stories and plays aimed at a radio audience. She became a scientist and teacher at all levels from preschool to postgraduate, then transferred to training workers in the care sector and, in parallel, started developing as an artist. Writing at work in education, training, and health and social care, took her into non-fiction and, after being made redundant, she started to write textbooks, learning materials and training packs on health and social care and management.

Shifting away from non fiction towards fiction proved to be a bit of struggle but the support of other writers has been invaluable and there are now files of uncompleted novels, short stories and poetry waiting to be finished. Meanwhile her artwork often incorporates words as well as references to science and care. Helen writes a journal every day and enjoys dancing, singing and growing her own food.

Alison Kenward

Alison grew up in Exeter where, at the age of five, she decided that acting was for her and everything else took second place. After leaving school, she spent three blissful years at Rose Bruford College. Fully expecting to become famous, she turned down a two year degree course from Kent University and continued working in rep, on TV and in Children's Theatre. Eventually she found a 'proper' job and began teaching, at the same time undertaking a degree with the Open University and a Masters at Goldsmiths. Alison has never done things the easy way.

Some years later, she returned to the acting industry, only to find that the Juliets and the Ophelias were beyond her reach and so she began writing plays with women at the centre of the action.

This year, her fifth play 'Politic Man' was produced in Bermondsey and included a short London tour. Alison's sixth play is a surreal piece about two crows in the desert who can both speak. Think Waiting for Godot with feathers. It will premiere in Basel Switzerland in 2018.

Other work includes short stories, poetry and a full length novel "The Clockmaker's Wife",which is still lurking on the hard drive and awaiting a huge re-write.

Alison lives in Whitstable and is Artistic Director of Kent Coast Theatre.

Kerry Mayo

Kerry Mayo is a writer and photographer who also runs a successful business in Canterbury. She has been published with the title Whitstable Through Time, a photographic/historic work looking at the development of Whitstable over the last 120 years, and has had serials and short stories published in the women's magazine market and online.

Kerry has written three novels and also enjoys writing screenplays. Her writing tackles contemporary issues with a large dose of black humour and irreverence.

Carole Mandeville

Once she'd discovered the joy of reading as a child and being transported to another world, Carole began writing stories for herself in small hand-made books. The writing has never really stopped from there though it slowed down when life interrupted, and a career and the children came along, apart, that is, from a pantomime which was performed by Minster Playhouse.

She has also contributed to a book on working with PTSD.

After retiring from the NSPCC as a play therapist and counsellor she joined a U3A creative writing course and she hasn't really stopped writing since then. Short stories and plays are her writing mediums of choice and she has had several recent successes. These have kept her sitting down time after time in front of a blank page waiting for the joy of inspiration.

Kim Miller

Kim is a new writer, joining the Whitstable group in 2015 to finally start writing after decades of prevaricating. So far she has concentrated on short stories, still trying to find her style and areas of interest. Naturally, she has an idea for a novel brewing in the background and will, hopefully, have the courage to start it soon(ish). She enjoys many kinds of books, classic and contemporary, and is in love with EF Benson's Mapp and Lucia.

Kim lives in the nearby coastal village of Oare and can see Whitstable from the home she shares with her partner, Andrew; their daughter, Daisy, is at university studying politics.

Ellen Simmons

Ellen became a true lover of literature when she read the Harry Potter series aged seven and has never looked back.

She went on to study English Literature and Creative Writing at university to see if she had any ability to write herself, and enjoyed being part of a group of writers so much that it made sense to find such a group when she returned home.

At present she has numerous novels on the go due to her inability to focus on just one particular story. Her latest project focuses on a small town very similar to Whitstable that delves into the secret supernatural community that dwells there.

Ellen writes mainly to break up the dull mundanity of everyday life, and will continue to do so until magic truly exists. Or her Hogwarts acceptance letter arrives in the post.

Lin White

Lin is an avid reader, and has been making up stories in her head for as long as she can remember. The Internet brought the realisation that others enjoy that sort of thing as well, and she soon discovered fanfiction.

Writing original fiction was the logical next step. To date there are three novels in various levels of completion, plus a bunch of short stories.

In her real life, she has been involved in publishing and education for many years and currently works as an editor and proofreader, helping other writers to polish up their work ready for publication. She has enjoyed helping the Writers of Whitstable to bring their work to print.

John Wilkins

John writes because it gives him an extraordinary energy to believe in whatever comes next. It is a very contagious opportunity to set down some of his thoughts and imaginings. Writing in two genres, mystery and fantasy, offers him a map full of routes to plot his stories and develop characters both inside and outside the everyday existence.

He is currently working on two novels. After writing the first fifty thousand words of each in 2014 and 2015 respectively, with the help of Writers of Whitstable he is editing chapter by chapter. The first novel is about a woman who discovers that the man who left her twenty-five years ago was an undercover police spy at the time. The other one is a fantasy novel about the quest of Martha to find the meaning of life, starting with her task of lifting the fog.

All of the above has been a journey of many footsteps since he persuaded Mick Jagger to lift his foot off the power cable at Earls Court back in the day...

David Williamson

David has been a long-standing member of the Writers of Whitstable and also designs their book jacket covers. David has received favourable reviews for his latest book *The Lovers of Today*, which will soon be followed by the sequel, *The Lovers of Tomorrow*.

Writers of Whitstable's first book, Beyond the Beach Huts, featuring stories set in and around Whitstable, is available from Whitstable booksellers Harbour Books, or online from Amazon.

Printed in Great Britain
by Amazon